Jessica Huntley

THE HANGING TREE

ISBN: 978-1-916827-14-1

First edition

Website: www.jessicahuntleyauthor.com

Cover Design: Get Covers

Edited and proofread by: Hayley Anderton at IndieVisible Services

About Jessica Huntley

Jessica Huntley is an ex-British soldier and Personal Trainer turned author of addictive psychological thriller books. She has spent almost five years writing and is now the author of twenty-one books. She is both self-published and traditionally published with Joffe Books and Inkubator Books.

She writes books for thriller readers who like their stories dark and twisty with complex yet memorable characters, who often suffer from relatable mental health disorders. When she isn't writing, Jessica is either reading, keeping fit, walking her dog or looking after her young son.

Sign up to her email list to receive news about upcoming book releases and download a FREE thriller short story (You Die...I Die) by visiting her website: www.jessicahuntleyauthor.com

Books by Jessica

Published by Inkubator Books

Don't Tell a Soul
Under Her Skin
The Good Parents
I Will Find You
Pretty Little Lies

Published by Joffe Books

Horrible Husbands
Room 21

The Darkness Series

The Darkness Within Ourselves
The Darkness That Binds Us
The Darkness That Came Before

My ... Self Series

My Bad Self: A Prequel Novella

My Dark Self

My True Self

My Real Self

Standalone Thrillers

Jinx

How to Commit the Perfect Murder in Ten Easy Steps

The Murder Maze

The Hanging Tree

Writing in collaboration with other authors

The Summoning

HorrorScope: A Zodiac Anthology – Vol 1

Bloody Hell: An Anthology of UK Indie Horror

Acknowledgements

This has been a labour of love for well over a year and I'm so proud and excited to have finished it, but I couldn't have done it without the amazing Hayley Anderton from IndieVisible Services, who not only edited it brilliantly and helped me hone the plot and ensure all the plot holes were filled, but has also shouted from the rooftops about this book from day one. She's not only a great author friend, but a professional businesswoman too and I'm so honoured that she's worked on this book with me. Thank you, Hayley!

Thanks also to my incredible narrator for the audio book, Candace Fitzgerald. I'm so glad you emailed me out of the blue two years ago and begged me to let you narrate The Darkness Series! What a journey we've been on since. I couldn't imagine anyone else narrating The Hanging Tree, as it brings in characters from The Darkness Series that you already know and love. Thank you so much for bringing them to life once again.

A huge thank you goes to the whole indie author and reader community, on Facebook and Instagram. I've truly felt like I've found my people there and I'm so grateful that you continue to read and support my books, even though I am now mostly traditionally published. This may be my last self-published book for some time, but I'll never say never!

Thanks to everyone who has been part of the ZooLoos Book Tour for this book and for Zoe for bringing it all together and getting 32 readers signed up! That's huge! I appreciate all your reviews and the time and effort you have made to support my book. Thank you!

Lastly, thank you to whoever is reading this right now. Not many people read the acknowledgements but thank you for picking up my book. I hope you enjoyed it, and I hope that whoever you are and wherever you are in the world, you can help illuminate the darkness by turning on your light. Just like Stephen.

Connect with Me

Sign up to my email list via my website to be notified of future books and receive a twice-monthly author newsletter and receive a FREE short story – You Die...I Die.

www.jessicahuntleyauthor.com

Follow me on Facebook: Jessica Huntley - Author - @jessica.reading.writing

Follow me on Instagram: @jessica_reading_writing

Follow me on Twitter: @jess_read_write

Follow me on TikTok: @jessica_reading_writing

Follow me on Goodreads: jessica_reading_writing

Prologue

JOHN

Bethgelert, Wales, 1925

The darkness drew closer with every passing minute. John didn't want to miss the sun disappearing behind the hill near the farm; the perfect vantage point to wave goodbye to another day. John closed the barn door, locking the ducks inside, and bid goodnight to the farm cat - Tabby - who'd woken up from her late afternoon nap. She was now ready to start her evening hunt for mice, which were plentiful among the hay bales and various animal food bags.

Chores complete, he turned towards the hill and began his ascent. The hill, though not very wide, was exceptionally steep, littered with divots and uneven ground, so one could easily twist an ankle if they weren't careful. Reaching the large, ancient oak at the very top was an arduous task for most other townsfolk, but having turned twenty only a month ago, John found it to be merely a gentle stroll. He'd worked on his family's farm since he could walk, developing his overall strength and endurance. He loved rambling to the top of the hill every day to watch the sunset and welcome in the darkness of the night. The surrounding countryside stretched as far as the eye could see on a clear day. He felt like he was standing on top of the world. The horses used to plough the land were grazing nearby, resting after a hard day of manual labour.

Tonight, he was due to meet Carys by the oak tree so they could watch the sunset together, something they did as often as they could. No day was truly complete until he'd watched the sun go to bed with his love. He already knew he wanted to spend the rest of his life with Carys Griffiths. At eighteen, she was younger than him, but it didn't matter to either of them. They were in love and had been since they were children, young enough to play together in the streams and run half-naked around the fields and barns.

Tonight. He was going to ask her tonight, even if his father and older brother, Rhys, who had come back from the war a changed man, didn't agree with his decision.

John jogged the final few paces up the hill, reaching out his hand and touching the tree, like a perpetual finish line he always had to cross. His heart raced, but it wasn't from the exertion. He stared up at the tree, closing his eyes.

The tree was the oldest living thing in the village, at over eight hundred years old. John's father, a member of the village order, had shown him old diaries and village documents of when the tree was first planted: back then, a symbol of life, strength and unwavering determination in the face of adversity for the local community. That was what the tree represented.

Some said the tree held mystic powers. There was a legend attached to it; that if you were to die near the tree, it would absorb the soul of the deceased and keep it alive within its bark and branches for eternity. When John pressed his palm against its gnarled trunk, he swore he could feel the tree pulsing with life. Perhaps it was the existence of souls nestled within.

It was just a legend, of course.

Most of the young people in the community used it for climbing. It was almost as if the tree had designed the perfect order of its branches to make it easier for people to climb. John had been a regular scrambler back in his teenage years. Higher and higher into the branches he'd climb, until the ground was so far away, his stomach would flip in exhilaration.

He often wondered what the tree would look like in another hundred years. Perhaps it would be even bigger with more limbs and climbing footholds. Technically, the tree belonged to his family as the hill it grew on was on their land. If he had the time one day, when he had taken over the farm and had children of his own, he'd love to build a treehouse in it. Nothing overly fancy, but enough to be able to sit in it and gaze across the fields below, or for his children to play to their hearts' content.

For now, though, there was a branch where he could sit and look out across the valley below. Sometimes, while he was on his break from working the land, he'd bring his packed lunch with him, usually a small block of cheese and meatloaf. It was hard labour, but he had never known anything else. His mind and body were strong. Farming was in his blood and, one day, he'd continue the family legacy and teach his children to live the same life. He didn't need to travel or go anywhere else. He knew he'd be perfectly content living here for the rest of his days with Carys by his side. Nothing else mattered to him.

The sun was setting. There was no sign of Carys yet. He didn't want her to miss it because today, the skies had been so clear; the perfect setup for a spectacular sunset. John looked down the hill, hoping he'd see her making her way up towards him. Perhaps he should have waited for her at the bottom. That would have been the gentlemanly thing to do. But no, she'd agreed to meet him at the top.

John took a deep breath as he sat at the bottom of the tree, his back resting against its rough trunk. The gentle wind whistled through the enormous branches above, causing a few loose leaves to cascade around his head. It was that time of year; a time when the abundance of green around him slowly faded to browns and oranges and yellows, Mother Nature preparing for winter.

He smiled as he took out his journal from the pocket of his light overcoat. A brown leaf floated in front of him, landing on the open pages, so he traced around its outline using his lead pencil. He enjoyed tracing leaves and sticks or drawing flowers and trees freehand. His journal was full of doodles, drawings, notes and ideas. To anyone else who opened and read it, the words and drawings wouldn't make any sense, but to John, they meant the world. The workings of his inner thoughts. He kept other journals too, but those he kept hidden. He made a lot of lists, made observations about a lot of people around him. He knew something was amiss in this village, but he wouldn't leave it for the world. His home. His community. He would do anything to keep it safe.

A large crack sounded above. He thought for a moment that something was jumping through the branches; a squirrel, perhaps, but he saw no sign of one as he looked up. The tree often creaked and groaned. A recent storm had damaged one of the larger branches and it was only a matter of time before the weight of it would succumb to gravity and crash to the ground.

Looking down at his journal, he began to draw a rough sketch of the sunset. It was a shame Carys was missing it. Perhaps she'd been held up by her parents. It was her job to feed the animals in the evenings. He loved that she was a hard-working woman, but she would often be solely focused on completing her chores and wouldn't have time to see him. He knew how difficult the past few years had been for young farmers and if they didn't work, then they didn't eat, since they wouldn't be able to sell their wares at market.

John's attention was focused on the page; the beauty of the sunset ahead of him. He looked up for a moment as the sky darkened.

No. It wasn't the sky.

A shadow passed overhead. He looked back down at the page, determined to finish the sketch before the light disappeared for the day.

At first, he didn't realise anything was wrong. He didn't notice the long rope with a noose at the end being lowered gradually over his head. Not until the noose caught around his neck and instantly tightened. The journal fell from his hands, landing on the ground as he reached his hands up to loosen the rope, pulling it away from the sensitive skin around his Adam's apple.

It was too late.

When the rope tightened again, it lifted him to his feet. His body jerked as the rope took his whole weight, cutting off his air supply. He kicked his legs. He tried to shout for help, but his voice was trapped inside his throat.

The rope remained tight.

He couldn't breathe, couldn't do anything other than stare ahead at the sunset as life drained from his body. It was so beautiful. Tears streamed from his eyes as he took in the magnificence of the world around him; a sight he knew he'd never see again. He knew it was over, so his final thought was of his dear Carys. He hoped she would be able to move on from his death and live a long and happy life. This was his fault. He should have left it well alone.

John's body twitched one final time.

His soul drifted from his body and sought refuge in the tree where it would hide in silence for the next one hundred years. The tree accepted its latest visitor, promising to keep it safe until someone came along who was willing to listen.

John would never know the significance of his death. About how the tree at the top of the hill, once a beacon of hope and strength, would now become a symbol of death and pain.

All because of him.

John's death would become infamous.

And so, started the story of The Hanging Tree.

Chapter 1
GRAHAM

Bethgelert, Wales, 2025

Graham takes his freshly brewed, stronger than average coffee and stands by the open barn-style back door of Rosemore Cottage, looking out at the picturesque fields and countryside beyond. Every morning for the past ten months, no matter the weather or occasion, he stares at the grassy hill opposite.

An ancient oak tree dominates the hill. In fact, it dominates the whole area, like an enormous lone statue standing guard. But what is it guarding? There isn't another tree or building anywhere near it. It's only a tree, yet it draws his attention every time he glances out of the kitchen window or steps foot outside the back door and into his yard. This morning is no different.

His home, Rosemore Cottage, sits on a small patch of land, once belonging to a larger development of Rosemore Farm. Over the years, the land had been sold off to neighbouring farms and the farmhouse itself was turned into a quaint cottage, which Graham bought almost a year ago after selling his place in Cherry Hollow. Living in that infamous town hadn't been an option for him any longer, not after the harrowing events of 2024 when he decided to retire from the police force early.

Now, he's enjoying his retirement, living in the rural village of Bethgelert in Wales, having put away a cosy nest egg to live on until his pension kicks in. He's never needed anything fancy. Just a roof over his head, food in his fridge and perhaps a nice whisky to enjoy in the evening while sitting by the open fire in his sitting room. He managed to buy Rosemore Cottage at a steal because it had been reduced in price several times, yet no one wanted to take on such a large project. The land and buildings in Wales weren't exactly hot property, especially when the nearest large town was over an hour away. It suited Graham perfectly.

He had even taken up a spot of gardening, since Rosemore Cottage came with its own vegetable patch. When he first arrived, it looked like it hadn't grown anything decent in years, so Graham decided to bring the patch back to life. He rolled up his sleeves and picked up his digging fork, ready for a challenge. His first attempt at channelling his inner Monty Don over the summer had gone surprisingly well with an abundance of runner beans, kale and oddly shaped carrots, not to mention enough courgettes to feed the whole village for the next few months. He'd had to resort to giving them away, taking them to the local farmer's market every Saturday and handing them out to the stalls. He didn't charge anything for them. He just couldn't face eating another courgette for dinner.

Now that the autumn has well and truly set in, there isn't a lot left to do, gardening wise. Gone are the light, warm evenings where he could stay outside working, picking through the weeds and pruning the straggling growth. The cold, late October wind whips around him and through the open door into the kitchen. He's letting out all the heat, but he's never been one to feel the cold. Graham tilts his head to the clear, grey sky, watching as a flock of birds circle overhead, having taken off from the branches of the large tree on the hill. He listens to sounds around him; the chatter of the birds, the babble of the nearby stream, a farm dog barking in the distance.

Is this heaven?

It sure as hell feels like it.

His eyes are drawn to the hill ahead, roughly a hundred or so yards away from the back door. The hill and the tree aren't part of his property, but they used to belong to Rosemore Farm. He's not sure who the land belongs to now, but Graham often sees local farmers and dog walkers up there, so presumably it's now part of a national right of way.

Graham has only climbed the hill once before to see the view from the top, but once had been enough, thank you very much. He isn't as fit as he used to be, having spent the past ten years or so chained to a desk, drinking vast amounts of coffee and binge-eating biscuits. Long gone are the days of his youth, running around solving cases and burning more calories than he can consume. Those damn biscuits have caught up with him. That hill is his nemesis. If his knees were in better shape, then he might be able to climb it a little easier.

Graham does like to walk, though. It's just the elevation that he struggles with. He walks every day without fail, come rain or shine. His body may ache more after a day on his feet, but it still allows him to get from A to B, albeit at a more leisurely pace.

Today, a Tuesday, is a crisp, late autumn day and he's already looking forward to a long walk along the river that flows through the village. There's a perfect path too, which stretches for several miles before circling back around on itself, crossing over the river via a delightful footbridge.

He finishes his coffee, rinses the mug in the sink and places it on the draining board to dry. Then, he grabs his flat cap and a waterproof jacket (one can never be too careful with the weather in Wales) before locking the back door behind him with his key; a proper old, rusty-looking one. He begins his trek across the field towards the hill where the path starts.

A friendly dog-walker waves at him from across the way, his golden cocker spaniel frolicking in the long grass, its ears flapping like it's about to take off in flight. Graham tips his cap to the man. Maybe he should get himself a furry companion. His two goldfish, Fred and Wilma, are great; easy, quiet, no hassle. Still, he thinks that when he has a glass of Scottish whisky of an evening in front of the roaring fire with his feet up on the ottoman, a warm lapdog wouldn't go amiss. He'll think about it. Or maybe a cat could be a more appropriate choice, since they need less looking after. They can even keep down the local mouse population.

'*Bore da*, Mr Williams!' calls the dog-walker as he strolls towards him through the long dew-laden grass.

'*Bore da*,' Graham replies, using roughly the only phrase or greeting he knows in Welsh. 'Lovely morning for a dog walk,' he adds, bending to stroke the excited dog. He's a little embarrassed that he can't seem to recall the man's name. He's seen him around, mostly from a distance. Everyone knows Graham's name, though. For what reason, he has no idea. He's still considered the *new guy*, he supposes, even if he has lived here ten months.

'This one gets me up at six every morning,' replies the man in his strong Welsh accent. A lot of the locals tend to speak Welsh with each other, but are happy to use English with the outsiders. 'You should get yourself a dog. Keeps you fit!'

'I was actually just thinking the same. It's not a bad idea.'

'Well, I won't keep you. Need to get to the butcher's bright and early before they sell out of all the good cuts. *Hwyl Fawr*.'

Graham smiles in response and watches the man walk away, his little dog running in circles around his feet and barking. He adjusts his cap as he looks towards the oak tree, squinting against the sun still sitting low on the horizon. It's taking its time rising this morning. He doesn't blame it. Sometimes an extra minute or two in bed is warranted. He brings his hand up to shield his eyes from the dazzling light, but the more he looks, the more he convinces himself that something isn't quite right with the tree.

Has a branch snapped overnight and fallen?

Curiosity gets the better of him and he veers off the path, beginning his slow ascent. Maybe his eyes will figure out what they are seeing the closer he gets. But he quickly realises he's wrong. With every step, his eyes continue to deceive him, continue to relay to his brain that there's something in the tree that shouldn't be there.

Graham's breathing becomes laboured as the hill gets steeper towards the top, more rugged and uneven. A narrow, well-worn path leads all the way up the hill, used by countless walkers and runners. Graham has sometimes seen the local running club doing hill sprints. He'll be damned if he's going to break into a jog to get up the hill. He'll probably drop dead of a heart-attack before he reaches the top.

Slow and steady, he climbs, his eyes never leaving the tree. Its cracked and fallen limbs make the perfect rustic bench, but the rest of it still stands tall and proud; an oak tree that must be at least eight hundred or so years old, considering its size. The bark has knarred, deformed and twisted over many years of enduring the notoriously bad weather in Wales. It could even be the oldest oak tree in Britain.

He's made it.

The hill levels out, but his heart rate doesn't. It keeps rising and rising, taking his breath with it. Dear God, he can barely take a decent lungful of air as his pulse thuds in his ears. With a sickening jolt, he realises what's hanging from the tree, tangled in the branches above his head.

A familiar stab of horror pierces his gut.

Not again.

Chapter 2
STEPHEN

Cherry Hollow, The Lake District, 2025

The great thing Stephen finds about being a freelance journalist is that he can work anywhere he likes. On top of that, being a freelance journalist who also happens to have helped solve the infamous forty-year cold case in Cherry Hollow last year, means he can now pick and choose which jobs he accepts. And he's bombarded with jobs every day from newspapers, online forums and podcasts, all salivating at the prospect of having *the* Stephen Mallow working for them. They can't get enough.

Stephen still works for the London Times, but his boss, Kevin, allows him to write whatever the hell he wants to write because he knows that whatever he writes will sell papers. Lots of papers. He writes one article a month for the company he's worked at for the past few years, but can now spread his wings a little and also writes for other publishing houses and newspapers when it takes his fancy.

Everyone wants to know what Stephen has to say. And they're happy to pay an extortionate amount of money for him to do it. Not that Stephen only writes the articles for the money, but it is nice to be able to pay the bills on time and not have to worry where his next pay cheque is coming from. It won't last forever, of course. Nothing does. But for now, he's revelling in his mild celebrity status.

A year and a half ago, no one had even heard of him. He was just some lowly journalist who wrote trashy articles in the paper; the ones that had no relevance or factual information. No one cared about them and he was paid next to nothing for his time.

But one viral article about The Creature and Cherry Hollow changed everything.

Suddenly, what he had to say mattered to people.

The general public couldn't get enough of the creepy small town in the Lake District that was supposedly haunted by an evil entity. Was it real or not? Nobody knew, but it was fun to speculate. After he helped Detective Graham Williams solve the case, his life turned upside down seemingly overnight and it hasn't been the same since.

Now, he is not only living in the creepy small town in the Lake District that was supposedly haunted by said evil entity, but he also has a girlfriend called Rachel.

Him.

Stephen Mallow.

The thirty-five-year-old man who has never had a girlfriend in his life and who has always been a laughingstock to most people due to his unique and eccentric mind that only a small portion of the population can relate to or understand.

It's only made him more popular online. Apparently, his quirkiness is alluring and he is, what everyone calls, *relatable* to a lot of people. He stays off social media because he finds it overwhelming, but from what he's heard, his articles are always *trending* or *going viral*. He knows what that means, but has never cared for the terms, and he's never been bothered about making it as a viral sensation. So much ridiculous stuff goes viral these days. Stuff that doesn't even make any sense, like TikTok dances and memes, or AI-generated graphics of people that end up having seven fingers on each hand. He doesn't understand it.

But he's glad that his article reached a lot of people, and he's glad that others find him relatable in some way, even if he'll never meet them.

Stephen knows he's different and a lot of people he meets find him too intense, too strange and too … *much*. But not Rachel. Not his girlfriend. Well, she maybe *does* think all those things too, but she also finds him endearing and cute (her words, not his) even though he often turns the light switches on and off seventeen times before entering a new room. It's something he is working on reducing. Sort of. Maybe. It's a work in progress.

At first, he tried to hide his quirks and eccentricities from Rachel, but the more he did, the more stressed and anxious he became. He couldn't hide who he was. As a child, his father tried to beat it out of him for years, convincing him that no one would want to be with a weird, OCD freak, but his father was wrong. Plus, he's now in prison for life, so it's hard to believe anything that criminal and murderer says. Stephen's mother had been kind and understanding about his so-called *behavioural issues*. Back then, mental disorders and mental health were not as well understood as they are today, but she'd still accepted him for who he was. Then his father had to go and kill her.

Rachel stirs, rolling over so her back is facing him. Stephen often wakes much earlier than she does and spends the time before his alarm goes off writing his next blog post or article or catching up on the daily events happening around the world. Not that he spends too long reading the news headlines. It's mostly all doom and gloom, but he likes to be aware of what's going on, even if he does feel helpless most of the time.

He clicks on his recent online article in the London Times, a piece about the ongoing struggles of homelessness. He raises his eyebrows at the number of comments that have appeared beneath it since it was published yesterday.

Love your articles, Stephen.

Great writing, dude!

Omg, I loved the Cherry Hollow story. Freaked me out! Couldn't sleep for weeks, thinking some dark creature was after me.

What a load of crap.

When are you going to write something else like the Cherry Hollow story?

Couldn't sleep after the Cherry Hollow story came out. Had nightmares!

Great story!

There's this weird dude who keeps stalking me. Maybe you could investigate him? Might make a good story?

Looking forward to your next creepy investigation. Stephen Mallow is on the case!

There are many more, most of which he skims over. Many of them mention Cherry Hollow or The Creature in some way, highlighting that the masses want more of the weird and unexplained mysteries.

You and me both.

He enjoys writing about real things that are important to him, but he also likes writing about deep and eyebrow-raising stories. The ones which make the reader truly think, not only about themselves, but about the world around them and the possibility of the strange and unseen forces that occur every day. Perhaps the story of Cherry Hollow had been a one off; one in a million. It certainly had changed his life and opened his eyes to the depths of the human mind, how far people would go to hide the truth from others and themselves. Not only that, but it's got people talking about mental health in a much more profound way and he's proud of that.

Stephen takes a deep breath and closes his laptop. It's time to get up and start the day. He and Rachel share a flat in Cherry Hollow and share the paying of the rent. Rachel has moved out of her parent's house to live with Stephen, something her parents had been both thrilled and shocked about. They'd met Stephen and had approved. That was all that mattered.

Stephen leaves the comfort of the double bed, rubbing his eyes as a blinding pain shoots through them. He staggers sideways as a severe head rush washes over him. He reaches for the nearest stable object; the bedside table. Rachel stirs again and looks over her shoulder at him. She's cute in the mornings with her tussled hair and blank expression.

Stephen rights himself once the dizziness has passed. 'One black coffee, coming up,' he says, pulling on his trousers over his boxers.

'Strong,' says Rachel, burying her face in her pillow. She isn't a morning person, the opposite of Stephen who often rises at five o'clock before the sun comes up. He does his best writing before the world surfaces and becomes too loud and obnoxious to function. His brain chemistry means he struggles with too much noise and confusion. It's difficult to compartmentalize his thoughts when there is so much else going on, but he's learning to adjust, alter his actions where he can, but not always. Sometimes he can't alter his actions. Besides, why should he have to change to suit the world? Why can't the world change to help others like him?

Padding barefoot to the kitchen, he flicks on the kettle and prepares the cups. His smart watch beeps with an incoming email. He takes a quick glance, then turns back to the cups. Several seconds pass before his brain catches up with what his eyes have just seen.

It's an email from an anonymous source.

The last anonymous email he'd received had started a chain of spectacular events, eventually leading to solving the case of Cherry Hollow. The young lad who'd sent that particular email was now in a juvenile holding facility for the next few years. Stephen feels bad about that, but it isn't his fault. The kid came forward of his own accord. He is serving his time, then will be allowed to re-enter society. Not everyone is happy about it, nor do they agree, but that's beside the point. The kid made the right choice and is paying his dues. Most full-grown adults wouldn't do the same.

Stephen ignores the email, turning instead to finish making Rachel a cup of coffee, and himself a cup of tea. He places the steaming cup on her bedside table and gently shakes her, knowing full-well that she often falls back to sleep. Normally, it takes several attempts to get her out of bed.

'Go away,' she says, her voice muffled against the pillow.

He shakes her again.

'If you don't stop, I'm going to break up with you.'

He smirks. Usually, he isn't good at understanding sarcasm, but Rachel has taught him a lot since they've been together. Arguments start because Stephen takes everything she says too literally, whereas most of the time she's only joking. But he likes to think he's better at understanding her sense of humour now.

He shakes her once more.

Rachel huffs and turns to look at him. 'Fine. You win. I'm awake.' She shuffles further up the bed so she's propped against the pillows and then picks up her coffee cup. 'Thank you.'

'You're welcome.'

His smart watch pings again. Seriously, another email? He's a popular guy today. But he ignores it, heading to the bathroom for his morning shower instead.

Afterwards, once he's dressed and shaved, he searches for his phone, finding it on the bedside table. Rachel pads into the bathroom, her empty cup on the side. Stephen picks up his phone and reads the anonymous email.

Ah, it's only junk. No threatening message (which he also receives rather frequently thanks to his constant speaking of the truth; people don't always like hearing the truth) or random requests to visit another cursed town. He finds himself mildly disappointed. Every day, he hopes someone will reach out with a mystery weird and creepy enough to tempt him into driving across the country for another adventure. It's not that he isn't interested in solving a missing person's case, but that's a job for the police. No. He wants to solve something the police can't, or something they aren't interested in.

Another email pings into his inbox. This one makes his blood run cold.

After he's read it, he swipes right, sending the email straight into the recycling bin.

That's a problem for another day.

Chapter 3
GRAHAM

The more he stares at the old tree, the faster and harder his heart thumps. His eyesight is far from being twenty-twenty, like in his younger days, but he's certain he isn't hallucinating and it's not a trick of the light. The eerie silhouette of the dark object swinging high among the branches is unmistakable. He's also sober, so can't blame his delusion on alcohol.

Graham stands under the enormous canopy of the tree and looks up, squinting as debris and brown leaves flutter down onto his face, caused by birds landing and taking off from higher in the branches.

Yep.

A body. There's a body hanging from the tree.

Holy shit.

He takes off his flat cap, readjusting his angle so the glare of the morning sun isn't in his eyes because, from where he's standing, the dazzling light is beaming through the leaves and branches, causing the body to glow around the edges.

Wait …

He's wrong.

No, it's not a body.

Relief sweeps over him, almost making his heart stop. The shock to his central nervous system causes a surge of adrenaline, which his aging body isn't used to. He places his hand on the rugged trunk and leans against it, sucking in air as he attempts to get his breathing under control. If there really had been a body hanging, he wouldn't have been able to get up to help them, not fast enough to save their life, anyway. It's impossible to tell how long it's been hanging here.

The point is, it's not a body, so he doesn't have to rush to save anyone.

But what the hell is it doing up there?

What even *is* it?

He stares up among the branches once again, determined to work out the origin of the body-shaped object. It isn't a real person, but it *is* humanoid in shape. Almost like a scarecrow, but crudely made, having no proper shape to the head, arms or legs, but enough of an outline to trick his eyes into thinking it was a person from far away. Just sticks, straw and possibly hay is stuffed into an old overcoat to pad it out. A rope wraps around the top part of the structure.

It looks like …

The scarecrow is hanging from a noose.

Graham scans the immediate area, almost expecting to catch whoever did this hiding and sniggering at the crude joke. Is that what this is? A joke of some sort? Perhaps it's a group of local kids having a bit of fun, but whoever they are needs a hard lesson in what's considered funny. Halloween is only a few days away, so perhaps it has something to do with that. Whatever happened to good old trick or treating? Now, kids go above and beyond with practical jokes and jump scares, determined to get the next viral reaction on their damn phones.

His mind races back to Cherry Hollow and what had happened to *those* kids from twenty-odd years ago. They had also started out just having a bit of *fun*. It hadn't ended well for them, had it?

Death. So much death.

Lives destroyed in a single moment that could never be taken back.

Graham shakes his head, forcing the old memories and dark demons out of his mind; the same ones which keep his mind active in the dead of the night when he's supposed to be asleep. It never bodes well to dwell on the past, and Cherry Hollow is most certainly a part of his past. This isn't like that, he's sure.

Not every small town is full of secrets, lies and twisted human beings …

Then again …

He looks up once more. He can't very well leave it here, can he? What if a poor unsuspecting dog walker or child comes along and spots it? He's surprised the dog walker he ran into earlier hadn't noticed it. Although, it seems to only be visible at certain angles. It's fairly well camouflaged otherwise.

It needs to come down. Graham's made of tough stuff. He can handle a bit of a fright, especially after spending so many years in the police force, but he isn't twenty years old anymore and climbing trees is a thing of the past.

He instantly thinks back to his childhood when he used to climb trees with his four best friends, only one of whom is still alive today.

Olivia Willows.

She's not able to travel and visit him anymore, so he makes the long trek to the Lake District every month to see her instead. Thankfully, he doesn't have to step foot into Cherry Hollow, as she now resides elsewhere. He stays the full two hours he's allocated during visitation time, and they speak about everything from the weather to what the latest news headline is, never running out of topics. They once spent the entire one-hundred-and-twenty minutes swapping their thoughts on the latest political catastrophe going on in the States. There is one topic of conversation they never speak about, and Graham is glad about that because his stomach turns and he feels physically ill whenever he even so much as thinks about it. So, they avoid it.

It's always bittersweet saying goodbye to Olivia. He knows she struggles with the isolation and being away from her family, but her daughters visit regularly with their husbands and children. When her husband, Frank, died last year, she'd coped surprisingly well, but Graham knew she was putting on a strong front like she always did. She has friends where she is, but having inmates as friends isn't the same as having a close childhood friend.

If Olivia could see him now, contemplating whether to scale a tree at the age of fifty-five, she'd laugh her socks off. He knows if he attempts to climb up and bring down the strange scarecrow, he'll most likely fall and injure himself, or worse, break his neck. But he can't very well leave it up there. However, there's a problem: even if he had springs for legs, he wouldn't be able to climb the trunk to reach the more climbable sections. There aren't any footholds. Maybe for a young spritely youth with strength and flexibility on their side, but not for him, someone who struggles to bend down and put on his slippers some mornings. Fifty-five isn't old, but Graham feels as if he's aging quicker than the average person of his age. Perhaps that's what the police force has done to him over the years: slowly caused his body to break down. He just hopes his mind stays intact.

There's no doubt about it. He needs a ladder.

Sighing heavily, he plods back down the hill towards his cottage, grumbling under his breath as his knees niggle with the steep decline. Nevertheless, he fetches an extendable ladder from the garage and a pair of clippers to cut the rope, then begins the arduous trek back up the hill, this time balancing the ladder on his left shoulder.

By the time he reaches the tree for the second time, his legs are on fire, his lungs feel like they may explode, and sweat is trickling down his back. He dumps the ladder against the tree, takes off his cap and wipes his brow with it before stuffing it into his jacket pocket. It may be late autumn but tell that to his body right now.

It takes several attempts to place the ladder in the right position. The tree is uneven, and the slope makes it difficult to centre it solidly, so it won't be at risk of toppling over when he's on it, but eventually he finds the right location, ensuring its feet are dug into the ground, anchoring it. The last thing he needs is for the ladder to slip either while he's on it or when he's up the tree. The idea of having to call the local fire brigade to rescue an old man from a tree is laughable. He's pretty sure if it happens, he'll make the local village newsletter headlines.

He takes a deep breath, cursing himself again, before slowly making the climb up the ladder, the shears in his pocket.

Damn it, the scarecrow is higher up than he first thought. How the hell did someone get it up here in the first place? Surely, it must have taken at least two people to do it.

He reaches the top of the main trunk where there's a natural shelf to stand on, the huge branches stretching in all directions. Even standing on tiptoes, he can barely reach the bottom of the scarecrow, fumbling with the crudely made feet, attempting to get a grip.

He needs to climb higher.

This is ridiculous. A man of his age shouldn't be climbing trees. But he's come this far. With a sigh, he continues.

Graham grabs a nearby branch and hoists himself up, wedging his left foot into a nook in the tree. He is now level with the scarecrow. It's an ugly-looking thing, that's for sure. Its face is made of sticks woven together and it has no eyes. But why does it still feel like it's staring into his soul? This is what nightmares are made of.

Graham holds onto a branch with one hand and reaches up with the other, holding the shears, stretching towards the rope.

Another two inches and he'll reach the top of the rope that's attaching the scarecrow to the overhead branch. His muscles burn with the effort of stretching that far. He's almost there, but positioning the shears on either side of the rope is proving tricky, considering the rope is bound so tight around the branch. He'll have to settle for cutting through the rope below the branch instead, leaving a circle of rope wrapped around it.

Damn it, the shears are almost blunt. He hasn't sharpened them since using them to prune the hedges around his cottage garden a few weeks ago. He uses every ounce of strength and effort to saw away at the rope; his arms stretched to the extreme.

The rope is beginning to fray. Then, with an almighty snap, it breaks, and the scarecrow plummets to the ground, hitting the branches of the tree on the way.

Graham's shoulders sag with relief as he puts away his shears and starts the steady descent back to the ground. The scarecrow lays twisted at an awkward angle beneath, but the overcoat surrounding it holds most of it together, aside from an arm that's broken off during the fall.

His feet touch the ground. He takes a steadying breath, straightening his own jacket before bending to take a closer look at the thing on the ground. The overcoat on the scarecrow is a size medium and has a noticeable rip in the arm seam. Whether that's been caused by the sudden drop, or it was there before, Graham doesn't know. The overcoat is faded too; a very old design, like something you'd find in a fashion museum with garments from a hundred years ago. There's a dark stain on the right cuff and more staining around the collar. He's seen enough to recognise what dried blood looks like.

'Shit,' he mutters, standing up straight. He shouldn't touch it anymore, but since the overcoat isn't on a human body, he decides it's safe to proceed with caution.

He checks the pockets.

In the left one, he pulls out two folded pieces of paper.

Holding his breath, he opens the bigger of the two.

It's a faded drawing in pencil. It's quite beautiful. It's a sketch of the tree, but it looks different than in real life. Slightly smaller, not as many branches. In the corner of the sketch are initials and a date.

JH – Oct 1925

He turns the paper over, but there's nothing else.

Someone drew this a hundred years ago, which explains why the tree looks different than it does today. How fascinating …

Graham opens the second piece of folded paper and reads the headline, his eyes widening.

At that exact moment, a cold wind sweeps across the top of the hill, rustling the brown leaves in the huge tree branches above. It sends a cascade of them upon Graham's head, and a familiar icy tingle makes its home at the back of his neck.

Chapter 4
STEPHEN

He works for three hours straight, barely moving a muscle, to get his latest freelance article written and sent off to the newspaper. That's the thing about Stephen; he has a highly focused, super attentive mind. Sometimes, it works to his advantage, and he can be the most organised person on the planet, complete all his jobs and goals before midday and still have enough focus and drive to start a new project. Other times, however, it can work against him and cause him no end of stress and headaches. During these times, he can't focus on anything for longer than a few minutes, or he'll get to roughly ninety percent through a project, lose focus and have to start something else. It's a quirk he knows drives his girlfriend insane.

A constant battle is always raging inside his head, and it often feels like he's being pushed and pulled in opposite directions. His diagnosed ADHD tendencies means he struggles to zone in on something, jumping from one idea to another at the drop of a hat while his OCD forces him to make everything perfect before moving on.

The political piece he's working on is going to cause a bit of a stir, but that's why people read his work. He writes things that are difficult to accept and digest. He writes about topics that others would shy away from for fear of causing a tidal wave. He says it like it is because how else is he supposed to say it? He's a man who sticks by his beliefs, no matter how uncomfortable they make people feel.

He closes his laptop at exactly twelve o'clock, leans back in his chair and stretches his spine. With an afternoon of freedom in front of him, he decides to turn his attention to research instead. He needs to find something to occupy his mind when it's not in work mode. He wants another case to investigate, but it can't be merely any missing person or mystery. He receives dozens of emails every day from people, reaching out to him for help in solving a multitude of cases, ranging from the disappearance of their children to the mystery of who keeps stealing their bins.

Stephen's not interested in any of them.

None of the stories have jumped out at him, not like the Cherry Hollow case did. Is he chasing some illusive story that doesn't exist? Searching for a high that may never come again? He hopes not.

After eating, Stephen rolls up his shirt sleeves and slurps his coffee, his second of the day, pulling his laptop closer from across the table. He types various keywords into the search engine. Oh yes, there's plenty out there to choose from, but to him, it's like searching for a needle in a haystack. But he'll know when he sees it.

The mystery of the cursed lake sounds promising. Apparently, dozens of tourists disappear every year while taking boats out to row across to the large island situated at the centre. He reads on, his breath catching in his throat when he sees the words *curse*, *bodies* and *witchcraft*.

The article is from a year ago, but as he reaches the bottom, he realises his mistake. It's a goddamn clickbait article, designed to lure in pathetic readers starved for some sort of juicy piece of news that has been warped and twisted into a story, delicious enough to keep them reading to the end. Exactly the type of articles he used to write.

Stephen tuts and scrolls to the next page of results.

A headline stands out.

Where do souls go when a person dies?

It's an interesting concept that has always fascinated him. Death, morbid as it may be, is fascinating in its own way. He does like the idea that souls stick around, though. Not like ghosts, because there's no such thing, but maybe some form of the human spirit remains on Earth even after death.

His phone buzzes on the table, disrupting his train of thought. Usually, he turns it over while he's working, ensuring it's on silent, but during lunch he's forgotten to do that, so the noise jolts him out of his focus zone.

It's the call he's been avoiding.

Sighing, Stephen answers. 'Hello, Stephen Mallow speaking.'

'Good afternoon, Mr Mallow. This is Jenny from Westmorland General Hospital. Doctor Simmons has asked me to call you to organise a time for you to come in to talk about your test results, which you should have received by email. The first available appointment is Friday at quarter past one. Will that be suitable?'

Stephen's heart thuds wildly in his chest. 'Erm ... sure. Fine.'

'That's perfect, Mr Mallow. I'll send you a confirmation email with the details.'

'Okay, thanks.'

'Goodbye, Mr Mallow.'

'Yeah ... bye.' He places the phone face down on the table after turning it to silent.

Great. Now he has to re-focus all over again.

Where was he?

A dull ache settles behind his eyes, then he feels the tickling inside his nostril. Slowly, a small drip of blood trickles down to his top lip. He takes a clean tissue from his pocket and wipes it away, tossing the tissue into the bin on his way to the coffee machine.

Chapter 5
GRAHAM

Graham stares at the crumpled poster in his hand; the one he found in the pocket of the scarecrow's overcoat, along with the sketch of the tree from a hundred years ago. It's a poster about a missing teenage girl called Sophia Hammel, who disappeared on the twenty-ninth of October, 2015.

Ten years ago, almost to the day.

There's no photo of her though and the poster is very crudely made. It looks as if no effort was put into making it. In fact, it's not even printed. It's hand-written and holds next to no details about the girl, nothing about what she looks like or what she was last seen wearing. Just her name, the day she went missing and that's it.

A horribly familiar ache forms in his gut, similar to when he found out about the missing teenage boy from Cherry Hollow all those years ago. Not a time he likes to think about. It's odd that he's lived here almost a whole year and this is the first time he's heard about any missing teenager from the area. That is, if she is from the area. He doesn't know yet.

Graham puts both the pieces of paper into his own pocket, then drags the scarecrow and the ladder down the hill, dumping both inside his garage. He lays the scarecrow down

on its side, but those oddly-shaped eye sockets give him pause
…

He shudders, quickly turning away from the eerie creature.

By the time he's done, he's drenched in sweat and feeling a little wobbly, so decides to skip his long morning walk and head into the village to grab his morning paper instead; another daily ritual of his. One he's come to enjoy for more than one reason.

He pushes open the door of the village newsagent, the bell dinging above his head. It's one of those run-down buildings that's crammed with far too many items, the shelves over-crowded with a mishmash of products. Graham's noticed that it's the only shop in the village. He can post items here, buy the paper, purchase small amounts of necessities such as bread and milk, and even scan papers or use the printers. Truly, a jack of all trades type of shop and since it's the only one of its kind in the village, he supposes that's why it's still doing well.

'Ah, *bore da*, Graham,' says the lady behind the counter, Karen; the owner of the shop. She told him once that she's worked here since she was fifteen and Graham wasn't sure whether to be impressed or feel sorry for her.

'*Bore da*. How are you, Karen?' he asks, handing over a copy of *The Guardian* to be scanned from the pile beside the front counter.

'Can't complain, although now the colder weather's here, my knees haven't got the memo. All they do is complain.'

Graham hands over £1.30 in cash, silently scoffing at the price, but he's too far gone to stop reading it now. It's part of his routine. 'Ah, yes, I'm with you there.' He's already feeling the after effects of his exertions this morning.

Transaction complete, Karen smiles at him, flipping her hair over her left shoulder. They play this game every morning. She's a little younger than him, he thinks, but not by a lot. Over the past few months, he's enjoyed getting to know her, swapping pleasantries and moaning about the weather, but it never goes beyond that. He doesn't even know her last name. It's never come up. That's fine with him because he's not interested in starting up a relationship, not concerned about having a girlfriend, or making a new friend of any kind for that matter. He doesn't attend the local village meetings, nor does he join in with the gossip he knows spreads around. It's a small village. People talk. He just doesn't care. He's never been one for getting involved in the local community, despite living in Cherry Hollow for his entire life until he moved away.

But there's something about Karen that ignites a very tiny spark inside of him, something he never thought was possible again, not after having his heart broken so many years ago. He's fifty-five years old, damn it, far too old to be thinking about such trivial things, such as how the morning sunlight beaming through the window highlights her naturally auburn hair, picking up the flecks of grey and making them dazzle like streaks of silver.

'How's your vegetable garden coming along?' she asks.

'Coming to the end of the growing period now,' he replies as he puts his left hand in his pocket. His fingers brush the two pieces of paper he found earlier. He wonders whether he should enquire after Sophia Hammel or tell Karen about the scarecrow he found in the tree this morning, but if he did that, he'd be here longer than he planned. Really, he just wants to get home and read the paper. A creature of habit is Graham Williams.

'Have a good day, Karen,' he says, tipping his cap.

'Oh, Graham, will you be joining the committee meeting tonight to talk about the new prospects and ideas for the village?' Her face reddens as she tucks a strand of hair behind her ear.

The bell above the door pings, followed by a couple of young lads who make a beeline straight for the snacks and energy drinks.

'Oh, er … I wasn't planning on it.' Village committees and the like have never been his type of scene. Back in Cherry Hollow, he'd avoided them like the plague, especially since most of the committee consisted of a gaggle of middle-aged women who mostly used the opportunity to gossip and drink copious amounts of tea during the morning meetings, and something a little stronger during the evening ones.

'I think it might be a good opportunity for you to voice your opinion on what you want to see happen in the village. I'll be there … and … um, I'm making my famous banana bread.'

'Famous, huh?' He doesn't want to burst her bubble and admit he's never heard of her so-called famous banana bread. 'Then that's sealed the deal for me,' he adds.

'Great. I think there's talk about cutting down that big old tree by yours.'

This piques his attention. 'There is? Good God, why would anyone want to chop down such a grand old majestic tree?'

Karen shrugs. 'It's been there a long time.'

'All the more reason to leave it alone.'

'The branches are rotting. There have been a few accidents over the years.'

Graham frowns. 'Hmm, well I for one will be voting to stop the destruction of the tree. It's a landmark of the village, surely?'

'I suppose so,' she replies with a sigh, 'but it does have a horrible history attached to it.'

'Which is?'

'You haven't heard?'

Graham shakes his head. The boys who entered earlier are now standing behind him, waiting for him to move. Graham doesn't like to be rushed.

'Would you tell me about the tree tonight at the meeting?' he asks, taking a step to the side to allow the boys to approach the counter, their arms laden with junk food and drinks.

'Of course. How about you meet me at five before it starts at six?'

'It's a date ...' His face instantly warms at his faux pau. 'I mean ... see you then ... then ...'

Karen giggles. 'I'll see you later. It's at the village hall.'

'Er ... *diolch*.' He holds up the paper awkwardly, stumbling over the Welsh word for thank you. He waves goodbye to Karen, who smiles at him while simultaneously scanning the teenager's items.

'*Diolch a hwyl fawr*,' she replies.

Graham walks home, the prospect of attending the village committee meeting already causing him to break out in a cold sweat, but perhaps it will be good to officially join in with the locals.

Or not.

He's mainly going to find out more about the tree, and why the hell anyone would want to destroy it. Plus, he may even discover the reason why he found a scarecrow hidden in its branches this morning. Hell, maybe it's a weird village tradition.

It wouldn't be the first time he's encountered one.

Chapter 6
SOPHIA

Bethgelert, Wales, 2015

Living in the darkest depths of Wales where there were three times as many sheep as there were people was hard work at the best of times, but add on to that the fact I was sixteen years old and I had myself a problem. Granted, I had friends at school, but to be honest, I was finding myself hanging out with them less and less as the years went by. It was a tiny school with only twelve students in my class, so the chances of finding anyone who I connected with was slim at best. The other girls my age (of which there were only seven) were more into boys, make-up and selfies whereas I preferred to sit under the massive tree on the hill opposite Rosemore Cottage - the cottage my dad owned and rented out - and draw.

The tree was an infamous attraction in the small village of Bethgelert; the village where I was born and raised. Well, it was infamous to the residents, but hardly anyone who lived outside of the community knew about it. That was what I liked about it the most. The tree held a story few people knew about. It all started with the death of a young farmer ninety years ago. A young farmer who just happened to be my great, great, great grandfather.

John Hammel.

In the years since his passing, the tree had become synonymous with death and bad luck. Several years ago, a bunch of kids climbed it and one fell and broke his leg. One time, like fifty or so years ago, way before I was born, it was struck by lightning and a massive branch fell down. Luckily, there was no one around at the time, so no one was hurt, but basically, as the legend goes, if you climb the tree or spend time near the tree, chances are you're going to die a very painful and horrible death. Or something along those lines. The legend seems to morph every few years.

However, I was still alive, and 'd spent the best part of the last decade visiting the tree every day, so … I assumed I was safe from the "curse" or whatever. Apparently, lots of people have died near the tree, even before John Hammel hung himself in its branches. There are village documents going back hundreds of years, across several generations, detailing the deaths. I haven't seen any of these documents, so I couldn't say if they were true, but sometimes, when I leaned against the gnarly trunk, I felt a pulse, like the tree was alive with the souls trapped inside.

I believed John Hammel used the tree to speak to me because whenever I put pen to paper, my drawings and sketches would take on a life of their own. That was the funny thing. In class, when I was asked to draw pictures, I sucked. Like, I *really* sucked at drawing. But sat underneath the canopy of the tree where my great, great, great grandfather died, I drew the most exquisite sketches. I couldn't explain it. It was my little secret, though. There was no point in trying to explain it to my dad or the teachers because they wouldn't understand, or they'd think I was nuts to think that the soul of a dead guy used my body to sketch pictures.

Anyway, I had my own sketchbook, a set of pencils my dad got me for my last birthday, and my own vivid imagination. What more could a girl want? Other than maybe a friend to share it with, but I was getting used to spending time by myself outside of school. I had the tree and the spirit of my dead relative channelling me whenever I drew beneath it, so … I was good.

My dad never understood where my love of drawing came from. No one else in the family liked to draw, apart from John, but he lived so long ago that it made no sense as to why I would inherit his passion. Dad said it wasn't a useful skill to have, especially as the only daughter of a farmer. I knew for a fact my dad was disappointed I wasn't a boy, so I could carry on the family name. But who said I was even going to get married and take someone else's name? Besides, I had no plans of marrying a *boy* anyway. Or maybe I did. I hadn't decided yet. I did love a boy once when I was seven, but then realised girls were much more attractive, but the girls at my school had personalities reminiscent of sparkle fairies, whereas I'd have preferred it if they were more like Lara Croft, my video game heroine.

With my sketchbook and pencils tucked under my arm, I opened the front door to walk the mile-and-a-half to the tree. We lived on the other side of the village from Rosemore Cottage on a smallholding called Blackberry Farm, but Dad still owned the area around the cottage and the tree.

Barney, our new sheepdog puppy, came bounding from the kitchen as soon as he heard the front door open. He still had a lot to learn with regards to herding sheep and learning the ropes, but he was the cutest thing, full of life and energy. Technically, he belonged to Dad because he needed him to pull his weight with the livestock on the farm, but Barney had taken a liking to me, following me wherever I went.

I bent down and tickled Barney's ears. 'You want to come with me, huh? You sure your little legs are up for it?'

Barney yapped his response.

'Where are you off to?'

I turned, casually plastering a sweet smile to my face. 'I'm going to draw at the tree for a bit. Can I take Barney?'

My dad appeared round the corner, dressed in his farmer's jacket and flat cap. 'What's with you and that bloody tree?'

I shrugged, pursing my lips. 'It's a cool tree.'

'It's a death tree, is what it is.'

'Yes, yes, I know the story, Dad. My great, great, great grandfather hung himself from the tree when he was twenty years old like ninety years ago, dooming the entire village to some weird, dark curse or whatever.'

My dad scoffed, narrowing his eyes at me. 'You should have more respect for the curse, my girl, or it'll come after you next. You spend so much time there, I'm surprised it hasn't got you yet.'

I wasn't worried about the curse. Maybe it was because I didn't worry about it that it left me alone. Besides, only the village committee members seemed concerned about the tree and its curse. The last family to be subject to the supposed 'curse' was the Davies family, roughly five years ago when all of their livestock tragically died of some weird disease in the space of two days.

'So … can I go to the tree and draw or not?'

'It's going to be dark soon. The sun is setting in the next hour.'

'All the more reason for me to hurry. I want to draw the sunset.'

'Fine, but be back by nine. Leave the dog here. You still have homework to do.' He looked at me for several seconds, then sighed. 'Would it kill you to grow your hair longer? You look like a boy.'

I grabbed a cap off the hook nearby and put it on, then waited until he turned his back on me before rolling my eyes.

I often allowed his insults to wash over me because I didn't care what he thought about me. I thought he'd be pleased I looked more like a boy than a girl, but perhaps my larger-than-average boobs offended him or something. There was no hiding those bad boys. Or girls. Whatever.

Saying goodbye to Barney, I jogged across the village towards the hill, my drawing pad tucked under my left arm. I didn't want to miss the spectacular sunset.

Chapter 7
GRAHAM

Graham's day drags, mainly because he's counting down the minutes before he has to leave to walk to the village hall to meet Karen before the town meeting at six. And he's not counting the minutes in a good way, like a little kid would do on the run up to Christmas, but in a very bad way, like a doomsday clock counting down to oblivion. It's not that he doesn't want to converse with Karen, because he does, but it's the whole talking to people in general he finds challenging these days. Perhaps it's because he spent so many years in the police force, constantly having to speak to people, trying to get the truth from them, to figure out what they're hiding behind their words.

Nowadays, he's all peopled out.

He knows how his old friend, Mr Mallow – or old nemesis, depending on how he looks at it – feels when in a room full of strangers. Graham has made many public speeches in his time, so talking with the lovely Karen shouldn't be a problem for him, but it is. Or at least, it will be. Because he knows she has an ulterior motive for meeting him early. She thinks it's some sort of date and that's because he made the absolute blunder of saying the word *date* during their last encounter.

Damn it. Even at his age, he still turns into a blubbering mess around a pretty woman. All he wants from Karen this evening is some information, but he also doesn't want to push her away and cause her to think he's not interested because he is, but just … not … right now.

Does that make sense? Graham's not sure.

He gets to the village hall bang on five and tries to open the double doors. Locked. He steps back, looking up at the tall building. Like the rest of the buildings in the village, it's showing its age with peeling paint on the doors and window frames, not to mention the crumbling bricks at the corners. The sign on the front of the hall says "Bethgelert Village Hall: Founded in 1875".

'Graham!'

The sound of Karen's voice startles him. He turns to see her waving at him from across the road. She walks up to him, twirling a set of keys around her fingers.

'Punctual as always,' she says.

Graham says nothing as she unlocks the doors. They enter side by side. The inside of the hall is no more impressive than the outside. Tired. Worn. Bland.

'Since you're here, Graham, would you mind giving me a hand putting out the chairs?'

'I didn't realise I was here to work,' he replies with what he hopes is pure comic timing. Apparently, it is because Karen chuckles as she switches on the lights, blasting the entire space into a yellow haze. 'So,' he finally says, once he knows where the chairs need to be placed. 'What can you tell me about the tree?'

'The Hanging Tree,' says Karen.

'The … I'm sorry, the *what*?'

'How long have you lived here, Graham?'

Graham places a chair next to another. 'Ten months or so.'

'And in that time you've never heard about The Hanging Tree, despite living opposite it?'

'I guess not.'

Karen shrugs. 'I suppose it's not surprising considering its history. People don't like to talk about it much. It carries with it a rather morbid topic of suicide.'

'With a name like The Hanging Tree, I'd be surprised if it didn't come with some sort of dark history.' He doesn't mean to sound insensitive, but if Karen is offended, she doesn't let on. 'What's the story then?'

'A hundred years ago, a local farm boy hung himself in the tree. He was only twenty. The locals couldn't understand the reason. His family were in shock, but refused to talk about it or draw any attention to the fact he took his own life. Over the past hundred years, as most stories do over time, the story has been distorted and warped and now no one really knows what happened. The residents have changed it to suit them. They started saying that the boy was evil, that his whole family were evil and that his death kickstarted a curse that's been sweeping through the village, attacking all the founding families.'

'The founding families?'

'Yes, there are several families who have lived in Bethgelert for many years, going back centuries, including the Hammel family. John Hammel was the boy who died.'

At this point, Graham looks up from straightening a chair so it's level with the one next to it. 'Did you say Hammel?'

Karen blinks several times. 'Yes, that's right.'

Graham wants to ask her more about the curse, but he needs to follow this possible lead. 'Do you know anyone by the name of Sophia Hammel?'

Karen's eyes widen. Graham's heart races at the prospect of finding some answers. 'You know who she is?'

'Certainly. She's Frank Hammel's daughter. Frank used to own Rosemore Cottage; your humble abode, I believe.'

'Used to?'

'It's changed hands a few times in the past ten years, but yes, Frank used to own it. The Hammel family lived there for generations, but eventually Frank rented it out as a holiday home before it was bought and sold several times. Then, you came along. Frank suffered through some tough times financially, so he was forced to sell it. It's not easy running a farm nowadays.'

Graham scratches his chin, running his fingers over his bristly beard. 'Was Sophia ever found?'

Karen's eyes narrow this time. 'Found?'

'I'm led to believe she went missing ten years ago.'

Karen stares at him for a moment, then bursts out laughing. 'Goodness me, Graham. Whatever gave you that idea?'

He's aware their topic of The Hanging Tree is long forgotten, but this puzzle of Sophia Hammel is enough to keep him pressing on. He delves his hand into his jacket pocket, ready to bring out the poster to show her, but something stops him. He's not sure why he doesn't tell her about the makeshift poster. Call it an ex-detective's intuition.

'No reason,' he says. 'Does she live around here then?'

Karen's eyes flick left and right and Graham notices a slight flush creep up her neck. He was in the police force long enough to learn how to read people, and this woman is nervous.

'She, uh … no.'

'Are you sure about that?'

'Quite sure.' She attempts a smile, but her jaw quivers. 'It was a difficult time for her family.'

'Why is that?'

Karen gulps. Graham can't help but notice that their job of lining up the chairs for the village meeting has also been forgotten. They're standing in the middle of the hall, facing each other.

'Ten years ago. She … well, she started saying some strange things and the village didn't like it.'

'The village?'

'The village committee, yes.'

'Who runs this village committee now?'

'Mostly the founding families. Frank is the man in charge, mostly, but Graham, I'm not sure you should be sticking your nose into this. Sorry, I don't mean to sound rude and insensitive, but Frank Hammel, Sophia's father, went through a very difficult time with his daughter, even before ten years ago when his … well, it's not my place to say. I shouldn't even be telling you this.'

Graham looks around. 'There's no one here but us, Karen. Tell me, if Sophia isn't missing and she doesn't live with her father in the village, then *where* is she?'

Karen bites her bottom lip. 'Um, you know, I'm not …' At that moment, the double doors to the village hall spring open and several people walk in with smiles across their faces, happily chatting, but when they see Graham and Karen standing in the middle of the hall, they freeze like rabbits caught in headlights.

One is an older man, roughly Graham's age, and he's wearing a flat cap and a tweed blazer. Very smartly dressed.

Karen snaps out of her trance and positively beams with joy at having a distraction. 'Goodness, we've got carried away, haven't we?' She starts placing the chairs out again, avoiding Graham's gaze.

The older gentleman in tweed steps forward, his hand outstretched. '*Noswaith dda*. It's about time you finally joined the village committee meeting, Mr Williams.'

Graham shakes the man's hand. His grip is firm. Maybe too firm for a friendly gesture. The men lock eyes and Graham can't quite work out whether he's about to get his head bitten off or invited into the fold.

'Yes, well, Karen promised me there would be banana bread.'

Karen gasps. 'Oh goodness, I've forgotten the blasted banana bread.'

Graham lets out a little chuckle.

'I'll just quickly nip back home and get it. I only live up the road.'

'Oh, Karen, please don't think that ...'

'Nonsense, Graham. I made it for tonight's meeting. It's my own fault I forgot it. I won't be a moment. I'll leave you in the capable hands of ... Mr Hammel.' She says the name firmly, without emphasising it, but she widens her eyes at Graham, who notices and nods his thanks.

So ... this is Frank Hammel, Sophia's father.

But clearly, he's a popular man because Graham doesn't get the chance to speak to him alone at all. Mr Hammel is soon swept into another conversation, so Graham finishes placing the chairs, by which time several more people have entered the hall and introduced themselves to Graham. Karen returns with her banana bread and everyone mingles, the volume in the hall gradually increasing until Frank Hammel's voice echoes above it.

'Ladies and Gentlemen, please all take your seats and the meeting can begin.'

Graham isn't sure what to expect from the meeting, but he sits and listens quietly, memorising people's faces. Despite having lived here a while, he doesn't know everyone by name, so it's certainly useful to hear people talk.

Frank appears to be the leader, guiding the discussions and topics to keep them on track. There is talk of expanding the village market square, which is met with a resounding yes, and there is also a discussion about what is happening with the empty shop in the centre of the village. No one seems to have the spare cash to rent it out, which doesn't surprise Graham. He's not sure how farmers get by as it is. He stays quiet and no one asks him for his opinion. But then, the tree is mentioned and there's a low murmur of disapproving voices when Frank explains how dangerous it is.

At this point, Graham raises his hand. The whole room turns and looks at him. 'If the tree is so dangerous,' he says, 'then why is it not cordoned off?'

A few murmurs follow his question. It's Frank who answers. 'We did try that several years ago, Mr Williams, but unfortunately a lot of kids around here still continue to climb it. You must have noticed since you live opposite the hill.'

'I can't say I've noticed kids climbing it, but I did find something interesting hanging in it this morning.'

The whole room descends into silence, like the mute button has been switched on. Graham holds Frank's stern gaze. Karen is sitting just off to the side of him, so he's not sure what she's doing, but he's assuming she's regretting her decision to invite him along right about now.

'You're talking about the scarecrow, I assume,' says Frank.

'Yes, I am.'

'I wouldn't worry about that, Mr Williams. It's a harmless prank the local kids like to play on the run up to Halloween.'

Graham thinks of the papers he found on the scarecrow this morning, burning a hole in his jacket pocket; one of which mentions Frank's daughter by name. It seems an odd Halloween prank to play, but he stays quiet, and listens to the rest of the village meeting.

There is talk of destroying the tree, but the majority of the people want to keep it. As Graham thought, it's an ancient monument of sorts, part of the village's history. Frank agrees to not have it cut down yet. Every once and a while, one of the residents shoots Graham a dark look, but he doesn't open his mouth again, and then, when the meeting draws to a close, Frank Hammel leaves quickly, exiting out the back door of the hall.

Graham says goodbye to several people, including Karen, though she doesn't seem as friendly as before. He grabs a slice of banana bread on his way out, biting into it as he walks back home.

Damn, that's good banana bread.

Chapter 8
STEPHEN

Wednesday passes by somewhat slowly. His research continues leading him to dead ends or random online chatrooms that he quickly exits when things get a little too weird. He's not into cults, murder plots or dark magic; doesn't believe in any of it. To Stephen, there's always a rational explanation for anything, whether it be a demon sighting or the myth of the Loch Ness Monster.

There is a potential case over in Ireland that holds his interest for longer than most, but after reaching out to the journalist who wrote the article, he finds out it's merely a hoax to draw in readers. Not his intention. He needs the real deal.

Rachel returns from work at eight, always a late shift at The Cherry Tree, the one and only hotel in Cherry Hollow, the place where they formally met and had their first date. Stephen likes to cook dinner, ready for when she walks in, along with a glass of wine waiting on the side.

Stephen opens the fridge and scans the shelves for ingredients he can throw together to form a healthy meal. He and Rachel like to eat healthy, preferring fresh vegetables to ready meals, but he hasn't been shopping since last week, so the shelves are looking a little bare. Didn't Rachel say she was doing the shopping this week? Perhaps he's misunderstood her. He's happy to go shopping and is also happy for Rachel to do it, but doing the shopping together is his idea of hell. The woman can't pack items into a bag to save her life, and she meanders up and down the aisles as if she's lost, casually perusing items as if she has no idea what she's there to buy. He, however, has a pre-prepared list which has everything he needs in the order he's going to walk down the aisle, which means he gets everything from the shelves in the right sequence so he can pack the bags in a correct and logical manner at the end. It just makes sense. Complete and utter perfect sense. The last time they shopped together, he ended up walking out and meeting her at the car. Sometimes, it's better to walk away than create an argument he knows he can't win.

There's fresh salmon in the fridge that needs to be eaten today, so salmon it is. He makes a quick spicy crumb and rubs it into the fish before putting it aside to allow the spices to infuse for an hour.

Next, he prepares basmati rice, which won't take long to cook, then chops up the last of the tender stem broccoli, ready to steam at the last minute. A quick and easy meal that Rachel is sure to enjoy after a long day stuck behind a reception desk answering calls.

Right on time, at eight, Rachel walks in and hangs up her thick coat, scarf and hat on the pegs by the door. Stephen fills her glass with wine and puts it on the kitchen worktop.

'Something smells good,' she says as she kisses him hello. 'Good day? Did you get any further with your research?'

Stephen shakes his head. 'Not really, no.'

'No creepy creatures lurking about then?'

Stephen allows his mind a few moments to understand her quip. 'No,' he says.

Rachel chuckles as she picks up her wine glass. 'That's a relief.'

Stephen flips the fish using the tongs in the frying pan. The aroma wafts into the air and the oil sizzles in the pan. 'Indeed.'

'Although, I bet you're wishing there was because you need a new story. Am I right?'

'You are. You know me so well.'

'And yet there's one thing I can't work out.'

'Oh?'

'Anything you want to tell me?'

Stephen puts down the tongs. This is one of those times he wishes his brain worked the same way as other peoples'. She clearly wants him to tell her something specific, but he has no idea what. It could be any number of things.

'You look very lovely today,' he says instead.

Rachel's expression doesn't change. Clearly, it isn't that. Her forehead furrows and the grip on her wine glass seems a little too tight. He's never been good at reading other people's emotions, but she certainly isn't happy.

Rachel takes a sip of wine. 'Don't try and avoid the subject. Why do you keep changing your pillowcase every morning?'

Okay, he certainly isn't expecting *that* question. He thought he'd been doing a good job of hiding it. Plus, it's not *every* morning. He hasn't had an overnight nosebleed for several days now, so why is she bringing it up today?

Rachel sips more wine, followed by some strong eye contact.

Stephen avoids her gaze. Eye contact is another of those normal human actions he finds difficult. 'Ah, yes, I can see why you're confused.'

Rachel sighs. 'Yes, confused is right, Stephen.'

'I've had a few nosebleeds. That's all.'

'When did they start?'

Stephen stares. He opens his mouth to answer, but the words get stuck somewhere along the way between his brain and his mouth. His brain can't quite connect the dots in time, but eventually, he can speak, albeit at a slower pace than usual. 'I'm not sure. Maybe ... six months ago.'

'Six months!' Rachel takes a breath. 'Why didn't you tell me?'

Stephen turns off the hob, allowing the salmon to sizzle and rest. He isn't prepared for this moment. In fact, he's done everything he can think of to avoid it, yet, despite having a higher-than-average IQ, he's failed to remember Rachel is a very intelligent woman.

'I'm sorry,' he says. 'But I didn't see the point in concerning you with it at the start. It happened so randomly. There was no discernible pattern to them.'

'And what's your excuse now? I've been hanging up pillowcases to dry every other day. You've been washing them without mentioning it, which means you're trying to hide it from me on purpose. I am your girlfriend. You don't think I deserve to know if my boyfriend is unwell?'

Stephen's head snaps up from staring at the countertop. 'I'm not unwell. Do I look unwell?'

'That's not the point, Stephen!'

'It doesn't concern you, that's all.'

Rachel clamps her mouth shut, turning away from him. He watches as her body rises and falls in time with deep breaths. 'Fine,' she finally says. 'If you don't want to tell me, then I'm not going to force you, but just remember something, Stephen.' At this point, she turns around and looks at him with softer eyes, slightly watery. 'I love you. I am here for you, but if you don't feel the same way, then please tell me now.'

Stephen frowns. How has she got the idea in her head that he doesn't love her? The female mind is a complicated thing to understand. 'Of course I love you,' he says. 'What does me not telling you about my nosebleeds have anything to do with whether I do or do not love you?'

'Then why haven't you told me you've been having nosebleeds? Have you spoken to a doctor?'

'What's that got to do with my love for you?' he asks again, purposefully ignoring her second question.

Rachel sighs. 'You really don't understand how relationships work, do you?' He knows she doesn't mean it as an insult, but it still stings.

'I told you I struggle to comprehend a lot of things, including the complexity of relationships and how I'm supposed to react. I just ... didn't see the need to tell you until I knew more. I didn't want to worry you, so I kept it to myself. You can understand that, can't you?'

'To a certain extent, yes. You have spoken to a doctor then?' Rachel takes a few steps closer, grasping his upper arms with her delicate hands. His skin tingles and the outline of her body blurs as he stares into her eyes.

'Yes, I have.' He stops.

'And?'

'I've had tests run and I am due to find out the results on Friday.'

'How are you feeling about them? The results, I mean?'

'I don't know. I haven't really been thinking about it.'

Rachel leans forward and wraps her arms around him, squeezing tight. Stephen hugs her back, relaxing into her warm embrace. He loves this woman so damn much, and his inability to understand simple human emotions and interactions is slowly ruining his chance to be in her life indefinitely. He's come to terms with his differences years ago, but when it threatens to push people away, people he cares about, he curses himself, wishing he were like everyone else.

'I'm sorry,' he says again. Should he ask her to come with him to the doctor's appointment? Is that the done thing? But does he want her to come with him? What if it's nothing and he's making a fuss over something that has a simple explanation?

'You can come with me to get the results if you like,' says Stephen.

'Do you want me to come with you?'

Oh God. It's a trap. Back out. Back out now.

Stephen holds his breath as he says, 'Not really.' Brutal honesty. Women like that, right?

Rachel smiles. 'It's fine. Just call me straight after though, yeah?'

'Okay.' Stephen nods. 'Let's eat.'

'Great, I'm starving.'

Chapter 9
GRAHAM

The next morning, he wakes up, aching like he's run a marathon and with a slight stomach ache from devouring the banana bread too fast. It had been a big slice. He really needs to do something about his overall health and diet. The local doctor has warned him that if he doesn't start increasing his exercise and decreasing his bad eating habits, he's at risk of heart disease, diabetes and all those other old-age conditions that he's sure are right around the corner, like a creature waiting to jump out at him in the night.

Eating cheap, quick food and drinking whisky every night isn't helping his mental state either. Still, he'd rather die early than have his mind waste away and forget everything that's happened in his life. At least he won't be leaving behind a wife or children who'd be forced to watch him decay and forget they ever existed. Graham isn't sure why he's become so morbid with his thoughts lately. Death is inevitable, he knows that, but he isn't *that* old. Hell, technically he's still too young to retire. What's the age of retirement now for a man? Sixty-five or sixty-six? It seems to go up every damn year. He still has a decade of work ahead of him. Maybe he needs to get himself a part-time job to keep his mind and body occupied because ten years is a long time. Plenty of years left, right?

Wrong. Not if he keeps eating crap and drinking whisky like it's water.

Last night, after he'd walked back from the village meeting, full of banana bread and overloaded with more questions than when he arrived, he sunk a couple tumblers of his favourite tipple as he stared absentmindedly into the roaring fire in his lounge. He always drinks his whisky with two ice cubes. No more. No less. He'd listened to the wind and rain pelt against the window next to him and it had lulled him into a deep sleep.

Woken with a start, hours later, he'd then plodded to his bedroom and passed out.

No wonder his neck aches this morning, having slept awkwardly. Or perhaps it was the previous morning's adventures up the tree that have caused his muscles and joints to seize up like a tin man in a rainstorm; another delightful reminder of his aging body. He doesn't want to imagine what he'll be like in ten or twenty years if he keeps going at this rate.

As he stands at his kitchen window, stretching his neck and back and waiting for the kettle to boil, he stares at the hill ahead, at the tree, thinking about what Frank and Karen had divulged about it last night.

The Hanging Tree.

A morbid name for such a spectacular living monument.

The rising sun is barely visible over the brow, sending a blend of orange and red cascading across the sky. Wow, it's a beautiful morning, made even more glorious by the glistening dew on the grass.

The kettle clicks off, but Graham doesn't make a move to pick it up because his eyes catch sight of something at the top of the hill.

No. Never mind. It's nothing.

His eyes are still puffy and full of sleep, and he's yet to officially wake up. He's seeing things.

He has no plans for today, other than to dig over part of the vegetable plot that's now mostly weeds. Clearing it now, pulling up the roots, will mean it's in the best condition come spring for him to be able to start afresh. He also wants to find out more about Sophia Hammel, but after sleeping on it, he wonders if diving headfirst into another small-town mystery is the best use of his time these days. He's over that now. He's got nothing left to prove.

Wait …

There's something in the tree again …

No way. It's not possible.

Without grabbing an extra layer to keep him warm, he yanks open the back door and makes his way up the hill towards the tree. His breath dances on the icy wind which rips around his body, but he isn't cold. Not yet.

He keeps his eyes fixed on the tree as he walks and the closer he gets, the more he doesn't believe what he's seeing.

Another scarecrow hangs in the same place as yesterday morning, dressed in the same overcoat. There's no frayed rope around the tree branch where he cut it yesterday. It's like it has been there the whole time and he never removed it.

But it isn't possible. Because he did. Remove it. Didn't he?

This time, yesterday morning, he had cut the scarecrow from its rope, dragged it down the hill and stored it in his garage, ready to chuck on the next bonfire he lit. He usually has one every few months to burn through the rubbish and cuttings from the garden. The scarecrow had spent the night locked in his garage, along with the ladder and numerous other boxes and items he has in there.

Yet here it is. Back in the tree.

Graham reaches the bottom of the trunk and cranes his head backwards. He then turns and scans the horizon, looking for anyone passing by, but it seems no one is up at this time of morning, not yet anyway. Someone is playing a trick on him. Some local kids are pulling a prank on an old man, just like Frank Hammel had said. Last night, no one had seemed in the least bit concerned about him finding a scarecrow in the tree. But why is it back here?

His body shivers against the cold. The wind is stronger up here than below in the valley, so he turns on his heels and heads back down the hill to his cottage. He bypasses the back door and walks straight to the garage, pulling the keys from his pocket and unlocking the door.

He flicks on the light.

The scarecrow is gone.

But the ladder is there.

Graham chuckles as he rubs the back of his neck. Is this the start of him losing his memory? It's his worst nightmare, the idea of losing who he is, of him forgetting everything that's happened in the past. Is that what's happening? Or have some local delinquent kids somehow broken into his locked garage, dragged the scarecrow back up the hill and hauled it up into the tree to mess with his head?

Neither scenario seems likely, but he does have proof that something happened yesterday.

His aching body. And the two pieces of paper in his pocket.

Graham slams the garage door shut, locking it. Double checking the bolt.

He looks up at the tree and sighs, the thought of repeating the retrieval process filling him with dread. No. The scarecrow can bloody well stay there this time.

Graham decides to go for his morning walk to clear his stuffy head and loosen up his stiff muscles. He usually finds his strolls calm and enjoyable; a time he can spend listening to the birds and admiring the beautiful scenery. Today is different. As the ground passes beneath his feet, all he can focus on is the damn scarecrow in that damn tree and what the hell a possible missing teenage girl and a drawing from a hundred years ago have to do with it.

It doesn't make any sense and, the more he thinks about it, the more confused and frustrated he gets. There's no logical explanation for how he had brought the scarecrow down from the tree yesterday morning, locked it inside the garage to be dealt with later, but then the next morning it was back up in the tree, with the garage still being locked.

He laughs. Perhaps he really is getting old. Is this truly the start of his downhill decline? He isn't old enough to have dementia yet … is he? The thought crosses his mind and then he can't get it out again. Maybe it's the start of something. Perhaps a visit to the doctor will provide some answers. Hell, maybe he'd been sleep-walking, even though he's never done that in his entire life and it hadn't happened during the night, but in the morning.

In his mind, he has two choices: either he goes to visit Frank Hammel and asks him questions about his daughter, questions he doubts he'll get answers to, or he goes back home and minds his own business. There is a third option: call and ask the one person who has the right mental capacity to deal with these sorts of conundrums, someone who thrives on complex and strange occurrences.

Mr Stephen Mallow.

A very strange man who, when Graham first met him, he didn't like one bit. Mainly because he was a nosey journalist. As a detective, Graham knew how meddlesome and difficult journalists could be, especia ly when they sunk their teeth into a juicy story, *especially* one that could potentially catapult their career into the stars. That's what he thought Mr Mallow was after and he'd judged him too quickly.

Mr Mallow was also rather peculiar and, as much as he regrets it now, at the time when they met Graham had no understanding of what ADHD or OCD was. He just thought the man was ridiculous, a menace and somewhat stupid, but once he understood the error of his judgement, he realised Mr Mallow was one of the most intelligent and unique individuals he'd ever met.

In fact, Graham wouldn't have solved his last case in Cherry Hollow without the meddling, questioning personality of Mr Mallow, whose mind just happened to be wired differently to his. Perhaps that was why they had butted heads at first, neither one of them willing to back down and Mr Mallow had that sheer determination to find out the truth, not caring who he pissed off in the process. Graham, included.

Mr Mallow had taught Graham a lot about mental health during their last case. Back in Graham's day, mental health wasn't spoken about as widely as it was today and Graham admitted that, to begin with, he thought of it as nothing more than people being weak. His father told him to never cry because boys, men, didn't cry, didn't show emotion, nor did they act weak or admit when they couldn't cope. They just got on with things. Now, it was more important than ever to talk about because the more a person kept their inner, dark thoughts trapped inside, the more the darkness took over, the more the creeping creature would torment them.

As an ex-detective, Graham knew more than most about that. There was always a dark cloud of pressure bearing down on his shoulders, never letting up for a moment. Everyone had expected so much from him. Ever since he was a young sergeant in the force, he'd wanted to help people, to solve crimes, bring people to justice, but it was never as simple as that. Often, crimes didn't get solved. Sometimes, people got away with murder or missing children were never found, or, if they were, they were found dead, and he had to deliver the news to their grief-stricken parents.

Some days, it had all gotten too much. But he never spoke about it with anyone. He carried that heavy burden all by himself. Until Mr Mallow showed him the error of his ways.

Graham shakes his head, dispelling the dark thoughts of the past, then turns and walks down another path, heading back home. Now he thinks about it, perhaps it will be nice to touch base with Mr Mallow. They had casually mentioned last year that they'd keep in touch, but seeing as they were both blokes who found friendship with other blokes a bit awkward, neither of them had taken the first step yet.

When Graham moved out of Cherry Hollow, he put the whole town behind him, including its residents. Nothing on God's green earth would make him go back there, but perhaps Mr Mallow fancied a trip to the middle of Wales to investigate a weird scarecrow found hanging in a tree, not once, but twice and to discover why the residents of this town didn't seem concerned about a potentially missing girl. Karen may have dismissed her disappearance, but Graham isn't so easily persuaded otherwise. There's something not quite adding up.

Graham arrives home, puts on a pot of coffee and scrolls to Stephen Mallow's number.

Chapter 10
STEPHEN

The next morning, once Rachel leaves for work, Stephen takes his coffee and sits at his desk, which overlooks the street outside. He and Rachel only live a few minutes' walk from the centre of the town. He likes to people watch, often seeing the same residents walking past at the same time of day.

Like clockwork.

Mr Clayton, heading off to open the shop at five minutes to seven; Penelope Forthright, a posh older lady who likes to be the first in line at the bakery when it opens at eight; and Katherine Mills, the woman who owns the local haberdashery store, which does surprising well.

He switches on his laptop and scans his emails, raising his eyebrows at several of the subject lines. He opens a few that catch his eye, all of which are pleas for help in discovering the answer to strange occurrences. Maybe there will be something worth looking into today.

One person writes that there's a weird noise coming from the bottom of a well in the Yorkshire Dales that demands his investigation skills. Another mentions a dark shadow that only appears on Wednesday evenings on a driveway in the Scottish Highlands.

While both are amusing, they don't warrant him travelling to visit the areas. Instead, he emails them back, asking a few questions and, within a few minutes, has easily busted the mysteries of both.

The strange noise at the bottom of the well turns out to be a gurgling water pipe in need of unblocking and the dark shadow on Wednesday evenings is revealed to be the woman's husband sneaking back after seeing the next-door neighbour. Nothing remotely challenging or interesting, but nonetheless, the email recipients are grateful for his help.

His phone vibrates, the sound amplified against the desk.

Stephen picks it up, but pauses when he sees the name on the screen. A small smile creeps across his thin lips as he raises the phone to his ear, leaning back in his chair.

'Detective Williams, to what co I owe the pleasure of your call?'

'Mr Mallow, good to hear your voice too.'

Stephen chuckles, enjoying their faint jibes at each other from the start. He hasn't spoken to him since the detective left Cherry Hollow last year. They parted ways, promising to keep in contact, but they never did. Just one of those things.

'Of course, it is good to hear from you, Detective.'

'It's just Graham now, remember? I've retired, as I'm sure you know, Mr Mallow.'

'Hmm, yes, I remember, but I'm afraid you'll always be Detective Williams to me, unless you feel the need to call me Stephen now?'

'Mr Mallow has a nicer ring to it, I've always thought.'

'Very well. I suppose this entire conversation so far has been moot, then.'

'Indeed,' says Detective Williams with a grunt.

'Were you calling about something in particular?' continues Stephen.

'Yes, as a matter of fact, I was. You're going to laugh about this, I'm sure, but I think I should tell you the whole story first. There's a large tree up on a hill near my cottage. Beautiful views, but the hill is extremely steep, too steep for me to walk up every day. The tree's been there for hundreds of years. Could even be a thousand years old ...'

'I'm sorry to interrupt, Detective, but is there a point to this story?'

'Yes, yes, I'm getting to it.'

Stephen sighs as the detective continues. Stephen really doesn't like long-winded stories, especially ones that don't catch his attention straight away.

'Yesterday morning, while I was having my morning coffee, I saw something hanging in the tree, so I went to look. I climbed up the tree and—'

Stephen almost spits his coffee out as he takes a sip. 'I'm sorry, but did you say you climbed up a tree?'

'I did.'

'You could have led with that little gold nugget of information. Anyway, my apologies. Please, continue. Consider me intrigued and a little confused.'

'It was a scarecrow,' says Graham bluntly, not bothering to backtrack. 'In the tree,' he adds in case Stephen has forgotten what they're talking about.

Stephen furrows his brow, slowly lowering his cup to the desk without checking if it's steady. 'A scarecrow?' he asks. 'How strange. They aren't known to hang in trees. Usually, they hang out in wheat fields.' He lets go of the handle of the cup. It topples off the desk and onto the floor, splashing hot liquid over the bottom half of his legs. He barely reacts, just ignores it. It's not that hot.

'Exactly my point,' says Graham. 'Anyway, after climbing the tree and bringing the thing down, I assumed some local kids had strung it up there to mess with me or as a prank. It was wearing an old overcoat. I put it in my locked garage, ready for the next time I had a bonfire, but the next morning - this morning - I woke up and it was back up in the tree. The lock on my garage hadn't been broken and there's no way the keys had been used because I keep them on a hook in the cottage and the doors are always locked. No one broke in.'

Stephen breathes in deep through his nose and then lets it slowly out of his mouth. His brain is doing that thing again when he can't find the words he wants to use in the right order. 'That's … perplexing,' he finally says. He closes his eyes against a wave of dizziness.

'Indeed.'

'Are you sure you weren't drunk?'

Graham bursts out laughing at the man's bluntness. 'It's a strong possibility, but I certainly wasn't drunk this morning.'

'Have you ever sleep-walked before?'

'Never.'

'Do you think you may have early onset dementia?'

Graham laughs again. 'Unconfirmed,' he says. 'But that's not all. There's more to this story. There was also a drawing of the tree from a hundred years ago in the pocket of the overcoat along with a poster of a missing teenager called Sophia Hammel from ten years ago. I left the thing hanging in the tree this morning, so I don't know if there's anything else in the pockets. I'm not climbing up a tree for a second day in a row. My body's already in clip as it is. I spoke with some of the local residents and no one seemed concerned. They said it was merely a prank by some local kids in the run up to Halloween. I also found out that a young lad called John Hammel hung himself in the tree a hundred years ago.'

Stephen rubs his forehead as a dull ache takes hold. 'Hmm, so the fact you're aching proves you did in fact climb the tree last night. You didn't dream or imagine it.'

'It would appear so.'

'And this John Hammel is related to the missing teenager, I presume?'

'Yes. A distant relative. I spoke with someone in the village yesterday but I was unable to confirm whether Sophia had actually gone missing. Her father seems to be the head of the village committee.'

'Have you spoken to Mr Hammel?'

'No. Not yet. I was ... I was rather hoping you might fancy a trip to Wales to assist me in my investigation. I'm sure I could solve this case on my own, but I wouldn't mind a little help.'

Stephen's ears prick up and he sits straighter in his chair, clutching the phone tighter. The spilled coffee is now cold against his skin and it's probably staining the carpet, but he doesn't care.

Detective Williams has just given him what he's been searching for. He wouldn't have called Stephen if he didn't deem it serious or if he wasn't in dire need of help.

'I have a couple of questions, Detective.'

'Okay ...'

'Is this a legal investigation involving the police or is this ... somewhat unorthodox?'

'This is the combination of a retired cop who's bored out of his mind and a smidge of rebellion against the police force, having spent so many years following rules and stuck behind a desk. Let's just say, this is a chance to work my potentially-dementia-ridden brain muscles.'

'But you haven't contacted the police.'

'No. This is strictly under the police radar until I deem it necessary to involve them.'

Stephen grins. 'Count me in, Detective. I'll leave right now.'

Chapter 11

SOPHIA

Bethgelert, Wales, 2015

Damn it, I should have brought my bike. It would have been quicker and easier than jogging to the tree because I had to keep stopping and starting every time I reached a hill. And there were a lot of hills in Wales. The last time I cycled in the dim light, though, I ended up riding head first into a fence that had come out of nowhere. Plus, there was no way I could ride up the hill to the tree. It was too steep and pushing the bike up was also pointless.

The sunset cast enough light on the surrounding fields so I could see them, but under the canopy of the large tree, I was shrouded in darkness. I'd made sure to wrap up warm before leaving home. As a farmer's daughter growing up in Wales, I knew about wearing the correct clothing for the elements and to be prepared for the changing weather. I was harder and tougher than most girls my age, not afraid of getting my hands dirty or climbing over a barbed-wire fence and slicing my shin open on the spikes. A muddy field was never a problem, not if I was wearing the right footwear. Mostly wellies. I lived in wellies.

I settled on the ground with my back against the trunk and opened my sketchbook and pencil set. Wow, the sky was particularly striking this evening. Yellows, oranges and reds cascaded across the sky, but since I only drew in pencil, I couldn't capture the colour. It didn't matter though. I doubt John Hammel had used colours or paints back in his day either. A pencil was all he required to create a piece of stunning art.

I began to draw, slowly moving the pencil across the page, closing my eyes every few seconds to feel for what I had to do next. Some might say it was creepy or weird that my dead relative was using my hand to draw, but to me it felt normal. Like he was speaking to me through the drawing. It brought me peace because sitting underneath the tree calmed me, despite it being a symbol of a very sad time in my family history.

It was true that John Hammel's suicide ninety years ago had set about a chain of unfortunate events in the village, culminating in my dad having to rent Rosemore Cottage to pay off his debts. Dad had made some bad decisions regarding finances and had the unfortunate knack of trusting the wrong person. It all started with John, if you believed the legend. Everyone blamed everything on the poor guy, who wasn't even here to defend himself.

There was a lot of bad luck in the area, which I learned more about a year ago, after I chose to research the tree and its history for a school project, which even got posted on the school's website. My father hadn't been particularly pleased with my choice, trying his best to get me to pick something else, like the mining disaster of 1992 in the quarry, but no, I wanted to learn about the tree and why John Hammel's death had kick-started a so-called curse upon the village.

In the end, I walked away with a B grade, which had been good enough.

Did I believe in the curse? Or was it just bad luck and a string of unfortunate coincidences? For my school project, I decided to go down the route of "curses weren't real" and that people made their own bad luck and just because a young farmer decided to end his life, it didn't mean everyone else was doomed. I was sure that was why I got a B and not an A. I put a lot of work into it, but my teacher was one of those believers. Most of the older residents in the village were. The younger generation, like me, were told to carry on the legend of the curse, but the more the years passed, the weaker the curse became. Eventually, when people like my dad and other village elders died off, there wouldn't be anyone left to carry on the legacy of 'The Hanging Tree.'

The pencil stopped moving on the open page.

I couldn't seem to get it going again, so I put it down and watched the sun set. I took out my phone and snapped a picture, but it didn't do the sight justice. I rarely used my phone, not for calls and texts, mainly because it didn't work unless I was within Wi-Fi range at home. Out here, even on top of the hill, there was limited to no signal, so it was basically a glorified camera.

It was time to head home.

I hadn't finished my sketch, but the sun had gone to bed now and the moon was making its appearance. I got to my feet, brushed the dirt from my bum and stretched my arms above my head. A rustle of leaves made me look up. A squirrel heading to bed, perhaps? Or a bird?

Another rustle, this one louder.

'Hello?' I called out, squinting my eyes, but the darkness was now too thick to see anything.

Another rustle; this one big enough to send a small cascade of dirt and dead leaves on my head. I coughed and stepped back, bumping into a solid object. I spun around, my heart practically leaping from my chest.

'Hello, Sophia.'

Fear ripped through my chest, taking my breath with it. How had he crept up without me noticing? Where had he come from? I was sitting there the whole time, looking up and down sporadically. Had he already been there, hiding behind the tree, watching me?

'Um, hi,' I said, instinctively stepping backwards and bumping into the tree. I felt safer touching it, like it was a barrier between him and me.

The man in front of me was dressed all in black and wearing a flat cap, blending in perfectly to the dimming light.

'Surprised to see me?' the man asked. 'I take it you were expecting someone else?'

'Um … yeah. I mean …' I recognised him as a friend of my dad. The man was roughly the same age as him and his cap was pulled low over his forehead, shielding his face. I'd never really liked him. He always gave me the creeps. Fear was almost strangling me. 'I'm meeting someone here. They'll be here any minute, so …' The lie slipped out easily. Maybe if he thought someone was on the way, he'd back off.

The man chuckled and tipped his cap back, revealing his face. 'Don't worry,' he said. 'I'm not here to hurt you. I'm here to deliver a message.'

'A message? What kind of message?'

The man took off his cap entirely now, holding it in both hands, squeezing it tight. He opened his mouth to speak, but a noise above in the tree stopped him. We tilted our heads to the tree at the same time. Something was moving up in the branches. Whatever it was, it was big, cumbersome. Not a squirrel.

My immediate thought was that John Hammel was distracting the man so I could make my escape. I pulled my eyes away from the canopy of branches above. Not giving him a chance to deliver his *message*, I saw my moment, leapt forwards, shoving the man hard in the chest, catching him off guard. His left leg stumbled over a nearby lump in the ground and he landed awkwardly, rolling several times down the hill.

Oh, shit.

I turned and ran down the hill, windmilling my arms to stop myself from going too fast. I ran all the way home, never looking back, only stopping when I reached my yard.

Chapter 12

GRAHAM

Graham says goodbye to Mr Mallow, smiling as he sets his phone down on the table. He knew Mr Mallow wouldn't be able to resist an intriguing case such as this. He hasn't even told him everything yet to do with the supposed curse that John's death started.

It isn't a life or death mystery, not yet anyway, but it's enough of a challenge, a mental workout, to lure Stephen here. Not that Graham's luring him here for anything sinister. Goodness, no. Graham's lonely, and he has a sneaking suspicion that Mr Mallow may be lonely too. Or bored. Mr Mallow always did like the strange and morbid, and a cursed tree is exactly his cup of tea.

Checking the fridge, Graham quickly realises he has nothing substantial to feed the man when he arrives, so he grabs his keys and drives to the local store, turning off the radio when a Christmas song comes on. It's not even the end of October, for goodness sake. No Christmas before Halloween. That should be the law. Why do the media and stores have to push the festive time of the year earlier and earlier? By the time Christmas eventually does come to town, everyone (meaning Graham) is so sick of the twinkling lights and the festive atmosphere that they want it to be over and done with already.

It's a strange time of year for Graham. Since working so much all his life, he's never made time for proper friends, and he has no family. His parents died over two decades ago within several months of each other. He has no wife. No kids. The only person he'd call a friend lately is Olivia, but her being locked up for life puts a dampener on them spending quality time together. He once pictured them entering into their old age as friends and going for long walks or learning new hobbies, like gardening. He and Olivia had been the best of friends as children and into their teenage years, along with Mary, Frank and Jack, all of whom are now dead. But something happened in 1980, and it drove them apart. Graham lost all his friends in one day, but now he and Olivia are back on speaking terms and closer than ever. It's a shame it took such a catastrophic event for it to happen and for them to have lost the rest of their group along the way.

Christmas is traditionally a time for friends and family to gather and celebrate. But Graham rarely celebrates the holiday, not like normal people do anyway. Once, many years ago, he accepted the kind invitation of old Mrs Price who'd lived her whole life in Cherry Hollow and spent Christmas Day with her and her husband. It had been pleasant enough, but thinking back on it, he was lucky to have survived the day, considering that same old woman had eventually admitted to poisoning her husband over the space of several years until he finally succumbed and dropped dead of a massive heart attack.

Nowadays, Graham books himself a table for one at the local pub and orders a full Christmas dinner, washing it down with a nice smoky whisky or perhaps a festive beer (if there is such a thing). This year, however, he's promised to see Olivia since it's her first year in lock-up, but he's also aware her family will be visiting, so he doesn't want to overstep the mark and encroach on their precious family time. He's so happy her two daughters, Brooke and Dorothy, continue to visit. Olivia deserves that. Graham would have done anything to keep her out of prison, but it was the way it had to be. She made her choice.

Graham enters the local supermarket and begins browsing the shelves for food he can easily prepare and cook. He's not sure what to buy, having never been particularly good at cooking for himself from scratch. He makes a mean curry, but Graham likes his spice to be on the high side. He's not sure if Mr Mallow likes to have his taste buds burnt off, so he opts for a milder sauce.

As he's perusing the alcohol aisle (an aisle he never misses), he overhears a couple of people talking on the other side of the shelves. It's a small shop, so it's hard not to overhear.

'What do we think about Mr Williams attending the village meeting last night, then?' asks a deep, male voice.

'It was a bit of a surprise to see him, considering he's been here almost a year and has never attended a single one. Apparently, Karen invited him,' says a female voice.

'I didn't like the way he was looking at Frank. Did you hear that he brought the scarecrow down from the tree?'

'Maybe someone should have told him to leave it alone. Now, we'll have a year of bad luck because of him.'

'You don't really believe that, do you?'

Graham can't quite hear what's said next, so he decides to push on. As he reaches the end of the shelves, he steps into view, but the two people who had been talking have moved further away. He only sees the back of them, disappearing round the corner, but he doesn't recognise them. The woman is wearing a dark purple jacket, though.

Once he reaches the checkout line, the cashier begins scanning his items.

'Oh, Mr Williams. *Prynhawn da*,' says a voice behind him.

He turns and looks at the older woman who is wearing the dark purple jacket. He's never been a fan of gossip, but finds it amusing that people are talking about him as if he's done something wrong.

'Hello,' he says, still having no idea who she is, but now that he's seen her face, he knows she was at the village meeting. She'd been one of the friendly faces who'd shaken his hand and welcomed him. It seems it had only been for show, though, as her less-than-friendly chat with the man he'd overheard earlier made it quite clear Graham hadn't been welcome there.

'Have you ... were you ...' She glances towards the back of the shop where she'd had the conversation. A blush creeps up her neck. 'Lovely to see you again,' she says.

'And you,' he replies. 'And don't worry, I believe we make our own luck in this world.'

The woman's mouth drops open.

'*Prynhawn da,*' he says, turning back to the checkout. He's not sure what the woman does when he bids her a good afternoon, but when he turns around to leave the shop, she's nowhere to be seen.

He drives home on autopilot, thinking about the scarecrow still hanging in the tree and what he'd overheard. Okay, so the scarecrow wasn't supposed to be removed, but so what? He meant what he said, about making our own luck. Besides, surely if he'd been the one to remove the thing, it would be *him* who would have the bad luck, not the rest of the village? But that's beside the point because he doesn't believe in any of it. Also, they didn't make it sound like it was a bunch of kids playing a joke the way they had at the village meeting.

He's hoping Mr Mallow will arrive during the daylight hours, so they can visit the tree and take a closer look at the scarecrow. Perhaps there's something else hidden in its pockets now that it's back in the tree. He is curious as to how someone broke into his garage and retrieved it in the first place. It looks like it's time to put his former investigative skills to the test once again.

Mr Mallow messages Graham an hour later with his estimated time of arrival. It appears he won't make the darkness cut off, so Graham decides to prepare dinner and light a fire to ward off the impending cold.

It takes several attempts for the wood to catch, thanks to the damp and lack of appropriate kindling, but once the flames get going, the small lounge fills with an ambient glow and a comforting warmth. He begins by sautéing onions in a pan, sweating them till they're translucent, then adds some cubed chicken breast and a selection of vegetables from his garden, including courgettes. He places the jar of curry sauce (he chose a tikka masala in the end) on the side, ready to add later. Some people may say using a jar of ready-made curry sauce is cheating, but Graham isn't one of those people.

While everything simmers, he grabs the village magazine that's delivered to the households for free each month. It arrived two days ago and he'd chucked it on the side, not giving it a second thought. If he had thought about it sooner, he could have read it, possibly finding some snippets of valuable information.

He was even briefly mentioned in the magazine shortly after his arrival in the village. Apparently, a retired detective was an exciting enough announcement to be included. He was awarded a short extract, right next to the news about a local prize-winning sheep who'd given birth to triplets.

The magazine is mostly a who's who of local businesses, reminding everyone to support farmers and to ensure no large, commercial compan es or shops make their way to the village and destroy it. Fair enough, but even Graham knows that without footfall and a constant revenue stream, it's only a matter of time before small villages fade away to nothing. It's sad, but it's the truth.

He scans the pages, searching for anything about the tree. Something catches his eye on page fifteen. As he reads the headline, his eyes widen in alarm.

Chapter 13
STEPHEN

An hour after saying goodbye to Detective Williams on the phone, Stephen's packed and ready to start his long drive to Wales. He stops by the Cherry Tree to say goodbye to Rachel and explain his plan to visit him, but when he opens the door and strolls up to the reception desk, she isn't there.

An older lady is where Rachel usually sits. 'Hello, Stephen,' she says with a kind smile. 'What can I do for you today?'

'Hello, is Rachel around please? I need to speak to her before I leave.'

The woman's smile falters slightly. 'Oh, where are you off to?'

'Wales.'

'My, my, quite the trek. I'm sorry, Stephen, but … Rachel isn't here.'

Stephen sighs, glancing around the small reception area. He recalls the two times he's stayed here fondly. His favourite pastime was sitting in the library in front of a roaring fire while sipping a whisky.

'Okay, please can you give her a message from me when you see her?'

'I … um …'

'Tell Rachel I'm sorry, but I had to leave to go and see Detective Williams. He needs my help. And tell her not to worry about my hospital visit. I'll rebook it.'

The woman nods her head. 'Very well.'

Stephen bids her goodbye and walks back out to his car. He scrolls to Rachel's WhatsApp and leaves her a voice note, telling her he's stopped by. It remains unread.

She won't be happy about him leaving without speaking directly to her first, but he's tried to find her, hasn't he? She'll be okay about it, right? If he doesn't leave now, then he fears … what? What does he fear? Nothing, really. Just that Rachel won't understand his true reasoning for going. He's going to miss his doctor's appointment on Friday too and he's okay with that, but Rachel won't be. She'll have plenty to say about it. Stephen's already annoyed that she found out about his nose bleeds. He thought he'd been sneaky and clever about it, but not a lot gets past Rachel.

There's more important things to worry about now than the state of his relationship. That's the thing with Stephen, he's either all in or he isn't. And right now, he's all in on this investigation that Detective Williams needs help with.

After leaving The Cherry Tree car park, he drives out of Cherry Hollow, towards his newest adventure. As he navigates the narrow roads through the Lake District, his phone rings. His car is too old to include Bluetooth, so he can't answer without safely pulling over. He lets the call ring out. It's probably from Rachel, wanting to tear him a new one for leaving so suddenly and leaving a message with the older woman on reception, but she should be used to his reckless decisions by now. He's impulsive at times yet also stubbornly set in his ways. It's part of his charm. Honestly, being himself is exhausting. He wishes other people could spend merely a single minute inside his head, then they'd understand why he is the way he is.

He's told Detective Williams he will be with him by six this evening, traffic depending. He had hoped to arrive before the darkness set in, but it doesn't seem likely now. He doesn't like to drive in the dark, or be outside in the dark, or have the lights off at night.

His nyctophobia is under control, to a certain extent, but it still likes to creep up behind him when he least expects it and scare the bejesus out of him. He's suffered from the phobia since he was a child. His father often locked him in their cold basement for hours on end. Sometimes it was longer than a few hours.

Before that started happening, Stephen had quite liked the darkness. He enjoyed the safety and comfort it would bring when he'd fall asleep tucked up in bed. The darkness was a fascinating creature. It used to be his friend, but that quickly changed when it began to give him nightmares, and his damaged subconscious created eerie creatures in the form of shadowy shapes.

A year ago, he faced his fear and won, but the darkness will always hold a power over him that he can't explain. He no longer fears the dark itself; he respects it because it is a powerful being. Nothing changes in the darkness. The same objects are there. They just can't be seen. It's the fear of the unknown that scares people. Phobias and fears may control a lot of people's lives, but it doesn't mean they should define who you are as a person. Everyone has the power to take back control, as long as you respect your fear.

As he drives, his vision blurs and a trickle of blood oozes out of his nose. He wipes it with a tissue from his pocket, but doesn't notice the small drops of blood now staining his shirt.

Chapter 14

SOPHIA

Bethgelert, Wales, 2015

I beat my record running from the tree back home by a full three minutes. I didn't stop to check if the creepy man was following me because I've seen enough movies to know that when people get chased, looking over their shoulder slows them down and then they get caught and killed. So I kept running and never looked back. I assumed that a man of his age wouldn't chase a teenage girl a mile across the village, but I didn't want to be too careful.

Upon arriving in my yard, I lent over the gate and finally took a full breath in, allowing my lungs to suck in as much oxygen as they could take, but then a wave of dizziness made me stumble sideways. I couldn't remember the last time I'd run that far, or that fast.

Once composed, I made my way to the front door, but before I could open it, my dad yanked it open, huffing and puffing like he was the one who ran over a mile in a personal best time.

'Oh. Good. You're back,' he said.

'Something wrong, Dad?'

'Yes, the electricity's gone out at Rosemore Cottage, and I have people arriving in the morning.'

'And that's my problem because …'

'Don't get smart with me young lady. You're the one who seems to have a knack for fixing things. I need you over there to sort it out right now. If I need to call in a professional, then I need to know ASAP. Lord knows I can't afford to, so I'm hoping you'll be able to sort it.'

I let out an extra-long sigh, making sure he knew exactly how pissed off I was, but to be perfectly honest, I liked fixing things almost as much as I enjoyed drawing. My sigh was merely a show of my stroppy teenage persona. I already knew what the issue was. Dodgy wiring. Thanks to my Dad refusing to hire an actual electrician, he relied on handouts from people in the village who liked to lend a hand, or who owed him a favour. It didn't matter if they weren't qualified. He hadn't had much luck lately, and I knew the farm was struggling to sustain itself. I wasn't sure what he had planned, but usually everything worked out okay in the end, especially for Dad. He knew a lot of people.

'I've just come from there,' I said with a whine.

'Then go back!'

I didn't mind going back to the cottage, but the idea of running into the old guy again was enough to set my teeth on edge. I hoped he wasn't hanging around. I was about to ask my dad why his creepy friend would be hanging out by the tree, wanting to deliver a message, but before I could, he shoved the bag of tools at me and slammed the door in my face.

'This is classed as child labour!' I shouted at the closed door.

No answer.

I hiked the bag over my shoulder and began my trip back across the fields towards Rosemore Cottage. My dad owned it, but rented it out to holiday makers, something he loathed to do because he hated the idea of outsiders infiltrating our community. But we needed the money.

He was in the process of selling it because it had become a drain on resources. The fact was that our family was broke, or at least in the process of breaking.

The curse continued …

Although, if my dad used his brain and projected blame onto himself instead of a ninety-year-old curse, he'd see that it was his own fault. But Dad didn't like to blame himself. It was always someone else's fault. My mother's. Mine. Whoever.

I cut across the path, deciding to take a shortcut instead. I placed a foot precariously on top of the wire fence and then leapt over, landing in the mud on the other side with a thud. My left foot slipped, but I managed to regain balance before navigating the muddy field and finding a track down towards a small river.

A few minutes later, I hopped over a low wall into the local graveyard, then weaved in between the gravestones that rose up out of the ground in zig-zag patterns. There were no discernible lines, but I knew exactly where I was going, having used this cut-through on numerous occasions. I used to hang out in the graveyard a lot with my friends, back when we bothered to see one another outside of school. It was the number one place to hang out and drink. We never made a mess or dishonoured the dead by spray-painting the stones or anything like that. I knew better. Besides, the whole Hammel family line was buried here, including John Hammel. His grave was a sacred place in many ways, yet also somewhere that was often neglected due to the sad memories it held.

The Hammel family had lived and died in the village for over a hundred and fifty years. Not only that, but my little brother was also buried here, having lost his life at five years of age. I'd been six at the time and now have very few memories of him, apart from the fact he used to make me laugh a lot and we'd put on crazy, made-up skits and dances in the living room for our parents.

His name was Tommy.

We didn't talk about him anymore. My dad, as usual, blamed the curse, but I knew better. It was a sudden illness that took him. One day he was fine, then the next he was in hospital fighting for his life, and the day after that he was gone. Mum couldn't handle it and, five years later, she walked out on us. Just up and left in the middle of the night. We hadn't heard from her since. It was one of those things that no one talked about. She managed to escape from here, away from the village, away from the horrible memories of losing Tommy so suddenly. It was never her dream in life to live here indefinitely. She wanted to move away, but convincing my dad to leave the village he was born and raised in was an impossible task. She gave up trying and decided to leave. I wished she'd taken me with her, but I hoped that wherever she was, she was happy. Maybe I'd find her, see her again one day. As soon as I turned eighteen, I'd be leaving this village too.

I said a quick hi to Tommy's grave as I passed, kissing my fingers and touching his headstone, then arrived at the far end of the graveyard where there was another wall which I hopped over. After that, it was a short trek across a field and I arrived at the cottage.

Dad always kept a spare key hidden behind a loose brick in the garage wall, so I took it and unlocked the door. The fuse board was upstairs, of all places, so I switched on the torch function on my phone and used it to climb the wooden stairs to the top floor.

It was only when I reached the top that I remembered the creepy old guy who'd been at the tree earlier. I scurried to the nearest window and peered out, scanning the gloomy yard below. It was too dark to see the tree, but I knew where it was, out there in the distance, ominously towering over the village. I made the decision to get home as quickly as possible.

I continued to the fuse board on the wall in the weird dead-end hallway at the top of the stairs. Bending down, I flipped open the small door and shone the beam inside. It looked fine. All the switches were in the right position. All good there.

Sighing, I dumped the bag of tools on the floor, then rummaged around until I found a screwdriver that fit. I held the phone in one hand and began fiddling with the various screws, ensuring they were all tight and in the right places, locking the wires in place.

Nope. That didn't work.

There was nothing remotely wrong from what I could see, so what was going on? It seemed like the problem might be with the main power console and if that were the case, then I wasn't qualified to fix it. I stood up, ready to go back downstairs where I knew the main power console was, to check it over, but a tapping sound stopped me.

Tap. Tap. Tap.

It was light, barely audible, but it happened again.

'Hello?' I called out. The dead-end hallway was ahead of me. It always confused me because there should have been another room there. It made sense that there would be, but there was nothing.

Tap. Tap. Tap.

'Is someone there?' I asked the darkness.

Silence answered back.

'Screw this,' I said, backing away towards the stairs.

Tap. Tap. Tap.

'Okay, what the hell? If this is Harry messing around … very funny. Ha. Ha. I told you not to sneak in here again.' Harry was the young boy around eleven who liked to break into people's homes and barns and leave graffiti everywhere. I'd caught him on several occasions with a brick in his hand. Annoyingly, he was the son of one of the local cops, so he seemed to get away with everything.

Silence.

'Harry?'

Silence.

'Not Harry?'

Tap. Tap. Tap.

'Shit …' I whispered, reaching to the bag on the floor and pulling out a big wrench.

I held the wrench above my head, ready to strike if necessary. I crept forwards, one small step at the time. I didn't understand. Where the hell was the sound coming from? I think it was coming from behind the wall, but … there was no door there, so how would anyone get behind it?

'Um … can you tap again?'

Nothing. Not for several long seconds, and then …

Tap. Tap. Tap.

It *was* coming from behind the wall.

I lowered the wrench, stepped close and pressed my ear against the wall, listening, waiting. I held my breath, but the tapping didn't come again. I scanned the area with my phone, searching for something that didn't quite fit. Anything.

I knocked on the wall three times.

Wait. How did I not notice that before?

The wall wasn't built from stone like the majority of walls in this old farmhouse. This was made from plasterboard. Someone had built a fake wall in the hallway, potentially covering up a whole other room I'd never seen before. Granted, I hadn't spent a lot of time at Rosemore Cottage recently, only popping in from time to time to help clean it ready for the next visitors or fixing bits for Dad, but even he hadn't noticed the fake wall. Had he? Did he do this?

Holy shit.

Was someone trapped behind it?'

'Don't worry! I'm going to get you out!'

I raised the wrench above my head once again and slammed it against the wall.

It went straight through.

Chapter 15

GRAHAM

He peers past the curtains at his yard just as headlights sweep around the corner, blinding him. Pulling the curtains back across, Graham releases the tension in his shoulders by rolling them back and clicking his neck from side to side. That's better.

It's late, much later than he expected. Perhaps Mr Mallow had car trouble or got lost along the way. If Graham remembers correctly, he drives a beat-up old banger that's probably better off going to the scrapheap, so the fact it's made it all the way to the darkest depths of Wales from the Lake District is a miracle in itself.

He flicks the kettle on as he walks past it to the back door. He rarely uses the front door. It's in an odd location, smack in the middle of the lounge, so whenever the door opens, the cold from outside comes rushing into the living area. Therefore, it's easier to use the back entrance located in the kitchen, so he can close the kitchen door; a barrier to keep the warmth trapped in the lounge.

Graham opens the door and watches as Mr Mallow's old banger (still has it then) rolls to a stop. He stays where he is while the man, who he used to find infuriating, gets out of the car and waves at him, a dopey grin across his face.

'Couldn't have lived a bit closer to civilisation, no?' calls out Mr Mallow. 'On a few of those hills, I thought my car was going to stall halfway up and roll all the way back down.'

Graham spreads his arms wide at the open fields surrounding his cottage, despite it being too dark to see them. 'It was the only place available.'

Mr Mallow smirks as he steps closer and extends his hand in greeting. 'Good to see you again, Detective.'

Graham shakes his hand firmy. 'And you, Mr Mallow.' He's about to offer a polite compliment, say that the man looks well, but truth be told, Mr Mallow looks anything, but well. The hollow, gaunt expression in his eyes and the paleness of his face stand out even against the dark backdrop. Perhaps he hasn't been sleeping. Graham knows how that feels.

'Wanted to get here before the darkness set in.' Mr Mallow glances around. 'But it looks like it beat me.'

'You'll find the darkness has ways of creeping up on you out here.' As soon as he says it, they lock eyes; a mutual understanding of their past flitting between them. They don't wish to speak about it, but they know it's there.

'Come on in. I've made the spare room up for you,' says Graham. 'You're the first person to use it.'

'Very kind of you.' Mr Mallow opens the boot and brings out a small suitcase and a laptop bag.

Graham steps aside, allowing Mr Mallow to walk past, but he pauses at the entrance on the doormat. 'Something wrong?' asks Graham, noticing the man's sweaty upper lip and twitching hands. He's nervous. Maybe not nervous, but ... agitated. Yes, agitated.

Mr Mallow crosses the threshold and closes his eyes for a moment. Seventeen seconds to be precise. Graham allows him his space to do what he needs to do to come to terms with walking inside a new place. When Mr Mallow opens his eyes, he smiles and walks all the way into the property, closing the door behind him.

'Nice place you've got here,' he says, setting his bags on the floor. 'A bit of a doer-upper.'

'Thank you. Yes, it's a work in progress.'

'Aren't we all these days.'

'Indeed. May I offer you a cup of tea? Or something stronger?'

'Something stronger wouldn't go amiss after the journey I've just had.'

'Whisky it is then.'

Graham turns and retrieves two glass tumblers from a nearby cupboard, then reaches down and pulls out a bottle of whisky from the bar area. While he pours, Mr Mallow wanders wordlessly around the kitchen, glancing at the various items on the sides and shelves.

Graham thinks back to when Mr Mallow made himself at home in his office back in Cherry Hollow. The man stepped behind his desk while he'd been out of the room and rearranged all the pictures on the wall so they were straight. Graham half expects him to do the same with the various knickknacks on the side, but he doesn't. He passes them with a quick glance and moves on.

'Ice?' Graham asks.

'Please,' replies Mr Mallow. 'Two cubes.'

Graham fetches four ice cubes from the freezer tray and pops two in each glass. 'I know what you're about to say,' says Graham, handing Mr Mallow a half-filled tumbler of amber liquid.

Mr Mallow takes it, smiling. 'What's that then?'

'It needs a woman's touch in here.'

'Not at all. What I was going to say was that you've done well in your retirement. It seems like the perfect place to settle down away from people.'

Graham shrugs and takes a sip of cool liquid. Anyone else would take Mr Mallow's words as a small dig or jibe, but Graham knows he's merely speaking the truth.

'How *is* retirement going?' Mr Mallow asks.

'I don't like it.'

'Bored already, huh?'

'Why do you think I decided to climb a tree yesterday and investigate a potentially missing teenager?'

Mr Mallow nods. 'I'm surprised you haven't got yourself a part-time job. To be honest, I've been looking for something similar to keep me occupied.'

'Writing articles for the newspaper not doing it for you anymore?'

'Not exactly. It pays the bills but doesn't keep my mind active enough. I'm lucky that I get to write whatever I want for the papers, but …'

'Nothing quite like a creepy small town mystery.'

'You got it.'

The two men stare into their tumblers for a moment.

'So … are we going to address the scarecrow in the room?' asks Mr Mallow.

Graham squeezes his lips together to force down a chuckle, impressed at Mr Mallow's attempt at a little humour. 'Actually, it's still in the tree. Fancy a nighttime trek? Dinner can wait.'

'Can't it wait until morning? I just got here.'

'We could, but the question is: will your curiosity last until then?' Graham knocks back the rest of the whisky in one big gulp and places the glass on the side. Then he grabs a torch from the hook on the wall next to his umbrella. 'Shall we? I'm afraid my own curiosity is running away with me.'

Mr Mallow sighs heavily before also draining his glass. He walks out the back door and follows Graham, the beam of the torch crisscrossing the yard.

'The hill's rather steep,' says Graham. Mr Mallow doesn't reply.

They fall into step beside each other as they climb the grassy hill. Graham pulls the collar of his jacket tighter against his neck as a strong wind whips around them.

'How've you been?' Graham asks. 'You know, in general ...' He admits he hasn't kept in touch like he promised he would. The fact Mr Mallow now resides in Cherry Hollow, the one place on this earth that still gives him nightmares, is probably part of the reason he's failed to keep contact. Couldn't the man have lived anywhere else? Why there, of all places?

Mr Mallow doesn't reply straight away. He seems to be struggling to keep up. Graham slows; not aware he's been walking fast enough for a fitter, younger man to struggle. And there he was thinking he was unfit.

'Good,' comes the late response from Mr Mallow.

'Still living in Cherry Hollow?'

'You know I am.'

'I can't believe after everything that happened last year, you're living there. You couldn't have found some other hellhole to call home?'

'Perhaps your idea of hell and my idea of hell are very different.'

'Indeed.'

Another silence stretches between them. It's not awkward, not like it used to be.

'Have you heard from Olivia?' asks Mr Mallow.

'Yes, I visit her as often as I can. Usually, once a month or so.'

'How is she?'

'Surprisingly, she's okay. Her family visit her often.'

'Crazy about what happened to Mary, right?'

Graham sighs. 'I'd rather not talk about her, Mr Mallow. I hope you understand.'

'I understand perfectly, Detective. Say no more.'

The way Mr Mallow speaks the words sends a shiver down Graham's spine, which has nothing to do with the chill factor. Mary is a topic of conversation he never discusses and luckily, Mr Mallow, after being told, honours his wish. He's a good man.

Graham slows as they near the top where the hill gets steeper. He stops under the canopy and shines the light up into the tree. 'Welcome to The Hanging Tree, Mr Mallow.'

Mr Mallow glances at him. 'You failed to mention that snippet of information in your previous phone conversation.'

'I thought it would be a nice surprise for you.'

'Indeed it is. The Hanging Tree. Nothing to do with *The Hunger Games*, I'm assuming?'

'You've lost me.'

Mr Mallow shakes his head. 'Never mind. I should have known you wouldn't get that book reference. I'm assuming there's a story behind the name?'

'You assume correct.' He directs the beam into the branches again, highlighting the outline of the scarecrow above. 'There it is,' he says matter-of-factly. He watches Mr Mallows' eyes travel upwards, but then they freeze when they reach the object swinging above.

'What the hell?'

'I told you … it's weird and …'

'Detective, are you seeing what I'm seeing?'

Graham frowns, returning h s gaze to the tree. He studies the scarecrow, but this time, something is there that hadn't been there before.

'Holy shit,' he says.

The scarecrow is *bleeding*.

Chapter 16
STEPHEN

He squints into the branches, through the gloomy darkness and the fluorescent torchlight. It must be a trick of the light, combined with the moonlight and his tired eyes. There's no way he is seeing what he thinks he's seeing; a bleeding corpse hanging in a tree.

'Holy shit,' says the detective. 'That's a body.'

Stephen's eyes widen. 'Are you sure it's not a scarecrow?'

Detective Williams lowers the torchlight and shines it right in his eyes. Stephen raises his hand, shielding himself as the detective says, 'I think I know what a dead body looks like, considering my previous career.'

'But you said you saw this thing up there this morning, right?'

'Yesterday, actually.'

'Right. And you're sure it wasn't a dead body then?'

'I'm sure. It was a scarecrow.' Detective Williams' voice is deadpan, clearly not in the mood to joke around anymore. Their previous chat had been on the lighter side, but now it has switched to a more sober tone. Dealing with a dead body had not been on his agenda for this evening. He'd been hoping to arrive and start his research straight away, but now things have derailed quite spectacularly.

Detective Williams returns the beam of light to the branches. He shakes his head. 'There's definitely blood dripping down the jacket. I need to call this in.'

'Wait.' Stephen holds up his hand like he's at school answering a question, even though it's too dark to see. 'You're no longer a detective, Detective.'

'I hope you're not insinuating what I think you're insinuating, Mr Mallow.'

Stephen glances up at the tree. 'Give me a boost?'

'Absolutely not. I am not going to allow you to contaminate a crime scene. *Again.*'

'Sounds to me like you already did that when you brought the body down the other day.'

'It wasn't a dead body then.'

'You're quite sure?'

Detective Williams stares at him, his eyes unblinking.

'Fine. You're sure. It might not even be a dead body, but there's only one way to be certain. Don't you want to double check before you call in a possible crime? I reckon the police in this area aren't exactly waiting by the phone for emergency calls. I'm sure they'd love to be called out late at night to what's probably more than likely a prank of some kind.' Stephen sucks in a deep breath after his long speech, winded. He's sweating, dizzy, nauseous. *Damn, that hill had been steep.*

The detective takes a moment before he answers. 'There's blood and it certainly wasn't there the last time I checked, which means someone has come back and done something to it.'

'Blood can be faked. Hence why I need a boost to double check before we start blabbing to the whole village that there's a dead body hanging in a tree. Rather poetic though, considering the name.'

Detective Williams sighs, relaxing his shoulders. 'Climbing a tree in the dark is suicide, Mr Mallow. Plus, no offence, but you look as if a stiff breeze could blow you over. Are you sure you're feeling well?'

'Never better. Here, hold this.' Stephen pulls off his thick wool hat and hands it to the detective, who takes it with a defeated look upon his face. 'Hold the torch so I can see what I'm doing.'

Detective Williams does what Stephen asks, directing the beam onto the trunk of the tree. 'It would be easier with a ladder, Mr Mallow. That's how I got up there.'

'Let's not waste time with ladders,' says Stephen, wedging his left foot into a knarred knot on the trunk. Luckily, the tree is old and disfigured enough to not have a perfectly straight trunk. There are enough broken sections, knots, other large branches and even old nails and pieces of wood to clamber up, probably put there by the locals to make it accessible to climb over the years. The detective gives him a boost by pushing on the bottom of his right foot. He grunts with the effort.

Stephen is looking forward to researching the name associated with the tree. He has a feeling that the detective hasn't told him the whole story yet.

Stephen gets halfway up the trunk before his arms start to burn, and his lungs protest. His mind casts back to the phone call from the hospital and his results that are waiting for him tomorrow morning, at an appointment he has no intention of attending. Maybe he should call and cancel, but then the doctor might try and tell him the results over the phone; results he doesn't want to know. Perhaps there really is something wrong with him, but whether there is or not, it isn't going to stop him from climbing the tree and finding out exactly what's hanging ominously above.

The higher he goes, the further his heartrate climbs with him. High and higher. He has to stop, his head swimming.

'Everything okay there, Mr Mallow?' the detective calls from the ground.

Stephen leans against a thick branch and glances down. 'Never better!' The ground zooms in and out of focus.

Now he is high in the branches, the torch beam isn't as strong, and it's getting more and more difficult to see which route he has to take to climb higher. He slips and catches his hand on a sharp branch, slicing through the skin on his left palm. A sting of pain electrifies his arm, but nothing he can't handle. The headache that's pounding behind his eyes is worse.

A couple of minutes later, he arrives at the bottom of the scarecrow. The top of his head is level with its dangling feet. One thing is for certain; it's *not* a dead body after all. It's a momentary relief, but where is all the blood coming from?

Doing his best to use the dwindling light from below, he cranes his head this way and that, trying to find the source of the blood that's dripping down the old coat. It isn't a lot. It isn't like there's rivers of the stuff running down into the branches below, but it's enough to stand out. In fact, the blood seems to glow against the faded jacket.

'Not a body!' Stephen calls out. 'Just a very creepy-looking scarecrow that's bleeding.'

'Good, but where's the blood coming from?'

'Hard to say! But I think … wait …' Stephen pulls on the legs of the scarecrow to get a better look at the front. The coat is done up with old-fashioned buttons, but not all the way. Twigs, leaves and dried mud make up the body and are sticking out of the top of the coat, but that's not what he's staring at.

'Um … it might not be a dead body, but …' Stephen pauses again, holding his breath. 'It's like something out of the *Wizard of Oz*.'

'What?' comes the gruff response from below.

'This scarecrow … he may not have a brain, but he does have a heart; a real heart.'

Chapter 17
GRAHAM

Graham stares. Blinks. Keeps staring. Up into the branches. He can just about see Mr Mallow's feet. Has he heard him correctly? Did he say the scarecrow has a heart? He knows Mr Mallow is a little peculiar, but he doesn't have him down as someone who'd play such a crude practical joke.

Graham's neck protests as he cranes it upwards, but he can't tear his eyes away from the scene as Mr Mallow unties the scarecrow with difficulty and drags it down through the branches, which snap and groan. Several dozen crispy leaves and a multitude of tree mites cascade into Graham's eyes.

He thinks back to what he overheard yesterday, regarding moving the scarecrow and bringing bad luck, but that was before he found out there may or may not be a human heart inside. As an ex-detective, he knows better than to mess with a potential crime scene, but all thoughts have now blown away on the wind.

There's something about this whole tree and scarecrow situation that calls to him. Like Mr Mallow, he has a passion for finding out the truth, no matter the cost. And now, this investigation has turned up a notch. If kids are playing pranks like this, then what else are they capable of doing?

Several minutes later, Mr Mallow finishes manhandling the scarecrow down through the branches and lets it drop through the final thinner ones where it lands with a thud at Graham's feet. While Mr Mallow navigates his way down the trunk, Graham steps closer, shining the torch beam onto the grotesque-looking heap on the ground.

The coat is covered in blood; a new development from yesterday when he last saw it. Now he thinks about it, he's pretty sure there hadn't been blood there this morning when he'd looked up at it either. Some of the blood is still fresh, glimmering as the light from the torch catches it. There's no way he would have missed it. Besides, due to the blood being fresh, it must have been left there recently, sometime in the last few hours. In the cold winter air, it will have taken longer to dry.

'What do you think, Detective?' asks Mr Mallow, joining him at his side. His breathing is laboured and a sheen of sweat sparkles on his forehead.

'You okay?' asks Graham.

'Never been great at climbing trees. I'm not exactly what you'd call the athletic type.'

'Join the club.' Graham returns his eyes to the scarecrow. He hands Mr Mallow the torch and then kneels on the ground. His left knee clicks loudly, and he winces in response.

Graham is careful not to touch the coat too much, so uses a stick to pull back the front of it. There, wedged inside the chest of the scarecrow, is a bleeding heart. Fresh.

'Is it human?' asks Mr Mallow, screwing up his nose.

Graham does the same. It's got that tangy, raw odour that most fresh meat has, yet it's also just on the edge of turning foul.

'Hard to say. Can't say I've ever been this close to an actual heart. Could be a pig's heart. They are remarkably similar to human hearts, especially to look at.'

'And you would know that, how?' asks Mr Mallow without missing a beat.

'After fifty-five years on this planet, you learn a few random facts from time to time.' Mr Mallow raises his eyebrows and Graham's face remains deadpan. 'I used to work in a butcher's shop when I was a kid. Fifteen. Something like that.'

'Huh.'

Graham meticulously checks the rest of the scarecrow, but he can't see any other body parts. He checks the pockets, but they're empty. He finds himself disappointed.

'Nothing in the pockets this time,' he says.

'Do you have the items you found on you?'

Graham stands up, his left knee cracking again. He reaches into his own jacket pocket and pulls out the sketch and the missing poster. He hands them to Mr Mallow, who studies them for several seconds, paying close attention to the sketch in particular.

'Someone is sending a message,' replies Mr Mallow matter-of-factly.

'That was my thought too.'

'I'm not talking about the sketch and the poster. I'm talking about the scarecrow. Has this happened before?'

'Apparently, it's a prank that the local kids play every year, close to the anniversary of John Hammel's death, which happens to be around Halloween. But nothing was said about there being an actual heart involved.'

Mr Mallow stares at the scarecrow. 'You said something about a curse?'

'It appears there's a superstition regarding the tree and John Hammel's death. Ever since his death a hundred years ago, the village has been plagued with bad luck. A curse, if you will.'

'Interesting.'

Graham shakes his head. 'What is it with these strange little towns in the countryside and their weird traditions and curses?'

Mr Mallow shrugs. 'Cherry Hollow didn't have a weird tradition or a curse.'

'No, just a dark, evil entity who tormented guilty people.'

'What do you make of the missing poster of the girl?' asks Mr Mallow.

Graham has always been mildly impressed with Mr Mallow's ability to change the topic of the conversation in a single breath.

Graham pauses before speaking. 'Hastily done. Not a professional job. No photo of the girl. Scribbled in pencil. Not exactly a decent attempt to look for her.'

'You say she's not actually missing?'

'Unconfirmed. I was unable to get a straight answer from anyone. She used to live on Blackberry Farm with her father, Frank Hammel. People seemed to be very sketchy with the details, almost like no one wants to talk about her at all, like she didn't even exist.'

'Sounds like this village is keeping secrets.'

'It's a high possibility. Yes.'

Mr Mallow pockets the sketch and the poster. 'Well, it's too late to start asking questions now. I'll spend tonight doing my own research. You have Wi-Fi, I presume?'

'I may be retired, Mr Mallow, but I still have the basic amenities.'

'Very well.'

Graham brushes some dirt from the knees of his trousers. 'Fine. Research it is. Let's get this blasted thing back into the garage. Hopefully, it won't decide to hang itself back up in the tree overnight.'

Chapter 18
SOPHIA

Bethgelert, Wales, 2015

It took several minutes to bust a hole in the plasterboard with the wrench. If I had something with a little more heft to it, I could have broken through in half the time, but the wrench eventually did the trick. I coughed and spluttered as particles and splinters of plasterboard flew into the air and danced around me, also covering me in a thin layer of grey and white dust.

My dad was going to kill me when he found out I'd busted a hole through the wall.

My dad. How was I supposed to explain this to him? Shit.

People were arriving tomorrow to stay in the cottage. Double shit.

How was I meant to cover up this mess? Triple shit.

I cursed my recklessness and lack of thought, but there could have been someone trapped behind the wall, so I couldn't leave them there, could I? It was too late to do anything about it now.

Once I created a hole big enough to fit my body through, I half expected a dirty head to pop out of the wall. I never had my dad down for human trafficking, but he was a member of the weird village committee who held their share of secret meetings, so I guessed anything was possible.

I used my phone and shone the beam of light through the hole, holding my breath to stop myself from inhaling the tiny dust particles. Beyond the hole was a spiderweb infested space, but further on it widened into a …

'No way!' I said, ducking through the tight hole.

Once I navigated the webs and dust, I crouched under a low beam and emerged into a room. An actual whole other room, complete with faded, outdated wallpaper and furniture. There was a bed, a chest of drawers and a wardrobe. The whole space looked frozen in time, like it belonged in a museum.

Shining the light around, I studied the simple decoration, the plain bedspread, the faded carpet. What the hell was this room? Did Dad know about it? Was he the one who boarded it up? There was even a window. I walked over and peered through the dirty glass, expecting to look out onto the yard below, but I saw nothing but darkness. The window must have been boarded up from the outside, or closed off somehow.

I'd never noticed an extra window before, but I'd always known there was something *off* about the hallway. It was a dead end and had always looked out of place, like there should have been a room attached. It was right there, as clear as day, and I'd missed it.

I wandered over to the low bed. Everything was covered in a thick blanket of dust. How long had this been boarded up? I couldn't explain it. I may have only discovered this secret place, but it felt as if it were a place just for me, to hide away from the world when I needed a little peace and quiet. But why was it boarded up in the first place? What was the reason? Did someone live in here once upon a time?

I cast my mind back. As far as I knew, my dad had always owned Rosemore Cottage. It was a family-owned farm, going back decades. In fact, John Hammel would have lived here.

That was when it hit me.

This was his old room.

I headed to the wardrobe, desperate for answers of any kind. The double doors were stiff to open, but after a bit of brute force, they finally gave way, revealing several hanging items of clothing, including an old coat, like a farmer would wear. Something about it drew me in, so I pulled it off the wooden hanger and checked it over, noting a rip on the left cuff and a few stains of red. I didn't return it, but took it with me as I walked across to the chest of drawers. I pulled at the top drawer, which, again, stuck, so I yanked it open.

The surprises kept coming.

In the drawer were several old books. They looked more like diaries or journals than ordinary books.

Setting the coat on the floor, I picked up one of the books. It was old, bound with worn brown leather. Not all of the books were brown. Some were black or grey. The pages of the one in my hand were full of sketches. They were really, really good and were shockingly familiar.

'Wow,' I said, taking my time to study each one. They deserved to be looked at thoroughly. The skill and precision were exceptional. The different pencil marks of varying strength, length and size made the sketches come alive before my eyes.

Animals. Trees. People.

The only other time I'd seen similar sketches was when I sat and drew them underneath The Hanging Tree. There wasn't anything that wasn't sketched. On every drawing, in the bottom right corner were the initials **JH** and the date they were drawn.

John Hammel, my great, great, great grandfather, drew these. A huge smile beamed across my face as I realised I was indeed standing in his bedroom, a room that had been blocked off from the rest of the house, sealing it shut, locking away all his treasured possessions for the past nine decades.

Why would anyone do that?

When John died, his family must have made the decision to board up his room. Had they been ashamed of him or were they trying to hide something? I'd never met the man, but when his soul entered my body when I sat beneath the tree, I didn't feel angry or sad. I didn't believe John had it in him to take his own life.

Holding the sketchbook close to my chest, I took a deep breath. 'What really happened to you, John?' I asked the empty room. 'I promise I'll find out the truth.'

Chapter 19
STEPHEN

Stephen watches Detective Williams move around the farmhouse-style kitchen, finishing preparing dinner. It seems he had already cooked most of it before he arrived. There's a large wooden table in the centre that acts like the kitchen island, a perfect base from which to conduct his research, so Stephen sets his laptop up there. Neither of them are particular outspoken individuals; both preferring silence to awkward small talk. It works for their friendship if they don't speak too much.

He doesn't want to waste a single minute. His mind races with endless possibilities as to the origin and background story of the scarecrow. Weird cult. Strange pagan ritual. Practical joke. Only time will tell, but the detective seems convinced it's a prank, having been told that by the locals. But if Stephen has learned anything in his time as a journalist, it's that people lie when they have something to hide. And this village certainly seems to be hiding something. What exactly that is is still open for debate.

His fingers dance across the laptop keys as they fight to keep up with his whizzing brain. He uses his knowledge of keywords to fine-tune his results using the search engine, but the detective is right about one thing; there isn't a lot of information on the world wide web with regards to the village and its history. It seems he has to search a little closer to home.

'Here, have a look at this,' says Detective Williams, chucking a small magazine at him. 'Page fifteen.'

Stephen reads the front cover first, never one to jump ahead of himself.

The Bethgelert Oracle.

A few baiting headlines pop out, bringing a smile to his lips. Even out here in the sticks, the people love a good catchy headline.

He flicks through the first few pages. It certainly holds a vast range of information regarding the village, its history and the goings on. The yearly aubergine competition makes his lips curve into another smirk. Apparently, when it comes to phallic-shaped vegetables, size *does* matter.

He navigates to page fifteen, curious as to what the detective has found interesting enough to warrant his attention.

Death to The Hanging Tree by Anonymous

The infamous tree atop the hill in Bethgelert has long been the subject of many a legend, myth and superstition, but it has also bred a very brutal and real curse. Those of us who have been around long enough, born and raised in the village, have grown up with the tree overlooking us, casting a gloomy shadow across the whole valley.

The time has come to say goodbye. There will be a petition going around the village over the coming months for those of you who wish to save the tree, but come December the first, if enough signatures are not collected, then The Hanging Tree will be set alight and burned.

The families of Bethgelert have lived with the curse for long enough. Our beloved committee member, Frank Hammel, has suffered the most over the years, losing his whole family along the way. He may wish to save the tree, but others may not. I hope you will join me in supporting the removal and destruction of the tree that has tormented our village for most of our lives.

This will be the last year the tree stands high.

May the souls of the dead trapped within its roots be set free.

Stephen lowers the magazine. 'Rather a morbid article for a village magazine, wouldn't you say?'

The detective nods. 'Indeed.'

'I wonder who wrote it and why they'd want to remain anonymous.'

'Your guess is as good as mine, but it appears that someone on the village council doesn't share Frank Hammel's views.'

'You said that there was talk during the village meeting about its destruction?'

The detective nods. 'Yes, but the majority of the village want to see it remain. Frank agreed.'

'Who were the ones who wanted to see it gone?'

Detective Williams is silent for a moment. 'No one in particular stood out.'

'Hmm.'

Stephen continues to search through the magazine, jotting down the names of the village committee, those in charge of running all the functions, and those in charge when it comes to land planning and building regulations. It even mentions the best person to ask for help with gardening, extensions and the local kids club, which runs on Saturday and Wednesday afternoons.

'Hmm,' says Stephen again, writing down the last name on the village committee list.

'Found anything else interesting, Mr Mallow?' asks Detective Williams, glancing behind him from tending the stove.

'Nothing yet, but it seems to me that the village committee members hold a lot of power in this village. Nothing goes ahead without their say so. Is that normal for a small Welsh village such as this?'

'Hard to say. We didn't have anything like that in Cherry Hollow, unless you count the weekly coffee meeting in the village hall. But yes, I got the feeling that Frank Hammel was the guy in charge when I attended the meeting last night.'

'It appears that the village committee members go back some way. The Hammel family have been members as far back as the 1900s and so have the Davies family. Do you know of anyone by the name of Davies in the village?'

'The butcher's shop is called Davies and Son.'

Stephen writes a note next to the name. 'So, that would mean that John Hammel would have been a member back in 1925.'

'I highly doubt that. He was just a kid. Twenty, I believe.'

'His father then, perhaps?'

'A likely scenario. Would you care for another whisky?'

'Please.'

Stephen ignores the detective while he refills his glass with ice and whisky and turns to the laptop, setting the magazine aside for now. He decides to turn his attention to Sophia Hammel and see what he can find out about her and her possible disappearance ten years ago.

It doesn't take him more than ten minutes before he runs into a problem. Quite a serious one.

'It seems Sophia Hammel doesn't exist on any social media sites. Not in the past ten years, anyway,' he tells the detective, who stops cooking and listens as he continues. 'She has an old Facebook account that hasn't been updated in ten years, almost to the day.'

He doesn't say anything else, and the detective doesn't press him further. Often, Stephen likes to speak his thoughts out loud, making them easier to decipher and organise.

'Hmm,' he says a few minutes later. 'It would be helpful if *The Bethgelert Oracle* published their articles online, but it seems they like to keep things very private. Too private. Would a small village like this hold physical records of old magazines they've published over the years?'

The detective shakes his head. 'Hard to say, but I can ask Karen next time I see her.'

Stephen doesn't ask who Karen is. He doesn't need to know the details, but if she can possibly help them in locating older copies of the magazine from around the time that Sophia Hammel supposedly went missing, then it would be very useful indeed.

'Ah,' he says. 'Here's something.' He leans closer to the screen. 'Apparently, Bethgelert made one of the national papers in January of 2015. Well, well, well ... looks like the village committee weren't able to keep everything offline after all.'

Detective Williams reads over his shoulder.

Ten years ago, there was a spate of disturbances in the village. A group of teenage girls were cautioned for loitering in the park and bullying another girl of the same age. No names were provided.

Stephen knows all about girls like them. When he was a boy, a group of four girls had picked on and tormented him from primary all the way through secondary school. His parents (mainly his father) refused to accept there was anything different about him and couldn't understand why he didn't learn at the same rate as everyone else. They called him disruptive, rude and lazy. Stephen wasn't any of those things. Quite the opposite. But those girls had been determined to make his life even harder by constantly belittling him in front of people and laughing whenever he got something wrong or made a fool of himself, which was quite often.

Nowadays, thankfully, society seems to understand learning difficulties a lot more, but from what Stephen has seen in the news and on social media, it doesn't mean people are any less sympathetic or accepting of it. In fact, with the explosion of social media since his school days, the bullying and harassment has increased dramatically. He's glad he didn't grow up in today's society where everything is posted online for the whole world to see and share. He's grateful his childhood and teenage years had been spent relatively social media free. The only reminders he has from that time are physical pictures hidden away at the back of his desk drawer. He didn't exist online before 2007.

'Do you think any of those girls were Sophia?' asks the detective.

'Unconfirmed, but as I said, she doesn't appear to exist online as of 2015. For all intents and purposes, she truly has disappeared, which raises more questions. The most obvious one being why is no one actively looking for her? There's nothing, anywhere online, about a missing girl from this village from that time.'

Stephen clicks a few more links in the search results. 'This could be something … it's a local school competition from eleven years ago. Sophia's name is mentioned and … it looks like she won. They have her winning entry right here and … Detective, you're going to want to read this.'

The Detective comes round and stands behind him, leaning over his shoulder as they read together in silence.

Death in the Trees by Sophia Hammel

Trees have always fascinated me. I've decided to turn my attention to the oldest trees in Britain. It's a well-known fact that the oldest type of tree in the United Kingdom is the yew tree, but determining the age of a tree is often difficult. This is because the trunks of ancient trees are usually hollow, so there's no chance of counting the rings.

However, the yew tree is different in this aspect. They have a remarkable ability to renew and continue to thrive, living for thousands of years. A yew tree can live for around 900 years before they are considered ancient, *whereas oak trees are considered ancient at around 400 years.*

Therefore, it's not surprising that most of the trees in the running for the oldest tree in Britain are yew trees. However, there are also several oak trees that deserve attention, including one that stands in the very village I live in. Situated atop a hill in the sleepy village of Bethgelert, in mid-Wales, is an oak tree, locally named The Hanging Tree.

This tree is somewhat of a mystery. It has a girth of just under 10 metres and is thought to be over 800 years old. What sets it apart from any other tree is its stunning location, growing on top of a large hill on the outskirts of the village. It towers over the valley below, like an ancient statue, guarding a secret. Unlike some large oaks, its trunk isn't hollow. It is an impressive beast of a tree.

It is named The Hanging Tree for a sad reason, but it's only had the name for the past 90 years or so. Back in 1925, a young man named John Hammel was found hanging from the tree after tragically ending his own life. He was my great, great, great grandfather.

He was discovered by his sweetheart, Carys Griffiths, who mourned him for several months before dying in childbirth; bearing his child and therefore continuing the family name. It's a sad story, but one that has moulded the village of Bethgelert for nearly one hundred years.

Old trees are usually symbols of strength, resilience and a beacon of hope in the surrounding community. The same cannot be said for The Hanging Tree. Since 1925, it has been left to its own devices, having even been struck by lightning in 1960, severely damaging the trunk and one of its thicker branches.

The land the tree stands on still belongs to the Hammel family, but hardly anything is known about John Hammel. He's now buried in the local graveyard with nothing but his name to show where he lies. It seems as if he has brought shame to the family name for ending his own life. Nothing is known about him, but his family have lived on until this day, including me.

The tree itself is over 100 feet tall; an impressive feat considering its location. It's a shame it has such a bad backstory. The question is ... why did John Hammel hang himself from the tree? Perhaps one day, someone will be able to learn more about the events of what happened in 1925 and why such a happy farm boy, who had everything to live for, decided to cut his life short one day.

The Hanging Tree knows, but who will be the one to reveal its secrets?

Only time will tell. That's the thing about old trees. In another hundred years, it'll still be here, watching over the village, hiding the secrets within.

Unless someone can uncover them first.

Chapter 20
GRAHAM

Graham reads the online article, which appears to be very well written for a teenager. It seems she knew a hell of a lot for someone so young and, since she was a daughter of the main man in the village, she probably had a lot more access to sensitive information than others.

But did she know too much?

There wasn't a lot in the article they didn't know already, but it did cement the fact that Sophia Hammel clearly had a fascination with The Hanging Tree and the untimely death of her relative. She was also searching for information; just like they were doing now.

Graham leaves Mr Mallow to continue his research. He quietly reads and scrolls on his laptop screen for several more minutes, his eyes barely blinking. If Graham didn't know any better, he'd have said the man is in some sort of trance. Graham returns to the dinner, now ready for serving, spooning a large ladle of curry into a wide-rimmed bowl, followed by a pile of fluffy, steamed rice.

He slides a bowl across the table towards Mr Mallow, along with a set of cutlery, then takes a seat opposite him and begins to eat, knowing better than to disturb the man. Graham is halfway through his bowl of food by the time Mr Mallow looks up from the laptop screen, taking a deep breath for the first time in a while.

'Okay, I think I'm getting somewhere.'

Graham swallows a mouthful of curry too fast without chewing the lumps of vegetables and a piece gets stuck in his throat. He coughs, then swallows it down. 'Enlighten me.'

'Where's Sophia's mother in all of this?'

Graham is silent, thinking. 'You know, she's never come up.'

'Exactly.'

'Which means?'

Mr Mallow sighs. 'I thought you used to be a damn good detective? I find myself disappointed.'

Graham tuts and spoons more curry into his mouth. He knows Mr Mallow isn't saying that to be cruel, despite it sounding exactly that. 'Fine,' says Graham. 'We'll ask around about her mother tomorrow. Wait .. there is one thing. In Sophia's written piece, there was nothing about a scarecrow.'

Mr Mallow looks at his laptop. 'Consider my disappointment in you revoked. That's a good catch, Detective. You're right, which means that the scarecrow could very well be a recent development. If Sophia is missing, then it only started being hung in the tree after her disappearance. It may not have anything to do with John Hammel at all, but rather Sophia Hammel.' At this point. Mr Mallow notices the bowl of food next to him and begins to eat, taking small bites and chewing a lot. Graham expects he has to chew his food a certain number of times before swallowing it.

'I have made numerous searches and there's nothing about her disappearance online. I think we need to know for sure whether she is or isn't missing,' says Mr Mallow after swallowing his first mouthful of food.

'Agreed. What do you make of the heart found inside the scarecrow?' asks Graham before spooning the last portion of rice in his bowl.

'Hard to say at this stage, but let's err on the side of caution and confirm whether it is a pig heart first. Let's head to the local butchers to see if they have sold any pig hearts lately or if any of the neighbouring farms have had any of their pigs killed. Considering the Davies family are also members of the village council, they may also have some useful information to share.'

'That's if they do share it at all,' says Graham.

Mr Mallow nods his agreement, then takes another small bite of food. 'It certainly is strange,' he says. 'The Hanging Tree is one of the oldest oak trees in the United Kingdom. It's possibly almost a thousand years old. It must have seen some amazing sights over the years.'

Graham watches as Mr Mallow stares off into space.

He admits, it's good to flex his brain muscles again with this mystery. A part of him wants this; no, needs this. He's been somewhat bored for a while and he's looking forward to investigating tomorrow morning. Someone somewhere must know something.

'Yet, they wish to burn it to the ground,' says Graham.

'Yes, which poses another question, doesn't it? Why now?'

Graham pushes his empty bowl away. 'Something is going on in this village. I've been blind not to have seen it before, but it all started when that scarecrow appeared in the tree. There's something that people don't want us to know. John Hammel seemingly killed himself a hundred years ago, but why? Another mystery is who wrote the short article about the burning of the tree in the Bethgelert Oracle?'

'Someone who wants that tree gone, along with all the secrets it holds.'

'But trees don't hold secrets, Mr Mallow. People do.'

Mr Mallow holds up a single finger in a point. 'Ah, but people also like to use deception and blame to distract others from their true intentions. The tree may not hold physical secrets, but it is a very large, very poignant symbol in this village and holds a lot of history. Whoever has made it their mission to destroy it is the person who has the most to gain from its destruction. Without the tree, this village is just an ordinary village. Perhaps they are hoping that with the tree gone, the history, the curse the residents have seemingly created, will disappear too.'

Graham lets out a long sigh. 'And here I was thinking this would be a straightforward investigation. I guess it's time to hit the hay, Mr Mallow. Tomorrow is a brand new day, and we have ourselves a lot of people to speak to, who may not appreciate our questions.'

'My favourite type of investigation,' says Mr Mallow. He reaches up and rubs his forehead.

Graham watches the man as he closes his eyes for a moment, as if in pain. Graham sees a trickle of blood drip from his nose. Mr Mallow quickly wipes it away with a tissue from his pocket and stands up, picking his laptop up from the table.

'Goodnight, Detective.'

'Goodnight, Mr Mallow. The spare room is the second door on the right just before the dead end hallway.'

Graham doesn't like the way Mr Mallow is holding himself. Something is wrong, but if he knows the man at all, he won't say a single word until it's worth mentioning. Graham must trust that he knows what he's doing. He isn't one to pry, but he'd also never forgive himself if something happened to his friend and he didn't do anything to stop it.

Chapter 21

STEPHEN

It's creeping closer to midnight, a brand-new day, by the time Stephen bids the detective goodnight, then climbs the stairs. He follows the detective's instructions and locates the spare room just before the dead-end hallway. The area intrigues him. A hallway that goes nowhere seems like a slightly pointless design of the cottage, but his intrigue soon turns to confusion. Something doesn't add up. What's the purpose of it? Surely, there should be some sort of window where the blank wall is, or even an extra room? It's only a two-bedroom cottage as it stands, but the downstairs is considerably larger than the upstairs.

He scratches his head, too exhausted to give it any more thought tonight. His brain needs to rest and recharge, ready for a big day tomorrow, and he's not feeling his best. A lingering headache is slowly weighing him down, to the point where all he wants to do is crawl into bed and pull the covers over his head, like he used to do when he was a child so he didn't have to listen to his parents arguing. He got good at ignoring that type of thing.

He's not sure if the detective noticed his bloody nose earlier, but if he did, he didn't remark on it. Stephen listens as the detective moves around downstairs, closing down for the night. Stephen then uses the bathroom and enters the spare room. It's pleasant enough. The single bed is like a warm, welcoming hug at the end of a long day. A simple lamp on a small table sits beside the bed.

Stephen dumps his case on the floor and searches his shoulder bag for his painkillers, popping two out of the blister pack. He checks his phone as he climbs into bed.

Damn it.

Rachel.

He hadn't messaged her when he'd arrived like he said he would. He'd completely forgotten about it. When his mind is busy like this, he often forgets simple things like keeping in contact with people and even eating and drinking. He has several missed calls from her and at least a dozen texts. Stephen is one of those people who will glance at a new text, make a mental note to respond soon, then forget about it and not reply until three working days later.

He reads through her texts, struggling to focus on the words, which blur together. The texts slowly get more and more concerned, then angry and annoyed. It's too late to call her now. She'll be asleep, so he sends her a text instead.

Stephen: *Sorry. Not much signal here. I'm fine. Arrived safe. Love you x*

She messages back within seconds.

Rachel: *I've been so worried. Please take care. What time are you back tomorrow? Don't forget about your hospital appointment. Love you too x*

He goes to type but finds he doesn't know what to say. There's no way he's returning to Cherry Hollow tomorrow. He's going to have to reschedule his hospital appointment, but Rachel won't like that, will she? She'll start nagging and telling him his health is more important than an investigation. But she's wrong.

He can't afford any distractions. Hospital appointments are included in that heading.

Nothing is more important than this case. Nothing.

He can't explain it to her. She won't understand. She's not like him. No one is.

Stephen turns his phone to silent and places it on the side table by the bed, face down. He'll deal with her wrath another time.

Like the detective said, tomorrow is a new day.

The Hanging Tree is calling to him.

He dreams about it. He's there, sitting beneath it, drawing a sunset, waiting for someone, but happy to be alone. The view is beautiful from up here. He looks down at his hands as they effortlessly sketch the view. Stephen's never been good at drawing, never had an artistic bone in his body, except when it came to words, but the drawing on the paper is beautiful. He recognises it.

Then, a tickle.

Around his neck.

A rustle of leaves from above.

A noose slithers down from the tree by itself, wraps around his neck and strings him up like an animal carcass. He jolts upright in bed, gasping and grabbing at his neck. It's sore – as if it really happened.

The tree is trying to tell him something.

For a moment, he was somewhere else, *someone* else.

John Hammel.

What happened to you, John? And why is your great, great, great grand-daughter now potentially missing a hundred years after your untimely death?

Chapter 22
SOPHIA

Bethgelert, Wales, 2015

I spent ages looking through the sketchbooks, taking in every detail, every torn and rotten page. A lot of them were damaged. They must have spent all this time in the room, locked away in these drawers hidden from sunlight, but in a perfect place for dust and mould to settle. I'd rescued them. They called to me, drew me into their pages. Each told a story, sketches of various sights around the village, most of them I knew well. There were even drawings of people; farmers, shopkeepers, neighbours, but most of the portraits were of the same young woman.

The fact that my great, great, great grandfather drew them, told me the woman must have been Carys, my great, great, great grandmother. According to the family history, she was the person who found John hanging from the tree all those years ago.

Carys was never the same, and she died eight months later in childbirth.

She told whoever would listen there was no way John would have done that to himself, but no one believed her. Back then, there was no way of gathering evidence to find out exactly what happened. There was no investigation. It was deemed an obvious suicide and John Hammel was buried without a special funeral provided by the church. In their eyes, he had committed the ultimate sin and didn't deserve a proper burial. No one came to pay their respects. That was why his grave was now overgrown and forgotten all these years later.

I was certain there was more to this story. The hidden room held all of John's secrets and I was determined to uncover them. Someone needed to speak for him. His voice had been stolen all those years ago. Someone killed him. I was sure of it.

Putting down the sketchbooks, I decided to keep searching the room, eventually finding a damp box hidden under the bed. I pulled it out and crouched next to it, opening its soggy, musty edges. The majority of it disintegrated in my hands. I gasped when I saw more books inside, but they weren't filled with drawings.

They were filled with writing. Diaries, perhaps?

Not only was there writing, but also cutouts of newspaper articles, all to do with the village and its residents from nine decades ago. Obviously, they weren't like the newspapers we had today, but it was fascinating to read. But the more I read, the more I understood why it was hidden.

John didn't want anyone to find these for a reason. He'd been collecting and collating information about everyone in the village at the time.

Listed on one of the pages in a well-worn book was a list of names, none of which I recogn sed personally, but the surnames were familiar. The names on the page were from generations ago.

Davies. Bevan. Hammel. Griffiths.

Those were surnames of some of the members of the village committee. I had no idea their family names went back so far, or that the committee had been around for so long. I knew my family had lived here for generations, but not the others.

Why had John listed them like this?

Was he watching them, keep ng an eye on them for some reason?

I flipped the pages faster, wanting to know the answers, but there was too much information here to absorb at once. It would take me hours to comb through it all. I dared not remove any of this stuff from the room. I had to keep John's secret, find out why he was compiling a list of information. Was it to be used agains: the village committee somehow?

Then, words started jumping cff the page at me.

Kill. Dead. Illegal. Underground. Heart. Human. Sacrifice.

Holy crap!

My eyes grew wider and wider the more I read. I was being sucked into the pages. Human sacrifice? Were the village committee into some sort of satanic ritual or something?

Then it hit me like a freight train.

John's death wasn't a suicide. I was right all along.

He was killed because he knew something; something the village elders didn't want anyone to know about. Now, somewhere in these pages was the truth, hidden for almost one-hundred years.

I decided there and then that I was going to fight for John Hammel. I was going to discover what was going on in this village. Maybe it had ceased since his day, or maybe it hadn't. For all I knew, my father was in on it. It was up to me now.

Those four families held the long-lost secrets of the village.

I decided to take John's coat with me, along with a sketch of the tree. He would tell me what I needed to do next.

Chapter 23

GRAHAM

He's awake, showered, dressed and nursing his second coffee of the morning before seven, having been tossing and turning, dreaming of scarecrows and bleeding hearts since six. No surprise there, he supposes.

He flicks the kettle back on when he hears the spare bedroom's door open and Mr Mallows' feet pad across the landing to the bathroom. Graham has never had a guest stay with him before, so it's an unusual situation. He's not sure whether to cook Stephen breakfast or allow him to fend for himself, so he settles for making a coffee, which he's sure to appreciate. He doubts Mr Mallow will have slept well if he's anything like Graham. Sleeping in a new place, a new bed, never goes well the first night.

A few minutes later, Mr Mallow appears at the doorway to the kitchen, his laptop bag slung over his shoulder. Dear God, the man looks positively sickly, as if he's about to keel over at any second.

'Morning, Detective,' he grunts.

'*Bore da*, Mr Mallow.'

'Have you checked to see if our little friend is still in the garage where we left him?'

Graham pauses with his coffee cup halfway to his mouth. Straight to business then. 'I locked the garage door last night.'

'That's what you did last time too, but someone still managed to get it back up the tree again.'

They hold eye contact for a moment and then, without another word, get their boots and jackets on and trek across the yard to the garage. The autumn sun is still waking up, so Graham holds his trusty torch aloft as he unlocks the garage. Without stepping a foot inside, he directs the beam into the corner where they'd left the scarecrow last night. The strange, ghostly figure lays haphazardly in a heap; the once-fresh blood now dried on the jacket.

Graham huffs and closes the door. 'Still there,' he says.

Mr Mallow shudders against the chill. 'So it seems,' he replies.

The men make their way slowly back to the cottage in silence.

Graham removes his boots and jacket. 'The butcher's shop opens early. Once we're ready, let's go there first and inquire about the heart.'

Mr Mallow closes the door behind him. 'Yes, and then we should visit Frank Hammel and confirm whether his daughter is living here, living elsewhere or is, indeed, missing.'

'If she is missing then something is definitely wrong in this village,' replies Graham. 'Back in Cherry Hollow, when

Kieran Jones went missing, the village was in an uproar for years. It was all anyone could talk about. Parents wouldn't let their children leave the house after dark. Small villages are notorious for banding together when a tragedy strikes the community, so why not here? Why wouldn't the village be more concerned about a missing teenager?'

'Hmm, I have a feeling there's a lot more to this than meets the eye. We have a lot of blanks to fill in today.' Mr Mallow sits at the table and switches on his laptop, typing ferociously while Graham finishes making coffee.

A few minutes later, Graham places a steaming cup of coffee next to Mr Mallow's laptop. Mr Mallow doesn't look up. His eyes are laserbeams on the screen.

'Can I get you any breakfast?' he asks, watching as Mr Mallow's eyes race back and forth, barely blinking or pausing.

There's no response.

Graham clears his throat. 'Mr Mallow?'

'Yes?'

'Breakfast?'

'I'm not hungry. Thanks.' A sheen of sweat beads on Mr Mallow's forehead. The cottage isn't overly warm. Graham keeps the heating on low during the autumn rather than turning it on and off whenever he needs it. Graham wonders if Mr Mallow is feeling okay. He has always seemed a little odd to Graham, but the way he's acting is rather out of character. The long pauses in between some sentences is not like Mr

Mallow, who usually speaks much faster than the average person.

Graham makes himself some toast and jam, eating whilst looking up at the tree that torments him. If it is indeed almost a thousand years old, it must have seen some incredible things. It may have been here before the village itself. Had someone planted it all those years ago on top of the hill, or had it sprouted roots on its own from a random acorn that was dropped by wildlife?

It's a mystery. Exactly like the curse and deaths surrounding it.

After breakfast, Graham gets ready to leave for the village.

'Are you ready to leave, Mr Mallow?' he asks.

Mr Mallow raises his head. 'Yes, just finishing off some work emails.'

'Everything all right?'

'I believe so.'

'I meant with your overall health,' Graham adds, hoping he hasn't overstepped the mark.

Mr Mallow coughs, using a tissue from his pocket to cover his mouth. 'Nothing to concern yourself with, Detective. I ...' He stops mid-sentence and stares ahead, straight out the window and up at the tree in the distance.

The early morning sun is rising behind it, giving off a pinkish, orange glow and Mr Mallow can't seem to take his eyes off it. Graham follows his line of sight, frowning as he does so, wondering what Mr Mallow is staring so intently at if it's not the tree. Then, in a blink of an eye, Mr Mallow snaps out of his stupor, shrugs into his jacket and heads out the door.

It's odd behaviour, but then Mr Mallow is renowned for being somewhat peculiar on occasion.

'I thought we'd walk as it's due to be a nice day,' says Graham, joining Mr Mallow in the yard. He prefers to walk when he can. Due to the narrow roads, parking is often a nightmare and there is no official carpark to use, so residents park wherever they can find a space, which causes chaos.

'Yes, yes, very good.' But Mr Mallow's gaze is elsewhere again. This time, looking at the cottage. Graham's not sure if he's looking at anything in particular, but doesn't question him.

Mr Mallow points at an area of the roof that's boarded up. Apparently, so Graham was told when he bought the place, there used to be a window there, but it was boarded over decades ago. Graham hadn't bothered looking at the plans or questioning it further. Things like that didn't concern him and, at the time, he'd wanted to complete the purchase of the house quickly so he could get the heck out of Cherry Hollow.

'Was there a window there previously?' asks Mr Mallow.

'Yes, I believe so.'

'In that case … there's something strange about its orientation.'

Graham looks up. Other than the boards looking a little out of place against the roof, he's not sure what Mr Mallow means.

'Which room would the window have belonged to?' continues Mr Mallow.

Graham opens his mouth to provide the answer but finds there is no answer to give. 'You know,' he says, scratching the back of his head. 'I'm not too sure. It must be the spare bedroom at the far end where you're sleeping. It only has a tiny window, so perhaps a second one was blocked off at one time or another.'

'No. That's not right. The spare bedroom doesn't look out over the yard. It's on the other side of the building.'

'I'm afraid I don't know then.'

'You never noticed there's a random blocked out window in your cottage that supposedly doesn't belong to any of the rooms inside?'

'No.'

'How long have you lived here?'

'Almost a year.'

'Hmm. Let's take a look when we get back.'

'What for?'

'To quell my curiosity.'

Graham can't argue with him there. He's curious now too, but now there are more important mysteries to solve than a misplaced window.

It takes fifteen minutes to walk to the village and arrive at the butcher's shop, by which time, a line is already forming by the door and down the street. People, it seems, like to buy their meat early in the day to purchase the best cuts. Graham has also noticed they do the opposite and arrive as the shop is closing to grab some cheap ones; the cuts that don't sell during the day and would otherwise go to waste. The butcher's shop is also the most popular place to buy meat, bone and offal for farm dogs. Most farmers around here seem to feed their dogs raw meat, so he's gathered.

'Mr Williams, good to see you,' says a man around Graham's age, who he recognises as the bank manager, but he can't remember his name. Graham often knows people by their faces, but is useless at remembering names. The bank is tiny and he's surprised it's still in business, considering most banking is done online these days.

'Hello,' says Graham, tipping his hat. Mr Mallow is standing quietly beside him. Graham recalls him not being very confident with general chit chat, something he can sympathise with.

'I don't think I've ever seen you in line this early for the butcher's shop,' says the bank manager.

Graham merely smiles, not giving anything away.

The line moves again and, this time, Graham and Mr Mallow squeeze into the small shop where a pungent odour of raw meat tickles Graham's nostrils.

'Uh, Detective, if you wouldn't mind, I'm going to wait outside. I'm afraid the smell in here is making me feel a little queasy.'

Graham nods. 'Very well. I'll see you in a moment.'

Mr Mallow sidesteps the other customers and heads outside, taking up a position a little way down the pavement, as far away from the door as possible. There's no doubt about it. Something is wrong with Mr Mallow. Something quite serious.

But Graham doesn't have time to worry about that now. He needs to find out as much information as he can about pig hearts from the butcher.

Chapter 24
GRAHAM

Graham waits patiently for his turn at the counter. He watches other customers as they mull over their choice of meats, sausages or joints for the day. Perhaps they have their usual order in mind, or maybe they have special visitors coming to stay and want to wow them with locally produced pork and lamb. He has to admit, the apple and mint sausages are appealing. They'll sizzle up nicely in a pan, alongside some thick gravy. Perhaps he'll get a few for dinner tonight, seeing as he has a house guest for the foreseeable future. There's also a nice selection of beef roasting joints, something he hasn't eaten in decades. His parents used to cook a beef joint for Christmas every year rather than the traditional whole turkey, and now, whenever he sees one, he is taken back to his childhood; the smell of beef fat, horseradish and a huge Yorkshire pudding or two, complete with a ladle of thick gravy, made with the drippings.

'*Croeso*, Mr Williams, what can I get for you, good sir?' asks Mr Davies. He has a blue and white striped apron on, stained pink in places, a butcher's hat and a see-through plastic wrap around his greying beard.

Graham hasn't realised he's reached the front of the line and Mr Davies is waiting for his order. 'Six of those apple and mint sausages please, and … a pig heart.'

Mr Davies stops as he reaches out his hand, using a piece of plastic wrap, to pick up the sausages in a clump. He only pauses for a moment, but it's enough for Graham to notice. He watches Mr Davies as he attempts to brush off the awkwardness and places the sausages on the scales.

'A pig heart, Mr Williams?' He places the sausages into a bag and prints out a price label, slapping it on the side where it attaches at a wonky angle.

'Do you not have any in today?'

'I'm afraid not, but what use would you have in buying one? Pig hearts aren't a common request for most customers, not on the whole. They mainly get used to make offal and faggots.'

'I fancy attempting to make some faggots.'

'I see.'

'Do you get many requests for pig hearts?'

'Couple times a month, I suppose. Mostly from Diane Bevan. She feeds them to her dogs. She provides me with all the pork products, you see, so I give her all the leftover parts of the animals, considering they were raised on her farm.'

Mr Davies hands the bag of sausages to Graham who takes it with a slight head nod. The men lock eyes. The whole butcher's shop has elapsed into silence. Graham looks around at the array of customers, all of whom have clearly been eavesdropping on their conversation, but then it is a small shop, and Graham hadn't been making an effort to lower his voice. Sometimes, it's worth speaking a little louder. You never know who might be listening.

'Can I get you anything else, Mr Williams?' asks Mr Davies, a fresh smile across his face.

'No, thank you, Mr Davies. You've been most helpful.'

'I'm sorry about the lack of pig hearts, but I'll be sure to let you know the next time I have some in. However, I do have some fresh faggots today, if you fancied trying some?'

Graham nods his thanks. 'Maybe another time. Thank you,' he says just before turning around to leave. Several of the customers behind him give him odd looks, but don't say anything.

'*Diwrnod da*,' says Mr Davies.

Graham leaves, feeling many eyes boring into the back of his head as he allows the door to swing closed behind him.

Chapter 25
STEPHEN

His headache is getting worse by the minute. It's unrelenting, like a sharp needle is piercing his brain, unlike anything he's experienced before. It isn't only his head either, but his neck and shoulders too. Even his eyeballs pulse in his skull, like they have their own heartbeat. Painkillers aren't touching it, about as useful as a grain of rice to hold off starvation, but he takes more anyway. He can't remember the last time he took some. It's more than four hours ago, though, the safe time frame to take more of the same type of painkiller. He thinks …

The stench of raw meat and blood makes him feel worse. Even standing outside the butcher's shop isn't far enough away for the odour not to claw at the back of his nose. Hell, he can practically taste it on his tongue.

The headaches started several months ago, seemingly overnight. One morning he woke up with one and it stuck around for five days before it finally went. Then, another. And another. Until he got fed up with them, so he visited the GP who asked him so many questions, he lost track of what he was even there for. Headaches. Yes, headaches. Mind-numbing, debilitating headaches. Not migraines. They were something else entirely.

His doctor told him it could be stress related, especially as he knew what had occurred in Stephen's life lately, but Stephen knew it wasn't stress or anything else like that. He wasn't being stubborn about it either, the way most men were these days when it came to their ailments, but he made it perfectly clear the headaches were not caused by stress, so the doctor booked him in for an MRI scan.

And that was the beginning of the end.

Now, he finds himself staring into the distance, seemingly waking up several minutes later, having no recollection of where he is. It happened earlier as well, back at the detective's cottage. He'd stared up the hill towards the tree.

He had seen something and hadn't been strong enough to pull his eyes away from the thick branches, no matter how hard he tried. Something was sucking him into the tree. Pulling. Drawing him closer, like it wanted a piece of his soul. Perhaps it was calling to him the way the ravine and the fallen tree had called to him back in Cherry Hollow.

Trees are living things after all.

They have life flowing through their veins, just like humans do. But a tree's veins were called vascular bundles, responsible for transporting water, nutrients and sugar to the tree itself. Not dissimilar to blood. Trees absorb nutrients from the earth, using whatever life source is around them to grow.

Perhaps …

No, it isn't possible. Even Stephen knows that a person's soul can't live inside anything else other than its host's body.

John Hammel's soul is *not* living inside The Hanging Tree …

But what a story angle!

His brain instantly starts drumming up story arcs he can use to write an article. Because there will be an article about The Hanging Tree. He's sure of it. Just like The Creature had taken over Cherry Hollow, The Hanging Tree has taken over the sleepy, quiet village of Bethgelert, holding its residents hostage to a curse formed a century ago …

The story practically writes itself.

Stephen blinks several times, realigning his vision. When he comes to, he sees a man standing on the other side of the road from him. The man is a farmer, complete with the cap and padded jacket and wellington boots. He even has a collie dog at his side off the lead because, apparently, farm dogs can roam free around here without the need to be constrained.

The man is staring at him.

The back of Stephen's neck bristles.

He is about to step across the road to approach the man, to ask him why he's staring, when the butcher's shop door opens, a bell sounds, and the detective rejoins him, carrying a bag of sausages.

'We have a lead,' he says. 'I suggest we head to see Diane Bevan. She lives at Pen-Y-Bryn, I believe, then we'll stop by Frank Hammel at Blackberry Farm.'

Chapter 26
SOPHIA

Bethgelert, Wales, 2015

I replaced the boards in the hallway as best as I could, using some leftover plasterboard I found in the garage, then hung a large picture frame over it to disguise the join. I stood back and admired my handywork. My dad would notice straight away if he came here, but hopefully the visitors wouldn't. I made a mental note to come back once they'd left and fix it properly. Perhaps I could create a door, so I could use it whenever I needed because I wasn't finished with the room behind the wall. Not yet. John Hammel had more secrets to reveal, more things he needed me to know, but I couldn't risk bringing the papers and journals outside. I didn't want them to be found by anyone. I still wasn't sure if my dad knew anything about it, but either way, I didn't want him to know that I'd found it. A little secret between me and John.

I slid my arms into John's overcoat and put his sketch into one of the pockets. It was a little big on me and it smelled musty, but it felt familiar and warm.

On my way out, I stopped by the power console and checked it over. The main switch had been tripped, so all I had to do was flip it back on. It must have been a massive surge that tripped it, but I was glad I'd been able to sort it, ready for the visitors to arrive tomorrow.

When I arrived back home, my dad was asleep in his chair by the fire with a bottle of beer balanced on the armrest, still clenched in his hand. I draped a blanket over him and removed the bottle from his grip in case it fell while he was asleep and smashed. That would only make him angry, and he'd find some way of blaming me.

As I placed the bottle on the side, I noticed a note lying next to an array of empty bottles. It looked like he'd been on a bit of a bender this evening since I'd left. He liked a drink most nights, but it wasn't often that he drank himself into a stupor. I picked the note up and read the words slowly, carefully. They were written in swirly, fancy handwriting.

The time has arrived. Hand her over. You got lucky once, but it won't happen again.

I glanced at my dad and then at the six empty bottles next to him. Who had delivered this note?

The note made it sound like whoever had given it to him had been waiting for a specific time or day, that it was significant somehow. The anniversary of John Hammel's death was coming up, so perhaps that was connected or relevant somehow.

It was also nearing the anniversary of my mother leaving us and the death of my little brother, but I doubt anyone else would care about that as much as my dad and I did. It had scarred us as a family and we were barely hanging on even now, but the rest of the world had moved on.

Dad was one of the founding members of the village committee, but I couldn't work out what that would have to do with anything either. John Hammel's journals mentioned a lot about the village committee and them hiding things, but from the tone of this letter, it seemed my dad was possibly keeping something from them. Something they wanted.

Hand *her* over.

Were they talking about me?

I turned the note over, frowning, and saw another short sentence scrawled on the back. This one made a lot less sense, but did answer the reason why my dad may have drunk himself into a stupor.

Oh, Dad, what have you got yourself involved in?

Chapter 27
STEPHEN

An unsettled feeling wedges itself in the pit of his stomach as he walks with Detective Williams up the road towards their next destination. Every step he takes, his gut tells him something is wrong. His body is sending him all sorts of warning signals, but his brain won't accept them. It just keeps shoving them aside, hiding them under a metaphorical rug like they don't matter at this point in time.

While the detective recounts what Mr Davies told him in the butcher's shop, Stephen fights with his brain to focus on the words. He hears them coming from the detective's mouth, knows what each of them mean, but none of them sink in, don't quite make sense. Just a mix of words, jumbled together, each one an individual rather than working together to form a coherent sentence.

They reach the end of the village; the houses and residents reducing in number now, more spread out. There's no longer any broken pavements to walk on, so they stroll down the side of the narrow country lane, keeping as close to the left as possible. There's even grass growing in the middle of it. Detective Williams says there's another mile to go before the turning to the farm. They must now walk in single file to avoid oncoming traffic. Not that there's a lot. A car every now and then. A tractor turning into a nearby field.

Slow, plodding footsteps sound behind him.

Stephen turns and glances over his right shoulder, spying a person following them about fifty yards behind. The person has a flat cap on, so he assumes it's a man, but it's difficult to tell for sure.

Is this the same person who'd been watching him in the village earlier? There's no dog with him, so perhaps not.

Stephen focuses his attention on the road ahead, continuing, but those warning bells are ringing again. Louder than ever.

He turns again, but the person behind him is no longer there. It makes no sense because there are no turnings they could have taken to get off the road and, unless they threw themselves into a hedgerow, there's nowhere to hide. Is he imagining things again? The hairs on the back of his neck tickle as he faces the right direction. Detective Williams doesn't seem to have noticed he's lagging. Stephen keeps his head down, his arms brushing against the hedgerows and the stinging nettles and brambles that are growing out into the road. The sound of an engine sounds ahead and he and the detective move in sync, pressing against the sides to give the vehicle plenty of space as it passes wide and slow.

'Not much further now,' says the detective.

Stephen looks behind him, back along the road towards the village where they've walked from. There's no sign of his secret follower.

The sign to the farm is nestled behind a thick bush, but the detective sees it just in time to stop from walking past it. *Pen-Y-Bryn*. Stephen wonders what it means in English.

It's a short walk up the track towards the farmyard. Along the way, they pass several fields filled with pigs of varying sizes and breeds. It appears that Diane is the owner of a pig farm. The closer they get, the more Stephen's nostrils twitch with an overwhelming stench of manure.

'Delightful,' says the detective, screwing his nose up.

'It's certainly an … interesting smell,' says Stephen.

The detective smirks as he heads towards the main farmhouse. Stephen takes a quick scan of the yard, noting the five separate barns surrounding it. It's a big area. Stephen can't imagine that Diane manages the farm by herself. She must have farmhands or helpers or whatever it is that they're called. He wonders how many pigs she has on the farm at any one given time. Hundreds, perhaps. How does one keep track of so many?

'Can I help you?' A woman's voice interrupts his thoughts.

Stephen turns and spies a mature woman striding towards them, carrying a shovel. While her manner doesn't appear threatening, she's clearly confused about who they are and why they're on her land. Stephen expects she doesn't get a lot of strangers visiting the farm. This is a village where everyone knows everyone, apart from the detective who clearly hasn't done much socialising since he's lived here. Not that he can blame him, but he does appear to know where both Diane Bevan and Frank Hammel live, so that's a plus.

'Are you Diane Bevan?' asks Stephen.

'Depends.'

'I'm sorry?' he asks with a stutter. 'Either you are Diane Bevan or you're not. It's a pretty simple question.'

The woman raises her eyebrows at him, just as the detective steps forwards and joins the conversation. 'I'm sorry about my friend here.'

'I didn't know you had any friends, Mr Williams, but that's quite all right. So, *is* there something I can help you with?'

Chapter 28
GRAHAM

Graham does a quick head to toe scan of the farmer who's roughly a decade younger than him, attractive and wearing green wellington boots, a scruffy-looking wax jacket and a pair of old jeans, her dark blonde hair messy and loose around her shoulders. He recognises her from the village meeting, but she'd barely said a word and hadn't introduced herself either.

'I didn't realise you knew who I was,' says Graham.

'A lot of people know who you are. You live at Rosemore Cottage. You're a retired detective, right?'

'That's right, ma'am.'

'My dad was a cop.'

Graham doesn't respond. It isn't one of those instances where 'Ah, that's nice' is considered the correct response. More like, 'I'm sorry' because Graham knows all too well the reality of having a father as a cop. His own father had been one and he'd barely had a relationship with the man. He'd always been too busy, too tired or too stressed to spend quality time with Graham. There was always a darkness behind his eyes that told a story not everyone could - or should - read. Being a police officer meant making difficult choices, seeing things that most people would have a breakdown over. It was one of the reasons why Graham had never married or had children of his own.

And now, it's too late for any of that. He made his choice many years ago.

It also strikes Graham as strange that Diane's father was a cop. He assumed that the farmers around here all worked in the family business, never stepping foot outside it to continue the legacy for future generations.

Diane wipes her dirty hands on an even dirtier cloth she has tucked into the pocket of her jeans as she looks Graham up and down. Thanks to his years as a detective, he's learned a thing or two about questioning potential suspects, getting them to trust him. Sometimes, it works in his favour to dive straight in and ask the inevitable and most important questions, but there are other times, like now, where he knows he has to take his time, gauge the suspect's responses and be a little crafty with his tactics. He just hopes Stephen cottons on and plays along.

Graham clears his throat and begins. 'May I ask how many pigs you currently have on this farm?' He knows the answer to the question isn't relevant to their investigation, but he thinks it may be a decent conversation opener.

'Currently, I have one hundred and twenty-one,' comes the quick response. Not even a whiff of a pause.

'Are you missing any?' Again, a question used as a point of interest.

Diane chuckles and shakes her head. 'I'm afraid I don't make a habit of counting my pigs every day, but the last time I checked … no.'

'When was the last time you counted them all?' asks Mr Mallow, stepping into the conversation.

Diane inhales sharply and pauses a moment before replying, 'A week ago, I guess.' She narrows her eyes at Mr Mallow. Clearly, she isn't as keen on him as she is Graham. She doesn't know Stephen like Graham does. He's harmless really, if you can put up with his abrupt manner and direct questions.

Graham decides to change the subject slightly. 'Do you buy pig hearts from the butcher's shop, Mrs Bevan?'

'Well, I don't really buy them, considering they are from my own pigs, but yes, Mr Davies keeps some back for me on occasion. Can I ask why you're asking me about pig hearts, Mr Williams?'

Graham clears his throat. He'd been hoping not to have to tell her the full story, but Diane doesn't seem like the type of woman who likes having the wool pulled over her eyes. She won't give up information without getting something in return first. That's fine. Graham can work with that. He decides to be honest with her and gauge her reaction from there.

'I think I found a fresh pig heart on my property yesterday and we suspect it came from the local butcher shop.'

'That has to be the strangest story I've ever heard.'

'Believe me, I've heard stranger ones.'

'How do you know it's a pig heart?'

'A very good question. We don't. We're making an educated guess based on the information we've gained.'

'I see. Well, I'm sorry I can't be of more help, Mr Williams.'

'There's one more thing, Mrs Bevan. I found this heart inside the chest cavity of a scarecrow hanging in the tree opposite my home. I remember from the village meeting the other night that Frank said the scarecrow was a Halloween prank, but a fresh pig heart inside its chest is taking things a bit far, don't you think?'

Diane gasps, then mutters something in Welsh. She makes the sign of a cross, a ritual that isn't lost on Graham. She fixes her gaze on Graham, barely blinking.

'I shall put your mind at ease, Mr Williams and tell you that the scarecrow is not a prank, but a respected village tradition that happens every year around this time, as a symbol. A pig heart is used as a reminder of the souls who have died near the tree over the years. Frank just didn't want to scare you, I suppose.'

'Are you saying that more than one person has taken their own life near the tree, other than John Hammel a hundred years ago?'

'That tree is almost a thousand years old, Mr Williams. It has seen the Black Death, the Tudor period, the Industrial

Revolution, the Napoleonic Wars, and both World Wars. I'd be shocked if it hadn't witnessed the death of more than one person in that time.'

Graham is silent for a moment. He hadn't considered that before, that the tree had continued standing throughout some of the worst times in history. John Hammel's death was merely a small blip on its radar.

'When did the scarecrow tradition first start?' he asks after reflection.

'Ten years ago.'

'And does that have anyth ng to do with Sophia Hammel's disappearance which also happened ten years ago almost to the day?'

Diane sucks in a breath and makes the sign of the cross again. 'I have answered enough of your questions, Mr Williams. If you wish to talk about Sophia, then I suggest you speak to her father. It's not my place.'

'I'll be doing just that. Thank you for your time, Mrs Bevan.'

Chapter 29
SOPHIA

Bethgelert, Wales, 2015

I wanted to ask my dad a million and one questions about John Hammel because, despite him being my ancestor, I didn't know a great deal about him. I knew about his death, but hardly anything about his life. From what I'd heard and what my dad had told me, the man who wrote in the journals was not the same man they described. My dad painted him as a layabout who had got himself into trouble, couldn't see a way out and decided to end it. I didn't buy a single word, especially not now. John wasn't like that, but everyone seemed determined to tarnish his name. Everyone except me.

My dad woke up with the devil of all hangovers, so I was forced to start the chores early without him, which was okay because it gave me time to gather my thoughts and decide which questions I'd ask him without raising too much suspicion. I didn't want him to figure out how much I knew.

My dad joined me in the yard as I was about to feed the sheep in the barn. He looked worse than he probably felt, or maybe he didn't. I had never had a hangover, so I didn't have a frame of reference. Barney was sniffing around next to me.

'Thanks, kiddo,' he said, ruffling my hair.

'Sure, Dad. What was with the beer binge last night? Normally you wait until the weekend to get shitfaced.'

'Oi, language. Bad day.'

'Uh-huh.'

'Those buggers who were supposed to be staying at the cottage cancelled last minute, so obviously I charged them the full amount.'

I had to admit, I was relieved because it gave me more time to make a better cover for the massive hole I'd bashed into the wall last night.

'Uh, Dad. Can I ask you something?'

'Sure. Make it quick. I need to go and see Diane.'

'What for?'

My dad paused, staring ahead into the distance. His eyes darkened in a way that told me he was holding on to a lot of things; things he probably didn't want me to know. 'Just … village stuff.'

It was typical of him to be vague. I knew better than to ask him to elaborate.

'Right. Anyway, I need to know more about John Hammel.'

Clearly, this wasn't the question he'd been expecting because he choked on thin air, quickly pulling out a tissue from his pocket and wiping his mouth.

'Why'd you want to know about that wanker? Thought I told you to stay clear of the past.'

'You never said that. No, it's for a … school project. An essay I want to write. I'm looking into the family curse as well as trying to figure out how he died. Do you know if he kept any … journals, or anything like that?' I held my breath. Chances were, if he knew about the secret room at Rosemore Cottage then he would have cleared it out by now and destroyed as much evidence as he could. Either that, or he did know about it and kept it hidden away like a forgotten relic of the past.

'No one keeps journals in this family.'

'Maybe ninety years ago they did. They didn't have computers and stuff, did they? Must have had to record information somehow.'

'I don't know.'

'Would the village council know?'

'I *am* the village council and I'm telling you; he didn't keep any journals.'

'Then how do you know he killed himself? Like … is there evidence that he killed himself? Maybe the village council kept records over the years. Where can I find details from years back?'

My dad took a deep breath in through his nose and held it. 'For your own good, please … just … stop. It will all be over soon.'

'What does that mean?' I asked.

He turned to me, and I could have sworn there was a tear in the corner of his left eye. 'I have to save the family.'

'Okay, Dad, you're starting to freak me out now.'

'I have to go and see Diane. Finish up the chores, then get to school. I expect you to be home on time today. We have work to do.' He looked me up and down. 'What are you wearing?'

Oh shit, I'd forgotten I put John's coat on again this morning. I should have hidden it.

'Uh, an old jacket I picked up from the market.'

'It stinks.'

'Yeah, well …'

He turned and walked away without another word, his shoulders hunched forwards, like the weight of the world was pressing down on them.

I watched him walk out of the yard, then dropped the bucket I was holding and ran into the house with Barney right on my heels. Dad didn't want me to find out answers, so I was going to look for them myself. He was lying when he said the village council didn't keep a written record of what happened in the village over the years. I'd seen him writing in a massive, leather-bound book several times. He just didn't know that I'd watched him.

I needed to find it.

Chapter 30
STEPHEN

'What do you make of that?' asks the detective while they walk back along the track towards the road. Their next destination is Blackberry Farm, home of Frank Hammel.

'She seemed quite helpful at first,' replies Stephen. He trips over a pothole, his feet not quite reacting in time, and quickly rights himself. 'But she did clam up rather fast when you asked about Sophia Hammel. We also confirmed we were correct in our guess that the hanging scarecrow is a new tradition, which started after Sophia's disappearance.'

'That's true,' replies the detective. 'The pig heart inside the scarecrow is obviously meant to represent the lives lost over the years, or just perhaps a way of honouring the dead, but it's a bit of a dead end now.'

'Yes, the whole scarecrow and pig heart thing does seem to have thrown us off a bit.'

'I think we now need to focus on Sophia's possible disappearance,' says the detective.

'Agreed.'

Once they reach the main road, they turn and walk back into the village. Stephen's feet are already beginning to ache and he's in dire need of a drink of water and a sit down, but now they have a solid lead, a strong trail of breadcrumbs to follow, he's like a dog with a bone. He's unwilling to let it go until he gets to the good stuff hidden inside.

The Blackberry Farm sign is engraved crudely with the name, in dire need of being freshened up. Clearly the wear and tear of the elements has caused degradation over the years. Perhaps a new one altogether would be more beneficial. Potholes litter the track leading to the farm; mostly filled with rainwater.

Stephen and the detective side-step the various holes and muddy areas, keeping to the left. It's another half a mile or so up to the farm itself, but there are various outbuildings, barns and stables in the fields surrounding the main farmyard. He often wonders how places like this are still going.

Out here, in the middle of Wales, he's noticed life moves at a much slower pace. Everything is less complicated and busy. Phone signal is almost non-existent, and traffic jams consist of sheep or cows being herded by a farmer and his dog, or a tractor turning in the narrow lane, blocking the way for cars. They either have to wait for the obstacle to move or find another way around, and that involves travelling for miles in a different direction.

By the time they arrive at the farm gate where another wooden sign tells them they are at the correct place, Stephen's shoes are covered in mud and sweat is beading on his forehead. Again. In fact, he doesn't feel all that well. Maybe the long walk hadn't been such a good idea. Does he have a fever? Or is he merely sweating from the exertion?

He wipes his forehead with the cuff of his jacket and unbolts the gate. A black and white dog rushes towards them, barking. It has tufts of grey around its eyes and muzzle. Stephen freezes, sliding the bolt back across, making sure there's a solid barrier between him and the animal. He isn't afraid of dogs, but he knows a warning when he hears one. Hopefully, the dog's barking will alert its owner.

The detective, on the other hand, takes a step away from the gate.

'You afraid of dogs, Detective?' asks Stephen with an eyebrow raise.

'On the contrary. I'm afraid of dog *bites*.'

They don't have to wait long before a gruff male voice from a nearby barn shouts, 'Hey! Barney, shut your racket!'

A man walks out of the barn wearing an old, checked shirt with the sleeves rolled up to his elbows. He looks to be in his late fifties, a similar age to the detective. His tanned skin is covered in deep set wrinkles, having clearly seen many years of hard labour working on the farm.

'Who are you?' he asks, catching sight of Stephen first, but then his eyes focus on the detective on the other side of the gate and he nods. 'Ah, Mr Williams. I did wonder if you'd be paying me a visit at some point.'

'We're here to ask you about your daughter, Sophia,' replies the detective. Stephen is taken back by his abruptness. With Diane, the detective had beaten around the bush a little, gauging her reaction before jumping in at the deep end, but with Frank Hammel, he seems to have taken the opposite approach.

Stephen's expecting some sort of aggressive reaction from Mr Hammel, or at least a standoffish one, but he doesn't expect the man to chuckle.

'Now, why on earth would you want to know about Sophia?' Mr Hammel glances down at the dog who is still barking. 'Quiet, Barney!' The dog stops and wags his tail instead.

'We've been led to believe that she disappeared ten years ago. Is that true?' asks the detective, increasing the pressure.

Mr Hammel frowns and stares at the detective. 'You live at Rosemore Cottage, right?'

'That's right, but you knew that already.'

'I used to own that pile of bricks, you know.'

The detective nods. 'I'm aware.'

'Fancy a cuppa?'

Stephen and the detective swap glances before Stephen nods. 'Thank you, yes.'

Mr Hammel unbolts the gate and pushes it open. They enter the yard and follow him towards the farmhouse with the dog, Barney, scurrying behind.

'I appreciate you taking the time to talk to us, Mr Hammel,' says Stephen as he steps across the threshold and into the building. The trio walk straight into a quaint farmhouse-style kitchen, complete with a log burner, an Aga and a large island. The warmth immediately defrosts Stephen's chilly hands, and his head begins to feel better, clearer.

'Call me Frank. Take a seat.' Frank gestures to a nearby chair. 'Tea?'

'Please. Milk, no sugar.'

The detective nods, but says nothing. Stephen is sure the detective is finding Frank's avoidance of his direct questioning infuriating, but they are here for answers, and if that means they have to go at Frank's pace, then so be it. If there's one thing Stephen has learned during his journalism career, it's that people will talk when they're ready. Not before. No matter how hard you push them.

Frank grabs an old-fashioned kettle, fills it with water and places it on the stove to heat up. Barney makes himself comfortable in his dog bed next to the Aga.

'So ... why do you want to know about Sophia?' he finally asks, proving Stephen's theory is correct.

'First, I'd like you to answer the question as to whether she's missing or not,' replies the detective. 'We've been getting a lot of mixed messages.'

Frank doesn't answer. Instead, he takes a deep breath and folds his arms across his chest. Stephen is no body language expert, but even he knows that the man is being confrontational and defensive.

'She didn't disappear,' he says quietly. 'She was killed.'

Chapter 31
STEPHEN

Stephen struggles to hide his surprise at how bluntly Frank had spoken.

'And you know that for a fact, do you?' Stephen asks. He has to tread carefully because he's known for putting his foot in it at the worst possible time, and the last thing he wants or needs is for Frank to turn against him. Perhaps he needs a lesson in tact from the detective sometime, but his forward approach has won him more battles than he's lost, so that's a plus in his book.

Frank appears to consider his answer carefully, rubbing his thick, greying beard for several seconds before replying, 'No, not for a fact, but what I *do* know for a fact is that Sophia wouldn't have run away. Therefore, she must be dead.'

'You don't think there's a chance she was kidnapped?'

Another long pause. 'No.'

Stephen wonders what's going through Frank's mind right now. The long pauses mean he knows the answer to the questions, but is trying to think of the correct way to say it without giving away too much. That's what Stephen assumes, anyway.

'Can I ask why you think she's dead though?' he asks. 'As far as we're aware, there was no news story about her disappearance and a body has never been found. No one in the village seems to be concerned with her whereabouts.'

At the mention of the word *body*, Frank flinches, almost as if he's been slapped across the face.

The kettle whistles, signalling the water has reached boiling point. Stephen is patient while Frank pours the water and makes the tea. He moves at a slow pace, not in any hurry.

Stephen glances at the detective who mouths, 'Tread carefully.'

Stephen nods in response, glad the detective is allowing him to lead this part of the interview. Stephen used to scribble notes in a book while questioning people, but now he likes to give the subject his undivided attention. Stephen has a very good memory when it comes to recalling facts, except lately he has noticed a decline in this particular skill. Something he hopes is only temporary.

Frank places a cup in front of Stephen and another in front of the detective, then takes a seat opposite them again.

'I take it neither of you have children.'

'No,' says Stephen.

'I do not,' replies the detective.

Frank sniffs loudly. 'Then you can't possibly know the pain of losing a child. No parent is supposed to outlive their child. It's not natural. Most people would think their child's death is the worst-case scenario; the most unbelievably painful experience you could endure. It's not. Not even close. When my son died at a young age, it hurt, but I could accept it, move on, in a matter of speaking. I thought that was the hardest thing I'd ever have to live through, and then Sophia disappeared. Trust me, it's the *not* knowing ... that's the worst possible scenario. Are they alive and suffering or are they dead, their body buried somewhere it'll never be found? Parents of a missing child can go either one of two ways. Either they constantly obsess over their disappearance, never give up the search of finding them alive one day, torture themselves day in and day out about their child's whereabouts ...'

Stephen waits while Frank stares out the nearby window at the fields beyond.

'... or they come to terms with the fact their child is dead and give up the search. I have chosen to do the latter and, because of that decision, I am now alone with only the damn dog for company. There was no other way for me to accept her disappearance, so I choose to believe she is dead.'

Stephen cups his hands around the warm mug. He understands where Frank is coming from. Not knowing the truth would drive him crazy too. His unique mind already causes him enough issues when it comes to leaving things unfinished, let alone never knowing what had happened to someone he loved, someone he cared about. It would be torture. Never-ending torture. That's why he likes to investigate and solve the unsolvable mysteries. Someone has to. Someone has to keep asking those difficult questions when everyone else has given up and moved on.

'I understand. What do you think happened to her? You said you believe she was killed, not simply dead. There's no online activity regarding her disappearance. Why is that? Why is no one in Bethgelert concerned about her?'

'Which question do you want me to answer first?'

Stephen takes a breath. 'My mistake. I apologise. My mind often races ahead and lists all the unanswered questions before I can stop it. I know you say she's dead, but truly … what do you think happened to Sophia?'

Another long sigh from Frank. He taps his fingers on the table. Possibly a soothing ritual. 'Sophia was a hard-working, stubborn and highly intelligent young woman. Many years ago, we lost her brother at a young age, as I said. Followed by her mother leaving us because she could no longer stay in this family. Sophia and I were all each other had. She loved me. I loved her. She wouldn't run away like her mother did. It makes no sense. Someone must have killed her.'

'Why? Did she have enemies? Was someone after her? Was she in trouble?'

Frank stares at Stephen for a beat.

Stephen closes his eyes, understanding. 'Again. I apologise. Please tell me why you think she is dead and not missing?'

'If she's alive, then I am the worst father in the world because I have given up searching for her.'

It's not the answer Stephen needs. It's not definitive. It's nowhere near good enough to satisfy him, but if he pushes Frank too hard, then he won't give them anything else and there's still plenty to ask. What Frank is really saying is that he can't bear to be the reason she's never been found. If she's dead, then he's in the clear.

'Let me ask my other question again. Why wasn't your daughter's dis-dis-a …' He stops, frowns, unable to recall the word he's after. What's wrong with him? What the hell is that word?

'Disappearance,' says the detective.

'Yes, thank you. Why wasn't your daughter's disappearance announced on any local news sites? Why does no one care that she's missing?'

Frank shifts awkwardly on his chair. 'I can't answer that question.'

'Can't or won't?'

'Can't. I told the local police. They asked all of their questions and did all their checks, but in the end, they told me she wasn't a high-risk case. There was no search. No investigation because one never existed. She's gone. They believe she left, just like her mother.'

Stephen sucks in a breath and holds it a moment, wondering if he's heard the man correctly. 'You did nothing, then?'

'I wouldn't say that. I did what I could, but no one wanted to know.'

Stephen doesn't believe it. There's a lot that doesn't add up with his answers, but he decides to make a mental note and do some further research first. Perhaps question some of the locals to get their point of view. Also, he's certain the detective will be able to shed some light upon the fact that the police force seemed to give no interest in the case of a missing teenager. The detective, however, doesn't appear to be in the questioning mood anymore.

There is one topic of conversation that Stephen wishes to learn more about, so he shifts his weight on the chair and dives straight in.

'Tell me about your wife, Frank. Why did she leave and when?'

'She left five years after Tommy died. That was fifteen years ago. Haven't seen or heard from her since.'

'Did you ever look for her?'

'No.'

'Why is that?'

Frank breathes in deep, holds it, then exhales slowly. 'She wasn't missing. My wife made a choice. Losing our son was the hardest, most painful experience, and I don't blame her for running away. I would have done the same, if I had the choice.'

'But you decided to stay here with Sophia.'

'Yes.'

'So then ... you're wrong ... you *are* a good father.'

Frank doesn't respond straight away. He looks out of the nearest window. 'That is yet to be confirmed.'

Stephen glances at the detective who gives the slightest of head nods. 'Okay,' says Stephen. 'Moving on. Can you walk me through that day? The day Sophia disappeared.'

Frank pulls his gaze from the window and stares into his mug. 'I'm afraid I can't do that ... not without drinking something a lot stronger than tea. Meet me at The Fox tonight; the pub in the village. Eight o'clock. I'm buying.'

'We'd prefer if you'd answer our questions now,' says the detective, finally speaking up.

'And I'd prefer not to talk to an ex-copper. I don't trust you people. Not after ... I'm not talking any more about anything until tonight.' He turns, looking directly at Stephen. 'And if you want me to talk freely, then leave your *detective* friend at home. Come alone.'

Chapter 32
GRAHAM

Graham and Mr Mallow walk back to Rosemore Cottage along the river route, passing over several quaint bridges and walking past numerous dog walkers. It's peaceful, pleasant, as these picturesque country villages are when you look at them briefly, but Graham always finds that the closer one looks and the more one uncovers, the uglier things can become.

'What do you make of the police not taking Sophia's disappearance seriously?' asks Mr Mallow after several minutes of silence. 'Especially now that she's been missing for so many years.'

'It's not unusual, unfortunately,' replies Graham. 'Often, some cases go unsolved. It depends on the workload and the severity of the case.'

'But she was under eighteen. Surely, that warrants further investigation?'

'Yes and no. It depends ... but I think that Frank is lying. That he didn't tell the police at all.'

'Why would he do that?'

Graham shakes his head. 'I'm not sure at the moment, but maybe tonight will reveal more. Are you sure you're happy to go alone to meet him?'

'It's not like I have much of a choice in the matter. He's openly said that he won't talk if you're there and I suspect he'll be on his guard in case you're hiding in the shadows. It's easier if I go alone and report back with what I find. It seems you haven't made many friends in the village since living here, Detective.'

Graham grunts in response. 'He must know you'll tell me whatever he tells you.'

'Perhaps.'

Graham frowns, kicking a small pebble across the path ahead. 'Meaning?'

'Meaning nothing, Detective. I find the mother's disappearance an odd occurrence too.'

'Parents leave their children all the time.'

'Do they?'

Graham ponders the question for a moment. 'Some do, yes.'

'Ah, but would *she*?'

'What are you getting at, Mr Mallow?' He always knows when Mr Mallow is skirting around a subject, attempting to summon information, but without asking for it directly.

'I'm thinking that Sophia's mother may not have walked out on the family.'

'You could be right. It's suspicious that both Sophia and her mother are no longer around, yet no one is looking for them. It's certainly worth looking at.'

Stephen sighs, as a wave of dizziness engulfs him. He blinks it away. 'Once we get back to Rosemore Cottage, there's something I want to check out at the tree, then I'll join you inside for a cuppa.'

Graham nods. 'An excellent idea. I'd like to take another look at the scarecrow while you're looking at the tree. I know we said it was now a dead end, but I want to double-check before putting it to bed completely.'

'Better you than me. That thing gives me the creeps.'

'You and me both, Mr Mallow. You and me both.'

Upon arriving back home, Graham leaves Mr Mallow to hike up the hill to The Hanging Tree and instead fetches the keys from the hook by the back door. He then heads outside again.

Now it's daytime, it's easier to see inside the garage, so the torch is no longer required. The garage lights have never worked. He opens the main roll up door to allow more light inside. But when he turns towards the scarecrow, he jumps back, clutching his chest.

The scarecrow is sitting up, staring straight at him.

'Son of a bitch,' he mutters. His heart rate has practically doubled in the space of ten seconds. What the hell is going on with this thing? It's almost like it's alive, but that's physically impossible.

Graham knows, without a shadow of a doubt, that he left the scarecrow lying on the floor, yet now it's sitting up, propped against some storage boxes as if it's been waiting for him to return. If it had eyes, it would have been staring straight into his soul.

Graham has experienced some hair-raising and unsettling experiences in his life, but this is certainly up there with the worst and freakiest of them. Someone is messing with him. How had they got inside his locked garage ... again? And why are they hell-bent on scaring the crap out of him?

There are three points of entry to the garage; the small glass window, the door on the side and the main roll down door, yet all of them are locked unless he's inside tinkering. Well, the window technically doesn't have a proper lock, but it can't be opened from the outside and it's still intact from what he can make out.

Graham sidesteps the various tools, boxes and the lawnmower and leans towards the window.

Damn it.

It's open. Not a great deal, but just a crack. Enough that it could be jimmied open from the outside with a thin stick or a finger. But the window itself is barely big enough to fit a small child through, let alone a grown person. Whoever has been in here is either, indeed, a child, or a slender woman. No way a grown man would be able to squeeze through the window, not without …

There's a mark by the window, just under the frame. A dark smear. Blood. It's unclear whether it's fresh because it's already dried, but he certainly hadn't noticed it before.

Leaving the blood smear and the window for now, he returns to the scarecrow. He still has the sketch and the poster he found in his pocket. He pulls them out, studying them. Again, he marvels at the skill involved in creating such an artistic and beautiful drawing.

John Hammel.

Found hanging in the tree one hundred years ago.

Now, a scarecrow is hung in his place, complete with a pig's heart; a warning, a symbol, a tribute.

He shifts the scarecrow, so it's lying on its back, then unzips the jacket, revealing the twisted sticks, leaves and various other pieces of foliage that make up the main body. The pig heart is still wedged inside, still oozing blood, but it has mostly dried. It's giving off a musty, unpleasant odour that makes him gag slightly. He needs to remove the heart and dispose of it or at least freeze it to avoid losing any possible evidence.

Graham grabs a cleanish rag from the work bench and uses it to pull the heart out of the chest cavity of the scarecrow. It doesn't come away easily. He wraps it up and places it to the side for now.

'What's your story then?' he asks the scarecrow. But, of course, it doesn't move or reply. It continues to stare at him, taunting him. 'I think I might be going senile,' he says with a sigh. 'Olivia would sure get a laugh out of this.'

Carefully, he searches the scarecrow from top to bottom, looking for anything else that may be a clue, but there is nothing. The pig heart, the drawing and the sketch are the only things of interest or relevance.

The cogs whir in his brain, clicking into place then straight back out again. Round and round. This whole investigation started with this scarecrow, but now it's grown wings and taken flight, leaving him far below, scratching his head.

Diane confirmed that it was a local tradition. He can accept that, but what about the sketch and the poster of Sophia stuffed into the pocket? Surely, they aren't part of the tradition?

Someone on the village council is trying to provide them clues, trying to tell the truth without actually having to say it out loud.

It's Graham's job to speak for them.

But who is it?

Chapter 33
STEPHEN

Leaving the detective to root around and study the scarecrow some more - something he's happy to avoid - Stephen makes his way up the hill again. It's a much easier task than it had been last night with the surrounding darkness closing in and trying to take his breath away. Now, in the late morning light, his trip up the hill is a delightful experience, enabling him to see across the valley below, as well as the village and neighbouring houses and farms. He feels as if he's climbing to the top of the world, the tree a large welcoming beacon ahead.

His head is still a little fuzzy, but the pain and dizziness comes and goes. Forgetting simple words is a new symptom though. Quite discon … discon … *confusing*.

Whatever he had seen earlier under the tree isn't there now, but how could it have been there at all? He'd seen a person standing at the base of the tree, staring down the hill at him, calling to him, beckoning him closer. He'd been too far away to make out any recognisable features, but the figure had been male, young, dressed in old farmer-type clothes. A local, perhaps?

He thinks back to the farmer who'd stared at him in the village and the eerie feeling of being followed as he'd walked along the road with the detective towards the farms. That farmer had been older, not young.

Detective Williams hadn't noticed the farmer boy under the tree, but then again, he hadn't been looking, had he? An odd sensation warms his chest as he thinks back to the moment.

Could it be …

Stephen reaches the top of the hill and the base of the tree. He scans the ground, littered with fallen acorns, not quite sure what he's looking for. He won't know until he sees it.

There's a fallen part of a large branch, which is perfect for a make-shift bench; a few beer cans and crisp packets discarded in the area. He hadn't noticed them last night. He picks them up and puts them in a pile, ready for when he heads back down to the cottage. There's nothing he despises more than littering. It's an insult to the landscape, to the beauty of the world. Those who litter, who discard their rubbish without a second thought, are as bad as petty criminals in his eyes.

Stephen circles around the tree twice, ensuring he checks further afield too, approximately twenty feet in every direction. Not only is he searching for rubbish, but for any clue he may have missed. He reaches the point where he's going to give up, but then notices a piece of wood sticking out of the ground, almost invisible behind a patch of long grass and a small thorn bush. The grass is fairly short up here, which means that sheep must graze regularly, but he can't see any close by.

Crouching, he grasps the wooden post and pulls, but for his troubles he comes away with a scratch across the back of his hand from an errant thorn. He yanks his hand away, cursing under his breath and tries again, this time using his foot to stamp on the thorn bush. The wood buried inside isn't coming out easily. In fact, it's buried deep in the ground too. Possibly a fence post, but there is no fencing or wire around to indicate that.

It takes the best part of five minutes before Stephen releases the post from the ground and frees it from the thorn bush it has been trapped inside for God only knows how long. The post is snapped at the base, close to the ground, clearly rotten and weak.

For his effort, all he has in his hand is a post, but near the top is a random nail stickling half out of the wood. It seems, at one point or another, another piece of wood has been attached to the post, like a make-shift cross. Perhaps this is a grave marker of some sort. Or, if not a grave, then a marker to commemorate someone. Sophia, maybe?

Using the post to stamp the rest of the grass and thorns away, Stephen searches further, eventually finding a second plank of wood, approximately two feet long, buried in the earth. It's rotten and covered in dirt, so he does his best to remove the grime.

The plank has certainly been attached to the post at one point or another, as it has a large crack down the centre, where the nail would have pierced it. There doesn't appear to be any engraving, but it's so filthy that it may indeed be hiding an inscription, so Stephen places it on the ground ready to take down to the cottage and clean.

He's not finished up here yet.

The tree has been pulling him in the whole time he's been close by. He can't explain it. It wants him here. The longer he spends around the tree, the better he feels. His headache is lifting, his head clearing. Words make sense again.

Stephen steps closer to the tree and places a hand on its rugged bark, closing his eyes. He takes a deep breath, listening, feeling the coarseness under his palm. He swears he can feel a heartbeat. He looks up, into the browning leaves and branches above, wondering if by some ridiculous miracle, the scarecrow is back hanging there.

It is not.

If only this tree could talk. It's Stephen's job to speak for it. There are a hundred or more stories waiting to be told, trapped within the trunk, its branches and leaves, yet bound to remain silent forever. Trees cannot talk. People can, yet they are the ones who willingly hold secrets and refuse to say a word.

Wait ...

There is something up there, among the leaves.

Stephen awkwardly grasps a large knot in the trunk and hauls himself up a few feet, just enough to reach where he needs to be. There's a hole inside the trunk, which isn't unusual for a tree of this size and age. It's full of holes, nooks, crannies, dark crevices …but he wants to know more.

Reaching inside, there are damp leaves and goodness knows what else, but then his fingers brush against something familiar. Solid, yet soft. Alien.

He pulls it out and jumps back down to the ground.

It's a sketchbook, wrapped in plastic.

Despite its protection, when he removes it, the book is worn and soggy at the edges. Too new to belong to John Hammel with its printed logo, but definitely not left here last week either.

He flicks through its delicate pages, smiling as he sees the drawings inside.

The initials S.H. are written in the corner of every page.

The sketches are delicate, breathtaking. Far too detailed and mature to have been drawn by a sixteen-year-old girl. She must have had an extraordinary talent. This is a refreshing new outlook on Sophia Hammel. A girl who loved to draw, to sketch the beauty around her, immortalise it on a page. He can relate to that. It's the same with his writing. It's not only scenery on the pages, either. There are a lot of sketches of women's bodies; their hands, breasts and curves of their bodies.

If he knows anything about this girl, it's that if she'd truly run away from home, she'd never have left her beloved sketchbook behind.

He's the same with his notebook and pen. He never goes anywhere without them. Most journalists, especially nowadays, prefer to use phones to take notes, either in written or audio form, but not Stephen. There's something about putting pen to paper that he likes. Yes, he types his notes on his laptop eventually and writes his articles online, but if he's on the ground, talking to people, then he likes to use a pad and paper. It gives him a greater connection to what he's writing. He hasn't used it recently though. Sometimes it's easier to memorise details.

A sharp pain pierces him like a hot poker between the eyes. He stops for a moment and squeezes the bridge of his nose, taking a deep breath. It seems the tree hasn't healed him after all. Perhaps it's time to head to the cottage and sit down to recover until he has to meet Frank this evening.

No. There's never time to sit down and recover.

At the sound of voices, he looks up, seeing a couple of walkers passing by along the path below. They see him and give a wave. It's odd. A lot of the people who live in the village are friendly, happy to give him a smile as a kind gesture, while others are the opposite, preferring to glare at him, as if daring him to do anything they wouldn't be happy with.

He doesn't return the wave, finding it very awkward. Social interactions have never been his strong point, especially with strangers. Putting him in a room full of strangers and expecting him to converse with them is like putting a lion into an enclosure full of lambs and expecting it to not eat them. Stephen would happily spend time by himself, be totally alone and never say a word for the rest of his life than be forced into a conversation with strangers.

The only time he likes talking with others is when it's a part of an investigation or part of his job as a journalist. Then, his mind switches into a different gear entirely and often goes the other way, where he'll come across as brash or rude to the person he's speaking to. Again, it's never his intention to cause issues or offence, but if difficult questions need to be asked, then he is the man who can ask them, something Detective Williams previously found out.

That's why he must do his best tonight when speaking with Frank.

Sophia is depending on him. This tree has revealed a clue and it relates directly to her.

He grabs the planks of wood, the sketchbook and the items of rubbish and heads down the hill.

Reaching the yard, he deposits the rubbish in the bin by the garage, then checks his phone. There are several missed calls from Rachel. He calls her back, hoping there's enough signal for a call to go through.

'Oh, so you are alive then,' she snaps as soon as the call connects.

Her rough voice catches him off guard and he flinches. 'What are you talking about?'

'No text. No call. No message. Nothing.'

'I sent you a text last night saying I'd arrived.'

'No, Stephen, you didn't. I've been worried sick.'

'But we have conversed via text message.'

'No, we haven't.'

Stephen frowns. 'I have to go. Sorry.'

'Stephen, wait! Don't—'

He hangs up and checks his text messages. Rachel is correct. He has a string of messages from her, asking him to call or to ask if he's arrived safe, but he has never replied to any of them.

What the hell is going on? He remembers, very specifically, that he'd replied. He wouldn't do that to her; make her worry about his safety, especially after their disagreement before he left.

Something isn't right.

Why is he seeing things that aren't really there or imagining things that aren't really happening?

He's running out of time. In more ways than one.

Chapter 34

SOPHIA

Bethgelert, Wales, 2015

I rarely ventured into my dad's bedroom. He said it was off limits. Always. He said I had no need to go in there, which was true before I found out he could be hiding something; something that could explain the origins of John Hammel and The Hanging Tree curse. Now, his room potentially held the answers. Somehow, he knew more than he was letting on.

I had always taken my dad's word as gospel. What he said was the truth in my eyes, but things had changed. I no longer trusted him. I needed to know more. Since finding John's things hidden in our old house, I was more convinced than ever that my dad and, quite possibly, some of the village committee members were covering something up.

But what?

I needed to find that book.

I was surprised to find my dad's bedroom door wasn't locked. More fool him, I suppose. He trusted me not to enter, which meant my betrayal would hurt him all the more if he ever found out I'd trespassed into his personal space. I had my own rules with my bedroom too. He always had to knock and wait for me to respond before entering. He was never allowed in there if I wasn't there. It was to protect both of us, not only him.

The moment I stepped foot into his room, the hairs on the back of my neck tingled, like my body knew what I was doing was wrong, and I had to watch my back. He was away. For now. But for how long was still up for debate.

Right. Time to search.

If I were hiding a secret book in my bedroom, where would I hide it?

I started with his wardrobe, chest of drawers and bedside cabinet. Clothes. More clothes. And medicine, some dirty magazines (gag – may need trauma counselling now) and general random items, like phone chargers and an old watch.

I checked under the bed, but there was nothing there except dust bunnies. The room was carpeted and I couldn't see any loose threads or evidence of the carpet being pulled up in a corner. I stood with my hands on my hips, scanning the whole room from top to bottom, left to right.

I couldn't see him hiding the book anywhere else in the house. This room was the only room I wasn't allowed in, so it made sense he would hide it in here.

The bed.

It looked higher than the average bed.

The mattress was almost waist height on me. Could be because he was getting old and struggling standing up out of bed in the morning, or it could be because he was hiding something underneath it. I pulled up the duvet which draped over the edge, covering the base of the bed.

Bingo.

There, underneath the mattress, the base of the bed had a small handle. I grabbed hold and lifted, but the weight of the mattress was too much for me. I struggled, unable to shift it. I had to push the mattress half off the base before it enabled me to lift the lid up.

Inside were more clothes. It was an extra storage space, but I knew I was nearing the final reveal. I could sense it. Smell it. I pulled the clothes out, keeping them as neat as possible until I found a second handle beneath them.

I was so close.

So close.

But then … the lid was locked.

'Dammit,' I said in a whisper.

Clearly, my dad was stupid enough to not lock the bedroom door, but he was smart enough to lock the actual hiding place under the bed. I needed his set of keys; the ones he kept on his person twenty-four hours a day, seven days a week, three hundred and sixty-five days a year.

It was time for me to get resourceful.

Chapter 35
GRAHAM

Graham takes a deep breath as he places a hand on his heart, feeling it beat under his palm. It's racing. He feels it, inside him, gathering momentum. He's close to the answers. He can feel it.

He walks out of the garage and raises his eyes to the tree at the top of the hill – The Hanging Tree; a morbid nickname by the locals or a literal representation of what happened there a hundred years ago? There is no local library in the village, so who will hold records of the area from that far back? Is there some sort of logbook?

Small, rural villages like this are often set in their ways, preferring old-school physical ways of storing information rather than digital options. Something tells him that Frank would know. He hopes Mr Mallow has some form of success tonight at the pub. It's all riding on him and his unique ability to read what people are saying beneath the surface. Graham thought he was good at that, after his many years on the force, but Mr Mallow has an exceptional talent for it.

Mr Mallow is standing in the yard, staring up at the tree, having walked down from the hill. The man looks as if he's on his last legs. Should Graham talk him into going to the hospital? It's not like him to forget words either, like they dropped out of his head. He knows the man is stubborn, but would he really put his own health at risk just to solve the case of Sophia Hammel?

He notices Mr Mallow is holding several items. Two planks of wood and a book.

'Found something, then?' he asks.

Mr Mallow snaps his attention towards him. 'It appears so. What do you make of this?' Mr Mallow hands him the book.

Graham flicks through it. 'A talented girl.'

'Yes.'

'Somewhat familiar in style to the drawing I found in the scarecrow's pockets. Seems like it was a prized possession of hers. I doubt she would have left town without it.'

'My thoughts exactly. You know, Detective, you and I are scarily similar.'

'Scarily similar?'

'Yes.'

Graham doesn't press further for what that may mean, but he's inclined to agree. Who knew that two people at opposite ends of the spectrum could share so many similarities?

'By the way, Detective, it appears your car has a flat tyre.' Stephen points towards it, parked next to the garage.

Graham frowns, walking over there. He reaches the car and stops dead in his tracks. Mr Mallow is mistaken. It isn't one tyre that's flat, but all four. In fact, they aren't just flat, but slashed, mostly like with a very sharp, very big knife.

A message is also scratched into the paintwork along the driver's side.

Stop. Looking. For. Her.

Mr Mallow joins him and they stare at the message. 'When the threatening messages start, you know you're on the right track.'

'Indeed,' replies Graham, scratching his rough beard. Perhaps whoever did this was the same person who'd crawled through the tiny window into the garage and propped the scarecrow into a sitting position to scare him. Someone is having fun at his expense.

Graham books a callout from the local garage to come and change all the tyres, but they won't arrive until tomorrow. It's too late in the day to visit now, apparently. He has one tyre spare, but not four. Strangely, Mr Mallow's car is untouched.

'Will you be driving to meet Mr Hammel later?' Graham asks.

'Yes. I don't know how late I'll be, so I don't want to walk back in the dark.'

'Fair enough.'

'So ... about your boarded up window,' says Mr Mallow, pointing.

Graham frowns. 'Ah, yes. I'd forgotten about that.'

'It doesn't belong there.'

'Yes, you said that before. I'm inclined to agree.'

'I have another hunch.'

Graham grumbles about what Mr Mallow can do with his *hunches*. Graham knows there are two bedrooms; one at the back and one at the front, as well as a bathroom upstairs and a small window on the main landing at the top of the stairs.

'Come on then, Mr Mallow. It seems we can't rest until we've figured out this next mystery.'

He heads inside and climbs the stairs two at a time, regretting his decision by the time he reaches the top one. He desperately needs to join a gym or an exercise class or something. Walking a few miles each day isn't cutting it. Not that there are any gyms around here, but he's always liked the idea of joining one. It's the thought that counts, after all, right?

He heads to the dead-end hallway; the area that has never made sense in his head. Footsteps sound on the stairs behind him, followed by a breathless Mr Mallow.

'As you can see, Detective, there doesn't appear to be a room up here which leads to the boarded-up window,' says Mr Mallow, gesturing at the hallway that leads nowhere.

Graham nods. 'It's certainly odd, I'll give you that.'

'Odd, yes.'

'A secret room, perhaps, that's also been boarded up?' Graham asks.

'An intriguing suggestion,' replies Mr Mallow. 'Do you have the title deeds to the property?'

'Somewhere, yes, but I've never looked at them.'

Five minutes later, Graham returns with the papers, all of which are dog-eared, faded and crumpled. They stand side by side in silence while he flips through the pages until he finds the design layout of the cottage. There it is, in black and white. An extra window with a room that Graham has never stepped foot in before.

'This makes no sense,' says Graham, flipping back a few pages in case he's missed something. 'Someone has blocked a whole room off.'

Graham watches, transfixed, as Mr Mallow bends to investigate the fuse box, which appears to be dead. Graham has never used it before as a brand new one has been installed downstairs underneath the stairs. Mr Mallow manages to get the small door open, revealing a bunch of twisted wires covered in dust, along with an array of switches.

Mr Mallow slowly moves his fingers around the area, pulls at a few wires, which come loose in his hand. He then knocks on the wall. A hollow thud sounds.

'I believe this is plasterboard,' says Mr Mallow. 'Might you fetch me a sledgehammer?'

Graham doesn't own a sledgehammer, but he does have a crowbar, which he keeps stashed under his bed in case of emergencies; a habit he's had from his time in the police force. Mr Mallow takes it from him, then wedges the pointed edge into the nearest corner of the wall. He yanks it out, pulling with it a chunk of plasterboard.

Graham steps forwards and peers through the hole in the wall. 'Mr Mallow, I do believe you are a certified genius.'

Chapter 36
STEPHEN

He can't quite believe his eyes, but the detective is clearly seeing it too. This time, he's definitely not hallucinating.

There's a secret room behind a fake wall. He uses the crowbar, prying off the rest of the plasterboard, enough to form a hole big enough to fit through.

The light from the hallway isn't enough to pierce the darkness beyond, so Stephen uses the torch function on his phone, holding it aloft as the detective steps forwards and attempts to squeeze himself between the wooden joists.

After several failed attempts, it's clear that Detective Williams is a little too large to fit between the joists and beams. It isn't merely a blocked doorframe, but a room hidden behind a structure built into the wall.

'Allow me, Detective,' says Stephen.

'Are you sure you're feeling up for an exploration?'

Stephen's touched by the detective's warmth and concern. 'I'm quite all right, thank you.'

'Because if you pass out in there, I'm not going to be able to come in after you.'

Stephen nods. 'Noted.'

The detective moves aside. Stephen takes a breath and holds it for a moment as his mind drifts back to his fear of the dark. The fear still lingers in the background, like an old friend, reminding him that it's okay to be afraid from time to time. It's what makes him stronger, more determined to succeed and fight those demons.

In he goes.

The dust particles attack his lungs and throat straight away, and the old cobwebs cling to his jacket and hair as he squeezes his slender body in-between the first joists. He ducks under the lowest beam until he reaches a wider space. It's a room; the third mysterious bedroom.

The barricaded window is at the back of the space, blackened by dust and grime. Along one side is an old bed and a pillow, a large pile of books that had probably once been stacked neatly, and a cardboard box that looks rotten enough to collapse if he picks it up. Every surface holds a thick layer of dust, enough to tell him that it's been several decades since the place was last cleaned.

He moves closer to the box and pulls back the lid, peering inside. Several books, along with various newspapers and photographs are nestled inside. He pulls the box closer, but the sides fall apart at the seams, unable to hold together against the pressure. The books and newspapers spill across the floor at his feet.

'Damn it.'

'Have you found something, Mr Mallow?'

'Yes, I believe I have.' Stephen bends and picks up the nearest book on top of the pile that has scattered. It isn't a book after all, but a diary. Its pages are filled with writing, diagrams, charts and drawings. Not a single page is clear.

The first page bears a name: John Hammel.

'Well, I'll be damned,' whispers Stephen. He grabs another, and another, flicking briefly through each one, finding more of the same. Drawings. Writings. Charts. All in black ink. Swirly writing. A lot of the penmanship is smudged, having suffered from the damp over the years it's been in here.

On the front page of each diary, along with John's name, is a date. 1920. 1924. Stephen even finds one from 1915. Stephen picks up as many as he can carry and passes them through to the detective who is waiting by the entrance.

'Diaries?'

'Lots of them. All written by John Hammel.'

'Interesting. Good work. Hopefully there is something in these diaries that can help us.'

Stephen returns to the room, retrieving the rest of the items. It takes him several trips, by which point, when he hands the detective the last of the newspapers, his arms are trembling.

'Go and sit at the kitchen table, Mr Mallow. I'll pop the kettle on. Is there anything else in the room of interest?'

'I don't believe so, but I'll do another quick sweep.' He takes one last look around at the long-forgotten room. Had Sophia found this space too? For a moment, when he first entered the area, a morbid thought had entered his mind. Would he find Sophia's body hidden in the walls?

There is no rotting smell, other than damp and mould. Thankfully, there is also no sign of a body.

Where are you, Sophia?

Ensuring the room is clear, he squeezes himself between the beams, exiting into the hallway, then joins Detective Williams in the kitchen where a mug of coffee is already waiting for him. The detective has also piled the diaries and newspapers onto the kitchen table. There are so many that barely a piece of the table itself is visible.

'I have a feeling this is going to be a long day,' says Stephen. 'Luckily, we have time before I need to meet Frank.'

The first thing they do is gather all the diaries together and work out the dates of each one. The earliest is 1912 and the latest is 1925. The diary from 1925 is only partially completed, stopping in October of that year.

The month he died.

The newspaper articles are next on the list to sort. They are crudely cut out, sometimes ripped. Nothing jumps out straight away, but there are mentions of residents who have died in the war. There are also a few notebooks, all with scribbles and lists inside. Stephen picks one up and reads through the first couple of pages.

Bethgelert Village Council

John Hammel Sr

Dafydd Davies

Margerie Bevan

Aled Griffiths

Then, it lists the names of their family members, including spouses and children.

'It seems young John's father, John senior, was a member of the village council,' says Stephen. 'Also, these surnames are all familiar. I'm not quite sure what the village council does, but I assume it involves knowing a lot of what goes on and giving the go ahead for planning.' He looks to the detective for confirmation.

Detective Williams nods. 'That's correct. They seem to have a lot of power within the local community. There's a meeting once a month, which I told you about. The day I moved in, a bunch of them turned up at my door and introduced themselves, explaining a few things to me regarding the cottage.'

'Like what?'

'Like … I wouldn't be able to change any of it, internally, or build an extension.'

'Surely, that's not up to them? That depends on whatever is said when you apply for the planning permission.'

'Not according to the village committee.'

'So this … village committee, or whatever you want to call them … they hold power over the village that goes back a hundred years, which means that whatever happened to young John Hammel was probably a result of him finding out what they were up to back then. Look at this …' Stephen hands the detective one of the journals.

Detective Williams looks over the page that's open. 'Human sacrifice?'

'A hundred years ago it wouldn't have been so unheard of.'

'Yes, perhaps, but … are you saying that the members of the village committee potentially sacrificed that poor girl ten years ago? For what?'

'Does it matter?'

'Yes, I'd say it does,' snaps the detective.

Stephen sighs. 'Human sacrifice may still be prevalent, even today. Most recently, a shrine of twenty-four human skulls were found in Uganda with injuries pertaining to human sacrifice. It was a widespread historical practice across many cultures for a multitude of reasons. The most obvious one was to appease deities, ensuring fertility or good harvests, but it could also be used to maintain social order, to terrorize lower classes, display authority, and maintain existing social hierarchies. It was also used as a means of showing devotion or to accompany the deceased into the afterlife.'

'But this is the twenty-first century, Mr Mallow. We're in the middle of rural Wales, surrounded by sheep and family farms.'

'I'd say that makes it even more likely. In some cultures, sacrifices were used to promote fertility in the land and ensure successful harvests. According to the village magazine, the same farmers win the village show every year.'

'Yes, but sacrificing a human is a tad dramatic, don't you think?'

Stephen shrugs. 'I've heard of worse reasons.'

Detective Williams nods. 'Hmm, you may be right there, Mr Mallow. I've also noticed that the most successful farms in the area are all run by members of the committee, including Hammel, Bevan and Davies, although Frank must have run into some financial trouble in the past.'

'It seems Frank Hammel, Diane Bevan and William Davies have just moved to the top of our suspect list.' Stephen swallows, attempting to dislodge the lump in his throat. 'To think … a father sacrificing his own daughter for the sake of the community.'

Detective Williams sighs. 'It wouldn't be the first time I've encountered such horrors. You remember Tyler Jenkins, right?'

'How could I forget? But what about Griffiths? Do you know anyone with that surname?'

'Not that I can recall. But I'll bet there's a Griffiths still in the village.'

Chapter 37

STEPHEN

Stephen parks in the pub car park and assesses his surroundings before moving another muscle. He finds country pubs odd places to hang out. They are mostly filled with a plethora of elderly locals who complain if anyone under the age of forty enters or if the noise levels raise above a certain decibel. And if it's not the elderly locals who take over the place, it's the youth who think it's suitable to laugh and swear really loudly right next to a family with a young child who are trying to enjoy a pleasant meal.

Stephen gets out of the car, walks the short distance to the entrance and then finds a quiet booth at the back of the pub, settling into the padded seat with his back towards the corner. He likes to have eyes on the exit and to be able to see who's approaching. He also enjoys people watching, fascinated by their behaviours. Yes, he's a person too, but he knows he's different somehow. Watching people is like watching television for him.

It's busier than he likes. He was expecting a quiet pub with a few locals and maybe a Labrador stretched out in front of the roaring fire, but it's exceptionally busy for a weekday evening. He prefers it when the background noise is a quiet hum rather than a loud roar. He can barely hear himself think. It's a struggle to form or organise any thoughts right now. He considers standing up and walking out, but no, he's here for information. The detective is counting on him to bring back vital details that will help them solve Sophia's disappearance. Not to mention the idea that people in this village are possibly sacrificing people for the good of their livelihoods and farms is a morbid thought if there ever was one.

What he really wants to be doing right now is combing through the heaps of diaries, journals and newspapers piled high on the kitchen table back at Rosemore Cottage with the detective. It's like a treasure trove of information spanning decades from a hundred years ago. Like looking into John Hammel's soul.

While he waits for Frank, he ponders his call with Rachel earlier today. It makes no sense. He remembers texting her as clear as day, but she'd never received anything. How odd. And yet, despite it being an interesting question that needs an answer, it isn't his number one priority.

'Mr Mallow, what can I get you?'

Stephen flinches as if burned as Frank Hammel speaks above him. He hadn't noticed him approach, despite his eyes being focused on the entrance the whole time.

'Whisky. The smokier the better.'

'Good choice. Won't be a moment.'

Frank turns and walks to the bar, weaving in-between various customers, all of whom greet him with a nod or a hearty handshake. Frank instantly engages in conversation with the barman. Stephen envies those who converse with others so easily. For him, it's a constant battle between the words that come out of his mouth and the words his brain wants to say. The ones from the brain, if he allows them out, would easily cause offence or make others uncomfortable with their bluntness, whereas the words that come out of his mouth sometimes aren't the ones he means to say and often leaves him feeling confused and disappointed.

Frank arrives a few minutes later holding two glasses. Stephen takes the one handed to him. He smells the smoky peat as soon as he brings the glass to his lips.

'Cheers,' says Frank as he takes a mouthful.

Stephen frowns. Doesn't one usually raise their glass and then clink them together to initiate a "cheers?" Or has he got that wrong? Battling against the words in his head, he remains silent and takes a sip instead.

'So … what would you like to know?' asks Frank. He leans against the wooden booth and spreads one arm out along the back of the bench. Stephen has been working on recognising body language and Frank appears to be relaxed in this environment. Stephen, on the other hand, is far from relaxed, crossing and uncrossing his legs and constantly shifting his position on the seat, unable to get comfortable. He may as well make a start. The sooner he asks the questions, the sooner he can get out of here.

'Run me through the events of the day of Sophia's disappearance. I need to understand her movements. Was there anything out of the ordinary? Tell me what she said, what she did, where she went. As much detail as possible. Don't leave anything out.' Stephen pauses for a moment and then adds, 'Please,' because it's the socially acceptable thing to say when asking so much of someone.

Frank clears his throat as he swirls the dark golden liquid around the bottom of his glass. 'Sophia and I had a falling out the day before, so we weren't on speaking terms.'

Stephen opens his mouth to ask what they had fallen out about, but Frank beats him to it. 'She was seeing this local bloke, Callum, and I caught him sneaking out of the house that morning. He was older. She was sixteen. You can imagine my reaction.'

Stephen catches himself before he repeats the words in his head. Something doesn't ring true.

'How much older was Callum?'

'Can't be sure, but he was at least mid-twenties. He was one of the local farm boys. Worked over at the pig farm with Diane.'

'Diane Bevan.'

'Yes.'

Stephen jots down his findings on his pad of paper. 'So ... the morning of the day before she disappeared, you found Callum sneaking out of her bedroom,' says Stephen.

'Yes. I told her she was too young to be engaging in ... that sort of thing.'

'She was sixteen. It's legal.'

Frank shoots him a stern look; clearly not the response he'd been looking for from Stephen. 'She stormed out of the house and didn't do any of her chores that day, so I had to do them, didn't I?'

'Um ... I suppose you did, yes.'

Frank stares at Stephen for a moment. Had Stephen said something wrong? Frank had asked him a question, so he'd answered it.

'Right ... well ... anyway ... Sophia didn't come back to the farm till later that night. I was angry. I'd had a few drinks.' Frank chugs the rest of his drink; the glass now empty. He signals to the barman for another two.

'You were angry and had a few drinks.' Sometimes Stephen likes to repeat the facts, to ensure he hasn't misunderstood the person he's talking to. Some might say it comes across as condescending, but he needs to ensure he knows exactly what is going on, that he has everything clear.

'That's right.' Frank doesn't seem at all fazed by Stephen's repetition.

Stephen watches as a waitress brings over two fresh drinks. He hasn't finished his first one yet. Stephen waits until she's walked away, a sudden idea springing to mind.

'Frank, were you aware that your daughter was attracted to other women?'

It seems he catches Frank at the worst possible time – mid gulp – because Frank coughs and splutters, grabbing a serviette from the table and dabbing his mouth where splashes of whisky are clinging to his rugged beard.

'Good God, man! Why would you blurt out something like that? Are you insane?'

Stephen shrugs. 'It's a perfectly acceptable question, Frank.'

Frank dips his head, glancing around at the bar, as if checking whether anyone is listening in on their conversation. 'Y-Yes, I was aware, Mr Mallow. She never told me as much, but … I was aware.'

'Stephen, please. So, would you now like to rephrase your previous answer about a young man leaving her room?'

Frank clears his throat and takes a breath before picking up his glass once again. He nods at the one remaining on the table, the one Stephen hasn't touched yet. 'Drink up, Stephen. You're already lagging.'

'Are you trying to get me drunk, Frank?'

'No, *I'm* trying to get drunk. It helps to have company.'

Stephen sighs, already tired of Frank's reluctance to answer a simple question. He picks up his glass, takes a large sip, holding the whisky in his mouth for a moment, then swallows. It burns as it travels down his throat. Once empty, he slams the glass on the table and picks up the second one. There. Maybe that will keep the old man happy. Doesn't look like he'll be driving back to Rosemore Cottage tonight.

Frank, after taking another sip, settles back in his seat and continues. 'Fine. There was no boy. We had an argument about something else.'

'Which was?'

'She kept asking questions about John Hammel, our ancestor who hung himself from The Hanging Tree a hundred years ago. He started the family curse, you see.'

'Tell me about this curse.'

'Like I said, John Hammel started it. He killed himself and, in the religious community, that's a big sin, especially back then.'

'Yes, but *why* did he hang himself?'

'Does it matter?'

'Yes, I believe it does.'

Frank stares blankly for a moment. 'I don't know.'

'You don't know why John Hammel hung himself?'

'That's what I said, but this curse ... it ruined our family for decades.'

Stephen stops scribbling words on the page and looks up. 'Interesting,' he says. 'Just your family?'

'No, a lot of families seemed to be affected by it.'

'Why's that do you think?'

'Good God, man, I don't know how curses work!'

Stephen bites his bottom lip. 'So … Sophia was interested in this curse. She was asking questions about it and you got into an argument. Then what?'

'Yes, she said it was for a school project, but I didn't believe her. I told her to leave it alone. I left the house that night and, when I came home later, I went straight to sleep.'

'Where did you go?'

'I'm sorry?'

Stephen looks him dead in the eyes. 'Where did you go after your argument with your daughter?'

Frank opens his mouth, but then closes it. 'I went to see some friends of mine. Someone in the village council. We had work to do before the next monthly newsletter came out. It was a late night.'

'Your friend's names are?'

'William Davies, Diane Bevan and Ceri Griffiths.'

Stephen writes them down, making a mental note to tell the detective that they finally have a full name for Griffiths; the fourth founding family of the village council. 'Anything else?' he asks.

'Yes. Sophia liked to spend time sitting underneath The Hanging Tree. She often went there. I saw her there the next morning while I was letting the ducks out into the yard. She often left her sketchbook up there hidden in the tree so it didn't get ruined. Not always, but sometimes she did. I get the feeling she didn't want me seeing what she drew.'

Stephen pauses, Frank's words not quite clicking into the right place again. It answered why Stephen had found her sketchbook hidden in the tree, at least. Frank's farm is all the way on the other side of the village, so if he'd been letting the ducks out into the yard, how the hell had he seen his daughter at The Hanging Tree, which was situated near Rosemore Cottage?

'Do you often keep your ducks at the cottage?'

'What?'

Stephen shifts in his seat, a warmth spreading across his chest. 'You said you saw your daughter while you were letting the ducks out into the yard in the morning, but how could you when your farm isn't anywhere near the tree? Who were you visiting at Rosemore Cottage? Or do you keep your ducks there?'

Frank drums his fingers on the table. 'You're very perceptive.'

'It's my job.'

'Very well. Yes, I was at the cottage. I didn't live there, but I still owned it at the time.'

'Were you letting the ducks out or visiting someone?'

'Neither.'

Stephen waits a moment, takes a sip of his drink. The heat is spreading. It's making him want to flap his hand in front of his face, the way people do even though it makes barely a bit of difference. He's getting irritated that Frank continues to lie to him.

'Like I said, I owned the cottage back then. I rented it out as a holiday let. I was there to double check the people had arrived. Normally, the visitors would send me an email or leave a voicemail to say they'd arrived, found the key and settled in, but they didn't.'

'Are you saying there was no one staying at the cottage at the time?'

'That's exactly what I'm saying. No one turned up.'

'What was their last name? The people who were supposed to rent it?'

'How the hell should I know? It was a decade ago.'

Stephen leans forwards. 'I'm really going to need you to remember their last name, Frank. It could be important.'

Frank grunts, staring straight past Stephen at the wall. Stephen checks over his shoulder in case he's looking at something in particular, but it appears he's merely doing that thing that most people do when trying to summon a forgotten memory: they stare blankly into space in the hopes it will help.

'Lankin.'

'Are you sure?'

'No, but it definitely started with L.'

Stephen's shoulders slump slightly. He's not sure what he was expecting. A lightbulb moment, perhaps. But the revelation of the name doesn't help him. There are still many questions to ask.

Stephen takes a sip of whisky to steady his racing mind. He's had two tipples now within a short period of time and is feeling the effects. Nausea, wonky vision and numb fingers. He reaches forwards for his pen, but he can't grab it quite right. It skids across the table and onto the floor.

'My apologies,' says Stephen, shuffling off the seat. He reaches to grab it with shaking hands, but his body has other plans. The last thing he sees is the floor hurtling towards him. His head bounces off the side of the table and the world turns dark.

Chapter 38
GRAHAM

Something keeps tapping against the window, as if someone is trying to get his attention. The more he tries to ignore the rustling and knocking, the louder it becomes. Mr Mallow has been gone for over an hour and he hasn't texted to say he's finished talking to Frank either. Graham hopes he will bring back some useful information. Nothing is making any sense lately.

Graham is stuck twiddling his thumbs. He never likes to be idle. He is more at home, more comfortable when he is constantly busy, never allowing his thoughts to settle. That's especially been the case before everything that happened last year in Cherry Hollow, but now it's behind him and he has finally learned the truth, he thought his mind might take the chance to reflect and rest. But it seems he's doomed to be restless. There will always be mysteries to solve in life. He knows what he really wants to do. He wants to speak to Olivia, but he isn't due to visit her for a few more weeks. Perhaps he'll call her instead. It will be nice to hear her voice.

Graham picks up his phone and dials the number for the prison. It's way past the hours allowed for calls to prisoners, but if he doesn't try, then he'll be mulling it over all night.

'Good evening, Ashmoore Prison.'

'Hello. Good evening. My name is Detect—ah, Graham Williams. Is it possible to speak to Olivia Willows, please? It's rather urgent.'

'All calls for prisoners need to be between the hours of nine a.m. and three p.m., Monday to Friday.'

'Yes, I'm aware, but this is important.'

'Are you a family member?'

'I … no, but …'

'I am sorry, Mr Williams, but unless you're a family member, then I can't … oh, it appears I was mistaken. Your name is on the list of trusted family members and friends.'

'Yes, that's what I was trying to tell you.'

'Very well. I shall get her to call you back, but please be aware that your call will be monitored.'

'I understand. Thank you.'

Graham stares ahead blankly as he lowers his phone to the table and places it down. He wonders how long it will be before she calls. He knows she will. It's not the middle of the night yet, but he knows she'll call him back no matter the time.

He drums his fingers on the table, his phone next to him. His breath threatens to run away like a freight train. To keep himself occupied, he looks through the journals of John Hammel again, but doesn't come across any new information other than Griffiths was the name of Carys, his girlfriend. Graham wracks his brain, attempting to remember if he's met anyone with that surname in the village, but he hasn't. He's sure of it. It's a piece of the puzzle they are missing, and need it in order to proceed.

He thinks of the room hidden upstairs. It shocks him that he hadn't realised it was there. Stephen had seen something was out of place immediately with the boarded-up window, but Graham had lived here almost a year and yet hadn't thought to investigate the odd dead end hallway in his cottage.

Sometimes he wonders if his mind blocks certain things from him. Mr Mallow explained in detail about mental health back in Cherry Hollow, about how one's mind can alter and make one see or hear things that aren't really there in order to protect oneself from the truth, which would likely cause more damage.

Four minutes later, Olivia calls.

'Graham, make it fast. I only get five minutes.'

'Olivia, good to hear your voice. I'm sorry for calling so late, but I'm in a bit of a bind. I could use your words of wisdom.'

'Now, I'm intrigued.'

'There's a missing girl who's been gone ten years and …'

'Stop right there. I'm not the person you should be talking to, Graham. Surely, Stephen Mallow is much more qualified for things like this?'

'Yes, he's here, but I'm a little worried about him. He's not himself.'

'Well, that's not surprising.'

Graham pauses before asking, 'Why's it not surprising?'

'Haven't you heard?'

'Heard what?'

'The poor woman he was seeing, Rachel. She died in a tragic accident a few months ago. It left him devastated.'

Graham clears his throat. 'I'm sorry, but can you repeat that?'

'Stephen's girlfriend, Rachel, from Cherry Hollow, is dead, Graham.'

'B-But ... how is that possible? Wait, how the hell do you know about it? You're in prison.'

'Tactful as always. I happen to receive the monthly gossip from Penelope and a couple of the other ladies in Cherry Hollow. It seems they enjoy writing to me. A few letters ago, Penelope told me about Rachel's death. She fell in the bathroom and hit her head. Stephen found her on the bathroom floor a few hours later.'

Graham covers his mouth with his hand. 'Oh, God ... I had no idea. Mr Mallow ... he ... well, he inferred that she was alive.'

'I see ... three minutes left.'

'This changes everything, Olivia. Don't you see what's happening?'

A pause stretches on.

'Yes, it appears that Stephen is suffering from intense grief,' says Olivia at last.

'Not only that, but I believe his grief is manifesting itself into something much bigger than he realises.'

'Why do I feel like I already know this story?'

'Because you do. We all do. The darkness … it's back. And it's after Mr Mallow for real this time.'

Graham ends the call, a dull ache settling in the pit of his stomach. How could he have not realised? The fact Olivia knows more about the man who's been staying with him for the past few days than he does, is ridiculous. Mr Mallow has never mentioned a single thing about his girlfriend passing away. In fact, he spoke about her as if she were alive.

Does that mean he truly believes she is?

Graham's mind reflects back to Cherry Hollow and the woman who moved there only a year or so ago, Emma Smithson. She'd suffered through the same thing. Seeing a person who wasn't there because of the magnitude of her grief. Because she wasn't strong enough to admit they were really gone. Grief is a powerful emotion in this world. There's a lot Graham doesn't understand about it, but he does know the power it holds over those who are struggling, who perhaps aren't strong enough to deal with it alone.

The darkness is continuing to lay waste to all those who aren't able to fight it. Mr Mallow needs help. Sophia will have to wait for the time being. He needs Mr Mallow in the right frame of mind before they can continue.

Graham looks up as a car pulls into the driveway. It's impossible to miss because whenever cars drive up the road towards his cottage, especially in the cark, the lights illuminate the kitchen. But it isn't Mr Mallow's car.

Curious as to who his uninvited guest is, he opens the door onto the yard. A man he recognises as the owner of the pub in the village steps out.

'*Noswaith dda*, Mr Williams. Sorry to disturb you, but I've had to escort Mr Mallow back here.' As he speaks, the passenger door opens and a weary Mr Mallow climbs out of the car, holding onto the door for dear life. 'He's a little disorientated, but otherwise seems fine.'

Graham rushes out to his friend. 'What the hell happened? Was he attacked?'

'Attacked? Good heavens, no. He's drunk, Mr Williams. Passed right out on the table while he was talking to Frank. He hit his head but doesn't appear to have a concussion. Just needs to sleep it off.'

Graham supports Mr Mallow's weight. 'Thank you for bringing him back.'

'No worries. He was a fool to try and keep up with Frank. That man can drink for Wales.'

Graham nods his thanks and holds on to Mr Mallow while they watch the barman get back into his car and drive up the road.

'Good grief, man. How much did you have to drink?'

Mr Mallow shakes his head. 'Not enough to make me pass out.'

'Then what …'

'Help me inside. I'll explain. I have something to tell you.'

'That makes two of us.'

Chapter 39

SOPHIA

Bethgelert, Wales, 2015

I came up with a plan instantly; the second I walked out of his room and closed the door after putting everything back exactly the way I'd found it. There was no way I was going to be able to steal my dad's keys from him without him finding out, so it was pointless in attempting to do so. No, I had to come up with a better plan, so I asked if I could join him at the village council meeting instead later the next day.

His immediate answer was a resounding no.

I was too young and I didn't need to concern myself with the village goings on until I was older and out of school. No children were allowed.

Fine. Whatever.

Plan B.

I would follow him there instead, then sneak in and listen. Yes, the book held vital information, but listening to a real live council meeting would be like striking gold.

A monthly village meeting was held at the town hall for all the residents to come and share their opinions, thoughts, feelings on whatever was happening. It was also where my dad could share any news and updates regarding building works, family fun days, and general all-round information. Coffee and cake were provided and everyone had a lovely time.

Then there were the weekly gatherings, which only my dad and a select few committee members attended. Why they needed a separate meeting, outside of the monthly one, I was yet to understand. The thing about the weekly council meetings was that they changed location every week. Not like the monthly one, which stayed the same. It was a secret that apparently only a select few were allowed to know.

Black coat and hat donned, I kept my distance on my bike as he walked through the village, meeting and greeting the community. Some shook his hand. Others merely nodded. My father was a well-respected man and people looked to him for advice and guidance. When my brother died and Mum left, the whole community gathered around him and ensured he had everything he needed. No one cared about me. As long as my dad was okay.

He always told me it was an honour to be a part of the Hammel family; an honour we had to uphold no matter what (meaning the embarrassment of having a past family member end their own life, even if it was almost a century ago).

Eventually, my father moved away from the busy street and into a small side alley. I parked my bike and waited a moment before popping my head around the corner, catching a glimpse of his back disappearing through a door at the end.

Checking behind me, I ducked into the alley and approached the door. There was no way for me to enter the building that way, but perhaps there was a window further round the side where I could climb through. I checked, but there was nothing, so I had to return to the door and keep my fingers crossed that the meeting wouldn't be held directly behind it. The building was part of a main shop, but I'd never been round the back before.

The door wasn't locked, so I pushed it open as gently as I could, keeping my ears pricked for any sounds. There were voices emanating from somewhere in the building, but not close enough to warrant a panic.

I found myself a small alcove down a hallway, outside of another door where I thought the meeting was being held. I was hidden enough that if anyone entered from the direction I'd come from, they wouldn't notice me. It wasn't ideal, but there wasn't anywhere else I could go where I could still hear what was going on.

I held my breath, worried I might be heard because my heart was beating so hard and fast, but the chatter and laughter from behind the door was so loud, I needn't have feared. Some of the voices I recognised.

Diane Bevan. Her laughter could be heard from a mile away. Unmistakably her.

William Davies. The local butcher who always added an extra sausage into the bag whenever I bought some for dad to cook for dinner. He was also the guy who'd given me a fright that evening at the tree. Strange how on one hand he could be so nice towards me, and then scare me half to death while attempting to deliver a message. I wondered what the message was about and whether it had anything to do with the note my dad had read, and then drunk himself into a coma over.

I strained to hear any other voices, but they blended together too much for me to pick them out. I didn't think there were any more people. Just the three of them. But above them all was my dad's voice. Commanding. Direct.

'Thank you all for coming. Let's sit.'

'Hang on,' said William Davies. 'Where's our fourth?'

'She's on her way,' replied my dad. Ah, so they were expecting someone else.

'Is everything ready?' asked Diane.

A long silence followed.

'You know it needs to be done,' William finally said.

'She's just a kid.'

'She may be, but she's the only one who can finally break the curse. Don't forget, Frank, it can only be a member of the Hammel family. Unless you'd like to volunteer?'

'I know but ...'

I didn't hear anything else because a shadow loomed over me and I stared up at the face of the woman I assumed they were waiting for. Their fourth. Holy shit. It was Ceri Griffiths.

'You're not supposed to be here, young lady,' she said.

I stood up, acting much braver than I felt. 'I was just ...'

'Never mind. It looks like we'll have to bring our plans forward.'

My eyes widened as she lunged forward and grabbed hold of my hair, tugging me towards the door. She shoved it open, then pushed me through it. I shrieked as I tumbled to the floor in front of my dad, who froze on the spot.

'I tried to warn you, *Cariad*,' he said as tears filled his eyes.

Chapter 40
STEPHEN

Detective Williams lowers Stephen onto a kitchen chair, checks to ensure he's not about to topple off it, and then turns to fetch a tea towel from a nearby drawer. He runs it under the tap, squeezes out the excess water and hands it over.

'Your nose is bleeding,' he says.

Stephen holds the towel against his nose. His pale shirt is stained with blood too, droplets that landed there during his trip back from the village in the back of the barman's car. Frank had offered to drive him, but he'd already had too much to drink, so had helped him into the car instead, chuckling that it was never a good idea to try and keep up with him while out drinking. Stephen bit his lip to stop his reply spilling from his lips. Frank had been the one who'd plied him with drinks in the first place! But little did Frank know that Stephen's dizzy spell had nothing to do with the alcohol he'd ingested. Not entirely, anyway.

Stephen doesn't say a word for a moment while Detective Williams makes them each a cup of coffee. For Stephen, it's too late for caffeine, but hopefully it will ease the pain and confusion in his head. Anything to be able to see and think straight.

Stephen waits until Detective Williams places a cup in front of each of them and sits down. 'So … care to explain why your nose is bleeding?'

'I hit my head.'

'Your nose is not your head, Mr Mallow.'

Stephen pulls the towel away and looks at the bright red blood soaking into the pattern. 'Sorry about your towel,' he says. 'I spoke to Frank. I drank four fingers of whisky quicker than normal, but I wasn't feeling quite right even before that.'

'What's going on?'

Stephen sighs. The time has come. 'I believe I had a seizure.' At the final word, Graham's eyes raise into his hairline. 'For several months, I have been experiencing distressing symptoms, but this is the first seizure I've experienced. I went to the doctor, they completed some tests and I found out the results the day before I came here via email.'

'What's the diagnosis?' asks Detective Williams, his voice calm, low.

'A brain tumour. I won't bore you with the details. It has a very long-winded name, but the prognosis isn't good.' Stephen lowers the towel to the table and picks up his coffee. He takes a small sip. 'But it does explain why I've been hallucinating lately and being rather … forgetful.'

'I see,' says the detective. 'What sort of hallucinations?'

'I seem to think I have been having conversations with people via text message, but I haven't. My girlfriend, Rachel, has been trying to get hold of me and I thought I'd responded, but I haven't. I also saw the ghost of John Hammel standing under the tree the other morning.' Stephen rubs his eyes, the dull pain behind them keeps forcing them closed. 'I don't know what's real or not anymore.'

Detective Williams stares at him from across the table. 'I hate to say it, Mr Mallow, but I think you may need serious medical help.'

'Not until this case is solved.'

'What's so important about this case? I can handle it. Believe it or not, solving missing person cases used to be my profession. I know I called you for help, but if I'd known you were sick, then I wouldn't have asked.'

'This is so much more than just a missing person case. I'm seeing things, hearing things that aren't really there. This is like Cherry Hollow all over again.'

'It's funny you should say that.'

'What do you mean? I'm not saying that The Creature is responsible. How can it be? This is a whole other town. The Creature was Amber's thing.'

'Yes, but do you remember what we spoke about that day in your office when you came back to Cherry Hollow for the second time? The Creature was so much more than one person's guilty conscience. Mental health disorders come in many shapes and forms. The darkness affects us all in one way or another.'

'Yes, I'm aware, but Sophia being missing has nothing to do with someone's mental health,' says Stephen.

'I'm not talking about Sophia Hammel here, Mr Mallow. I'm talking about you.' The detective points at Stephen.

'Me?'

'Your brain tumour. When did the nosebleeds, hallucinations and other symptoms start?'

Stephen narrows his eyes, unsure where the detective is going with his line of questioning, but he knows better than to fight against him on this. The detective has many more years of experience with questioning people than he does.

'I ... I suppose it was a few months ago.'

'Did anything substantial happen around that time that you can remember?'

Stephen tents his fingers in front of him and stares at his nails, studying them one by one. He always likes to keep his nails neatly trimmed and clean. You can tell a lot about a person by the state of their nails. He takes a moment and looks at the detective's nails, which are also clean and tidy. Figures.

He needs his mind to work the way it usually does. Why can't he focus and think straight? Something is blocking his memory, his special way of thinking about things.

'I … yes, I believe something did happen, but I'm unsure what it is.'

The detective takes a deep breath in through his nose, then slowly exhales. 'Mr Mallow, what I'm about to reveal to you may come as a bit of a shock, but I mean no harm. I believe you need to be reminded of something and then your mind will start to clear.'

Stephen nods. He understands and is fully aware that the detective is being serious. 'Please, continue,' he says.

'Very well. Mr Mallow … I spoke with Olivia Willows again earlier, while you were with Frank at the pub. I originally called her to speak about Sophia Hammel and this case. I thought she may be able to shed some light on things, but as it turns out, she shed some light on something else instead. Something involving you … and your girlfriend, Rachel.'

At this point, Stephen forgets how to breathe. He holds his breath, feeling his pulse increase with every passing second.

'I'm afraid to tell you, but … Rachel is dead. She died months ago from a sudden fall. She hit her head and it killed her. You found her on the bathroom floor hours after it happened. There was nothing you could have done to save her.'

And then everything makes sense again.

It hurts. Of course it does. It's been hurting ever since it happened. The pain was too much to contain. That's why he's shoved it all into a box in his mind, locked it up tight and thrown away the key. But the detective has just found that key and opened the lid, revealing the horrors lying within. Stephen now has no choice but to stand up and face it.

Now, the hurt, the grief, is loose again, but it means there's a possible answer to his illness. Perhaps he isn't sick at all. Not in the traditional sense It's been his grief, masquerading as an illness, a brain tumour, to trick him. He understands.

'Yes, I remember now,' says Stephen, lowering his line of sight to the floor. His vision is blurring again, distorted around the edges.

It *did* happen.

Rachel is dead. She has been all along.

His mind has been protecting itself from the pain, from the terror of what it would be like to face this world without her in it.

The detective reaches out and covers Stephen's shaking hands with his own. 'Grief is a terrible burden to carry alone, Mr Mallow. Don't let the darkness win. Not again.'

Stephen looks up at him through hazy, tearful eyes. Something in him breaks into a million pieces in a way it's never done before. Is that his heart breaking or his mind? Whatever it is, it's a relief. For so long, Stephen has forced the barriers to stay up, to remain strong and stoic in the presence of others.

Not anymore. Not today.

Today, he's allowing his barriers to come crashing down around him. Sometimes, it's okay to grieve and show weakness. It's what being human is all about.

'Thank you, *Graham*. For rescuing me,' he says with a weak smile. He wants to tell him that he's wrong, that it's not only the darkness that's causing his illness. But he wants to protect his friend a little longer. Just a little longer.

'Any time, *Stephen*. Any time.'

Chapter 41

GRAHAM

Graham hands Stephen a cup of coffee to help clear his whisky-infused head, but he has a feeling that Stephen's already thinking a little clearer since he revealed the truth. He doesn't mean to upset the man, make him re ive the tragedy of what happened to his girlfriend, but revealing the truth was the only way he was going to get his friend back, thinking with a level head.

Graham takes a slurp of his own coffee, but it's still too hot, so he places the mug on the table in front of him. 'I am sorry, Stephen. About Rachel. She was a lovely young woman.' His voice catches on *Stephen*. It's always been their thing, to not use first names. It's a form of respect between them, and a small in-house joke they've continued. But at the moment, it feels right, more personal.

Stephen nods. 'Thank you. Yes. She was. It was a shock when I found her. My mind ... I suppose you could say that I didn't handle it very well. I found her ... in the bathroom, dressed in her pyjamas, getting ready for bed. They say, even if I'd been there, I wouldn't have been able to do anything fast enough to save her after she fell and h t her head, but it didn't help. She died instantly, they said. She'd have felt little pain. My mind shut down. I let the darkness in.'

'It's understandable ...'

'No, it isn't. I, of all people, should know how powerful it is, especially living in Cherry Hollow. The grief was too much. Why does it happen? Why does death happen so suddenly?' Stephen looks out the window towards the hanging tree, but it's too dark to see anything. 'One second, she was alive. And then she was gone. Just like that. I would understand if it was a bullet or she was hit by a car or something, but it was an accident. She slipped on a puddle of water which she didn't clean up after taking a shower. There was no warning. Nothing.' Stephen shakes his head, covering his face with his hands.

A silence looms around them. The darkness outside feels as if it's trying to squeeze the cottage tighter and tighter. The air is thinner.

'I think we've spoken about this enough for one night, wouldn't you agree?' says Stephen.

'Yes, if you're sure. I'd still like you to be careful though, considering you've had a seizure. Real or not, your body is recovering from severe mental and emotional trauma.'

Stephen nods, feeling his eyelids growing heavy. 'I think we're being watched. Maybe not right this minute, but ... I've seen several people around the village keeping a close eye on us. Tonight, at the bar, before I face-planted the floor, I also felt many pairs of eyes on me.'

'Speaking of which, how did the talk with Frank go before you … you know?' asks Graham.

'He tried his best to lie, but I saw right through him. He told me about a curse on the Hammel family that started with John in 1925. Also, Sophia and Frank had an argument the day before she disappeared because she kept asking questions about John Hammel.'

'We already know a lot of this.'

'Yes, but I did find out one new piece of information. Ceri Griffiths.'

'Ah, the infamous name we've been after.'

'Do you know anyone by that name?'

Graham shakes his head. 'Unfortunately, no.'

'Did you ever speak to that friend of yours? Karen, was it?'

'No, it slipped my mind. When I fetch my paper in the morning, I'll be sure to ask if she knows who that is. It must have been one of the women at the vi lage meeting the other night. I have a feeling it may have been who Diane Bevan was talking to most of the evening.'

'Would you recognise her if you saw her again?'

'Yes, I believe I would.'

Chapter 42
STEPHEN

He trundles downstairs the next morning, wishing he felt better, but even a decent sleep hasn't done him any favours. He's surprised at how quickly he did fall asleep. Maybe it's his body's way of telling him he doesn't have to fight against his grief anymore. He's not sure if the symptoms will disperse now or whether they will continue to get worse.

Grief doesn't disappear overnight after a good sleep and a wake up call. It stays with you, raising its ugly head at the most inappropriate and random times. Deep, pure grief is for life. Stephen knows this, so there's a chance he may never feel normal again. But accepting it and understanding grief and its effects is the first step. That's what therapists and doctors always say, isn't it?

It's later than Stephen usually gets up, but his body and mind must have needed the rest. Graham is awake and has coffee brewing. Stephen could smell it the moment he stepped outside the bedroom door earlier. Warm and inviting. Stephen takes a seat at the kitchen table and lets out a long sigh.

'Well, Graham, what's on the agenda today?' It feels strange to call him Graham. Maybe he should go back to calling him Detective just for old times' sake. Stephen always feels better when he returns to the familiar.

'Hmm, well ...this investigation has taken a somewhat detour off a cliff lately. I believe the journals and diaries from young John Hammel may hold more clues. What we need is solid evidence tying Frank Hammel, William Davies and Diane Bevan to the crime, or evidence of Sophia Hammel's disappearance. It would also help to find out who Ceri Griffiths is, but things seem to have come to a slight ...' While he's been talking, Graham opens the back door and stares into the early morning gloom, squinting his eyes, but then he stops. 'Ah, bugger. It seems our hanging friend has returned.'

Stephen gets to his feet and joins Graham at the back door. It may still be relatively dark outside, the sunrise barely cresting the brow of the hill, but there is, indeed, another scarecrow hanging from the tree. This one is much further down, the feet of the scarecrow skimming the earth. There's something different about it. Somehow more ... life-like ...

'Um ... I don't think that's our hanging friend ...' says Stephen.

'Shit ...'

Before Stephen can react, Graham takes off up the hill, moving at an alarming pace for an older gentleman. Stephen follows, attempting to catch him, but failing miserably. By the time he reaches the top of the hill, Graham is already there, standing next to the swinging body of a man who is very clearly dead.

'Frank Hammel,' says Graham with a long sigh. 'Goddamn it!'

Stephen stares at the hanging body of the man he spoke to last night. A rope is pulled tight around his neck, dark bruising already forming. The man's eyes are open, bulging and streaked with red veins. There's a ladder propped against the tree trunk.

It seems Frank climbed it, tied the rope around one of the thicker branches, then slipped the loop over his head and stepped off.

'I'd better call this in,' says Graham. 'I think this investigation just went from casual to severe. This is no longer about a missing teenager.'

Stephen nods, agreeing. He watches while Graham takes out his mobile and calls the local police. He paces back and forth while he speaks, using terminology and phrases that sound professional. Stephen leaves him in peace.

Stephen has a hunch and he's hoping he's right. While Graham's back is turned he reaches up and checks the pockets of the jacket that Frank is wearing. It's the same one from last night. Stephen even catches a whiff of whisky. His fingers find a piece of paper, tucked into his inner jacket pocket. Stephen quickly scans it.

I'm sorry. I tried. 568962-1925

Stephen looks up as Graham approaches. 'What's that?' Graham asks.

'A clue,' replies Stephen.

'Please tell me you did not just touch a dead body and remove a vital piece of evidence?'

Stephen shoves the piece of paper at Graham. 'We don't have time to hang about while the police arrive.'

Graham nods. 'Okay, but what's the clue? What are these numbers?'

'I've seen numbers displayed like this before. I think the first six numbers are a grid reference. I need a map. Now.'

Chapter 43

GRAHAM

The officer on the phone tells Graham to move away from the body and a team will be there within fifteen minutes to cordon off the tree. What a mess this has turned out to be. When he woke up this morning, he was expecting to continue investigating Sophia Hammel's disappearance. Now, her father has been found hanging from the tree outside his home.

Then, Stephen goes and contaminates the crime scene by removing a vital piece of evidence from the victims' pocket. Despite his recent retirement from the force, his training and discipline still kick in from time to time. He's not sworn to uphold the rules of the police force anymore, not like he used to be (not that he followed the rules every time, even then), but he doesn't want to do anything to jeopardise the safety of a young woman. It's highly likely they won't find her alive, but there is hope of finding out what happened to her, maybe even finding her body.

Stephen has found a grid reference.

And Graham has a map inside his cottage somewhere.

Stephen is right though, about the police force not being trustworthy around here. If Frank Hammel took his own life, then there was a reason. They could be closer than ever to finding out what happened to Sophia. Frank left the paper in his pocket for them to find. He's sure of it. Clearly, the man was done hiding secrets and didn't see any other way out. Perhaps he was the one who left the sketch and the poster inside the jacket pocket of the scarecrow in the first place, kick-starting this whole thing. Had Frank Hammel been trying to tell them the truth from the start?

Graham starts his walk down the hill towards the cottage. Stephen is urging him to get a move on, needing to find a map, but Graham is knackered after running up the hill only moments before. He's out of puff, but going downhill is always harder on his knees and he's more likely to take a tumble. That's the last thing he needs.

He's going to be speaking with the police for a long time, so he needs another cup of coffee before the whole process starts. He'll have to leave Stephen to find where the grid reference leads to. He can't be in two places at once. Frank's body needs to be dealt with. He knows only too well how many questions the officers are likely to ask him, especially when he explains about the scarecrow and the pig heart, still currently laying in the garage. He wonders whether word has already got around, though. It seems the village residents are notorious for spreading rumours and the most recent gossip.

Graham heads straight through the door and into the lounge where there's a coffee table in front of the sofa. He pulls out the drawer underneath the low table and rummages around until he finds the local map of the surrounding area. He always buys one when he travels to a new location, preferring to explore the area with a physical map rather than using his phone. Most of the kids nowadays wouldn't know how to read a proper map or find a grid reference to save their lives, depending solely on Google maps to get them out of trouble and to their destinations. Call him old-school, but learning to read a map is a necessity in his mind.

He hands the map to Stephen who's standing right behind him. Graham can practically feel the nervous energy radiating from the man. He's glad he's feeling better, more himself, more focused.

Stephen grabs the map and, without heading back to the kitchen first, bends down level with the coffee table and spreads the map open across it. It seems Stephen also prefers physical maps.

Graham watches silently, keeping an ear out for the crunching of gravel outside, indicating the police have arrived. There isn't a police station in the village, so they'll be coming from several miles away at least. Perhaps they won't be corrupt if the officers don't work in Bethgelert, but they may live here, for all Graham knows. He has to be vigilant.

Stephen scans the numbers, using his fingers to trace across the map, eventually stopping at a single point. He stops and stares up at Graham.

'What is it?' Graham asks. He knows it's bad.

'This grid reference. It shows the location of ...'

The sound of gravel crunching makes them both stop and turn, looking towards the back door leading out to the yard.

Graham sighs. 'I need to go and handle this, Stephen.'

Stephen nods, turning his gaze back to the map. 'And I have to go and check this place out again. More thoroughly, this time.'

Graham heads out the door, meeting two officers as they get out of their police car. One is a middle-aged man with a head of thick, black hair and the other is a younger woman with cropped blonde hair.

'I'm DC Tanner and this is PC Franks,' says the male officer.

After confirming Graham's name and that he is the owner of the property, the officers turn to look up the hill towards the tree, which is now highlighted by the rising sun.

'Did you say the body was hanging in the tree?' asks DC Tanner, shielding his eyes against the glare.

'Yes,' replies Graham, mimicking his action.

'Are you sure?'

'Quite sure.'

'Because from what I can see, there's no body hanging from that tree.'

Chapter 44
STEPHEN

Stephen watches while Graham takes the two officers up the hill. He stays in the yard, unwilling to climb that damn hill again in his still weakened state. He knows what he saw. Both he and Graham had seen, touched, the body of Frank Hammel, so he knows it's nothing to do with his delusions, or whatever is going on in his head with regards to his grief and brain tumour.

Frank was very much dead. There's no doubt about that. He couldn't have faked his own hanging. Stephen had seen straight through his deceit when he'd spoken with him in the pub. The man couldn't lie to save his life, let alone stage a fake suicide.

Something else, much more sinister, is at play here.

There *had* been a body hanging from that tree. He could still smell the musty aroma coming from the corpse, still see the glassy look in Frank's eyes, even in death, as he hung there, gently swinging in the breeze.

It doesn't make any sense. Dead bodies don't get up and walk away. Someone must have taken it down in the time he and Graham had been in the lounge looking at the map and waiting for the police to show up. It hadn't been more than five minutes, ten at most.

But who would remove a dead body from a crime scene? Is this still about messing with their heads or is someone, whoever is behind this mystery, trying to make he and Graham look stupid? If Frank did hang himself, then who removed his body? Did they know he was going to do it? Had they been watching while he carried the ladder up the hill, propped it against the trunk, slipped the noose over his head and jumped?

Another thought pops into Stephen's head. One that makes him shudder.

Perhaps someone has set it up to look like a suicide, just like a hundred years ago with John Hammel. Were he and Graham meant to see the body, or was it a silly mistake, one they quickly tried to rectify by removing the corpse before the police arrived?

It's all one big sticky mess.

Stephen groans, rubbing his eyes again as a dull pain settles there. He goes into the kitchen, pops more painkillers and slurps the rest of his now cold coffee. The map is still clenched in his hand, his grip barely loosened since he grabbed it.

He has a place to be. He needs to leave soon. He can't waste another minute here when whoever it is who's messing with them is already one step, if not two steps, ahead. They always have been. Stephen and Graham have been playing catch up this whole time, but clearly they've reached a point of no return.

Here they were, thinking Frank was the kingpin behind everything going on in this village, but what if it's not been Frank who's been leading the charge against them, against this curse? What if Frank was also the victim to some extent? Someone else has a lot to lose, and they aren't about to let two out-of-towners mess up their plans.

It doesn't take long before Graham and the officers walk back down the hill. A few heated words are exchanged and Stephen sees a glimpse of the old Detective Williams for a moment. Then, Graham bids the officers goodbye. Once the police car is gone from the driveway, Graham storms into the kitchen, a little red in the face.

'That's it,' he says roughly. 'I've had just about enough of this bullshit. Someone in this village is messing with us, and I want to know why. Dead bodies don't just get up and walk away.' Stephen smirks. He'd been thinking the same thing not a few moments ago. Graham grabs his jacket from the hook by the back door. 'Let's go and find that location on the map.'

'Right you are,' replies Stephen.

'All this time, we've been thinking that Frank is behind this, but he's clearly been trying to tell us something all along. Hell, maybe it was him who put the clues in the pocket of the scarecrow from the start. He wants us to find his daughter. Now, he's dead.'

'And gone.'

Graham grunts as he nods his head. 'Yes, but in death he has provided us with a vital clue. One that, whoever has stolen his body, doesn't have. He warted us to find him first. Let's go and see what he's been keeping on his farm besides ducks.'

Chapter 45
SOPHIA

Bethgelert, Wales, 2015

My knees stung with pain from where I crashed into the concrete floor. Refusing to show weakness, I allowed the tears to fall, but held back a sob. I turned and looked over my shoulder at the woman who had kicked me through the door. Something didn't feel right. The way she kept staring at me, her dark eyes boring into me, watching my every move. My body was betraying me, shaking in fear. I knew I'd never liked her.

'Sophia ... what are you doing here?' asked my dad.

My dad's voice made me turn around to face him again, but I stayed on the floor, unsure if my legs would be able to support my weight if I tried to stand. 'I ... I needed to ask you something.'

In the dim room, the outline of my dad and his friends looked like dark shadows. Wait, no, they weren't shadows. They were wearing black robes, which made them look like shadows.

What the ...

My dad stepped closer to me, the faint light from above highlighting the rugged contours of his face beneath his dark hood. He wasn't pleased to see me, but it wasn't anger spread across his facial features. There was another emotion etched onto his face, one I'd barely seen before from him.

Fear.

My dad was terrified to find me here. He glanced behind me at the woman. Ceri Griffiths. She stepped around me on the floor and stood next to my dad, holding his intense gaze. The tension between the two practically crackled.

'You ... you shouldn't have come here,' said my dad, his voice low, his eyes never leaving mine.

'I'm sorry, but ...'

'They're going to ...'

'Enough with this,' snapped Ceri. 'Diane, grab some rope, would you?'

'What?'

'We're doing this now.'

My dad gasped. 'No, you can't!'

'You've had long enough, Frank.'

I'd forgotten about the other people in the room who were standing behind my dad. He locked eyes with me. I knew that look. He was trying to tell me something. He wanted me to run. I glanced behind me. The door hadn't been closed yet. I still had a chance to escape.

I took my chance, summoned strength and coordination from somewhere and threw myself towards the half-open door behind me.

'Stop her!'

The pounding of shoes on concrete sounded behind me as I ran, tripping over my own feet as I wrenched the door open and ran at full speed down the dark corridor the way I'd come. They were closing in fast. I didn't have enough of a gap, enough of a headway.

I made it outside. Since I'd been in the building, it had started raining and dark clouds had formed overhead. Streetlights were on, but there was no one around. Empty streets.

Heart pounding, I ran straight out onto the road. My legs burned, my lungs heaved. I couldn't hear footsteps anymore. Had they given up already? I didn't dare look back to check.

I only stopped running when I reached the graveyard. There was still a way to go to reach Rosemore Cottage, the only place I could think to run and hide, but I couldn't keep up the pace any longer, not without passing out or puking.

There were no raised voices or footsteps following me, so I thought I was safe. For now.

Sucking in deep breaths, I made my way through the gloomy headstones towards John Hammel's lonely grave. I needed to pass it to reach the other side where I'd then continue to head towards my destination, but a twig snapping made me stop in my tracks.

Was that me? Or was there someone behind me?

Every muscle and reflex wanted me to turn and check behind, but I forced myself to keep facing ahead.

'Sophia, stop,' said a familiar voice.

I did stop. I did turn.

'Dad?'

I stared at my dad, standing amongst the headstones, a plank of wood clenched in his hands. The rain was pelting down, soaking us.

'Dad, what's going on?' I asked. 'Are they following me?'

'No, you're safe,' he replied, stepping forwards.

'I don't understand what's going on. Why do they want me?'

Dad hung his head, his chin grazing his chest. 'I'm sorry,' he said.

'Dad ... what ...'

I didn't get a chance to finish my question before he lunged at me, the plank of wood held high over his head. I shrieked and stumbled backwards, tripping over a fallen headstone. The last thing I saw was my dad's face full of tears, seconds before he brought the plank of wood down on my head.

The world went dark.

I woke up an unknown amount of time later in a dark, cold room. Nothing made sense. My dad had wanted me to run, then followed me to the graveyard and knocked me out with a plank of wood. My eyes ached. They practically pleaded with me to remain closed, but I had to keep them open. I had to know where I was and what had happened. The back of my head throbbed and the swirl of nausea in my gut made me want to retch.

I forced my eyes open, only to be met with darkness. I may as well have kept them closed. I allowed a few seconds to pass for my eyes to adjust, but all I saw were dark shapes. I inhaled, smelling damp soil. Was I underground, perhaps? Or in a cellar? The farm did have one. It was where my dad stored food items that needed to stay cold.

Speaking of cold: it was freezing. Goosebumps sprung to my exposed skin. John's old jacket I was wearing was soaking wet from the rain I'd run through to get away from the village council members. I went to pull the jacket tighter across my chest to protect against the bracing cold, but I couldn't move.

My hands were attached to something in front of me. A thick rope bound my wrists, biting into the delicate skin. Leaning forwards, I reached out my hands, feeling for the rope and followed it until I found it attached to a metal ring in the wall, which itself was damp and cold. Earth. I *was* underground, in some sort of large hole.

It was proving difficult to get my bearings. All I knew was I couldn't move more than a few feet in any direction and my hands were bound together. As I sat in the darkness, my ears picked up a scuffling sound coming from nearby.

'Hello?'

Nothing, but silence followed my voice.

It was most likely a mouse or a vole, digging in the soil around me.

'Good, you're awake.' The familiar voice of my dad came from the darkness beyond, but it made me feel anything, but safe and warm.

'Dad?' I yanked the rope, but all the movement did was cause it to bite into my skin even further.

'I wouldn't pull too much, or you'll do yourself damage.'

'What's going on? Why have you brought me here and tied me up?'

My dad stepped forward just as a light flickered to life nearby. It illuminated only one side of his face, causing him to look menacing, evil. He didn't look like my dad.

'To save you, *Cariad*. To save you.'

Chapter 46
GRAHAM

'Should we show the police what we've found?' asks Stephen as he grabs his coat from the hook by the door. 'I know they just left, but ...'

Graham huffs. He knows it's counterproductive and hypocritical of him to think so, but involving the police right now is the last thing he wants to do. After their earlier visit, even if he does call them back to explain what they found, he doubts they will believe a word he says. Dead bodies don't disappear from trees. They would accuse him of tampering with a crime scene. He knows that, but without solid proof, the police are often blind to whatever is in front of their eyes, especially if it suspends disbelief. He used to be like that too. Things change.

Graham scratches his chin. 'Let's leave the police out of this now,' he says. 'Let's move. We'll have to walk into the village to fetch your car, since mine is still incapacitated and I don't fancy walking all the way to Blackberry Farm again. We're on a deadline now.'

'Wait, I need to grab something first.'

Once Stephen has grabbed what he needs, they waste no time in walking into the village to The Fox pub where Stephen had been forced to abandon his car last night. He has to admit that while Stephen still looks a little pale, he does appear more *with it* this morning. Graham is glad there's another explanation for Stephen's odd symptoms. He would hate to think there was something genuinely, medically wrong with him. He doesn't want to lose another friend.

Upon arriving at the car, Graham drives while Stephen searches through the pages of one of the diaries he grabbed before following him out of the door, but Graham is having issues with the gear box. Every time he changes gear, it makes a loud, clunking noise.

'Go easy on the clutch, Graham,' says Stephen. 'It needs a light touch.'

'This car is bloody ancient. Have you had it serviced recently?' Graham grumbles as he shifts into third, accelerating down the narrow lane.

'It's slipped my mind.'

'Clearly. What are you looking for exactly, Stephen?' asks Graham, only taking his eyes off the road ahead for a moment, but it's not long enough to catch what Stephen is doing.

'These diaries we found in the hidden room at Rosemore Cottage ... I saw some blueprints somewhere. Not blueprints, but drawings. I didn't take any notice of them before, but now I keep thinking about them, what they could mean ... here.' Stephen stops talking for a moment. He's using the light from above the passenger side visor to see better as the gloomy early afternoon is playing havoc with his vision.

'At first, I thought they were sketches of barns, but I think they're more than that.' Stephen leans closer to the page while Graham navigates the car around a tight corner.

'Talk to me,' says Graham. 'What are you getting at?'

'John Hammel's family also owned Blackberry Farm that now belongs to Frank Hammel. It's been in their family for years. The place we're driving towards this very moment.'

'Okay ...'

'And they had a barn where they kept animals and hay or possibly farm equipment.'

'That's not exactly ground-breaking stuff ...'

'But it had a secret room underneath the floor.'

Graham sucks in a breath as he slams on the brakes to avoid a collision with an oncoming car, which sounds its horn. 'Come again?'

Stephen holds up the pages so Graham can glance at them. 'I don't know what I'm looking at here ...'

'Well, I do ... when we get there, we need to find a barn that looks like this and I think that's where we'll find the answers we've been looking for.'

'What are you expecting to find down there?' asks Graham.

'I believe we'll find Sophia.'

'Her body ...'

'No, I believe Frank has been keeping his own daughter locked away underneath h s barn floor in a secret room for the past decade.'

'You can't be serious.'

'I am.'

Graham mutters a few indecent words. 'What about the scarecrow and the clues we've found inside the pockets of the coat? What does your unique brain think about that after everything that's happened over the past few days?'

Stephen is silent for a moment. 'How heavy would you say the scarecrow was, Graham?'

Graham frowns at his odd question, but knows better than to question him. 'Not that heavy. Just … cumbersome.'

'Hmm. Would a man be able to get it up high into the tree by himself?'

'Not unless he had some sort of pulley system set up to help. Even a full-grown man would struggle to haul it up into the tree without a rope.'

'So, what you're saying is that it would take at least two adults to drag that scarecrow up into the tree without a rope or a pulley system?'

Graham nods. 'I'd say that's a fair assessment.'

'Hear me out for a moment.' He holds up his hand to signal silence, even though Graham hasn't made a move to speak. The tarmac is rushing past them, the white lines a blur. 'According to John Hammel's diaries and journals, he was collecting information about the village council and wrote it all down, which he then hid behind a secret wall in your cottage. Sophia also hid her drawings in the tree. The diaries and the secret room were never found, which means that none of the members of the council knew about it, not even Sophia's father who owned the cottage at the time. Or, perhaps he did, and decided to keep it hidden, away from the other council members, I don't know.'

Graham's aware that Stephen is repeating what they already know, but saying it out loud obviously helps him compartmentalise all the pieces, which, at the moment, are flying around his own brain with nowhere to go. He, like Stephen, needs to catch them all and force them to be still.

'A hundred years ago, this all started because of one man – John Hammel. He was the first to be hung in the tree. Someone killed him, but why? Because he knew too much. I believe that other members of the village committee wanted to do the same thing to Sophia. To hang her in the tree as a human sacrifice to help stop the curse on them and their farms and livelihoods. But Sophia knew too much and you can't just string up a person in a tree anymore without any repercussions – so Frank made her disappear instead, but I don't believe he did it with malicious intent.'

'How is locking someone up in a barn for a decade not considered malicious intent?'

'Because I think he did it to save her from her fate ...'

Chapter 47

GRAHAM

Graham parks the car in front of the wooden farm gate of Blackberry Farm. It's locked with a chain and padlock, heavy duty, so he and Stephen climb over it, then walk through the yard towards the barns.

'No police presence, so I'm assuming word hasn't got out that he really is dead yet,' says Graham.

Stephen holds up the drawing of the barn. 'There are a lot of barns here,' he says. 'The grid reference is roughly over there.' Stephen points to the other side where there are several buildings.

Graham scans the yard and checks the drawing in Stephen's hands, scanning the outlines. 'If these were drawn a hundred years ago by John Hammel, then it's safe to say that a lot will have changed since then. The original structure may not even be here.'

'Then there must be another way to access the underground bunker. She's here, I just know it,' says Stephen.

'How about we search each barn in turn?'

'I think that's as good a plan as any. I don't think these drawings are going to be of much help anymore, but the grid reference will at least narrow down our search area.'

Graham sighs, realising it was never going to be as simple as following a map, and takes a step, but as he does, a dog growls nearby. He puts his hand out, stopping Stephen in his tracks. 'Stand perfectly still.'

The old dog rushes forwards, barking hysterically, baring his teeth, hackles up. Graham shows his palms, revealing he's no throat, keeps his tone of voice low, calm as he talks. 'There, there, Barney. Remember us? There's a good dog.'

'I'm not sure the dog understands English,' replies Stephen.

Graham ignores his ignorance, slowly bending level with the dog who has now moved on to creeping forwards, nose twitching to sniff his outstretched hand. Graham holds his breath as Barney seems to wrestle with his basic instincts to protect his home. He eventually gives Graham's fingers a lick and allows him to tickle his neck.

'There, you see,' says Graham. 'A kind voice and a bit of trust goes a long way.'

'Hmm,' says Stephen.

They approach the first barn, but both stop when Barney starts barking again. Graham spins to face him, expecting to start placating him again, but Barney runs away to the far end of the yard. Stops. Then barks again.

'Why, I do believe our new friend wants us to follow him,' says Stephen, leading the way.

Barney leads them to a small barn tucked behind the largest one. It's a solid structure, but not big enough to store farm equipment or anything larger than a car. Graham reaches for the door handle, but finds it locked, bolted with another padlock.

Stephen steps past him. 'Allow me.' He crouches, his face level with the padlock, then reaches into his pocket, pulling out a small leather case, roughly the size of a pencil case.

Graham watches silently as Stephen slides a thin metal stick into the keyhole of the padlock.

'You continue to surprise me, Mr Mallow.'

'What happened to Stephen?'

'What indeed. I never took you for a lock picker.'

'It's one of my lesser-known skills.'

It takes less than two minutes for Stephen to get the door open. Barney whines and rushes through the door, scurrying behind a stack of boxes.

Following him, Graham steps into the small building. He searches for a light switch, but there's not one he can see. Stephen pulls out his phone and switches on the torch function. The outside light is fading fast.

There are several boxes, along with a lawn mower in the far corner. There's also a small table with a radio resting on it, along with a microphone. In the middle of the one-room building is a clear space with an old, tattered, circular rug in the centre. Barney reappears from behind the boxes and starts scrabbling at the rug, pawing and whining.

Graham and Stephen move as one, grasping the edges of the rug and dragging it along the dusty, concrete floor. Barney hops out of the way, then returns to the centre.

Stephen directs the beam of light onto the floor where Barney is furiously digging.

'Well, well, well,' says Graham. 'Time for you to use those lock-picking skills again.'

He looks down at the fairly new-looking wooden trapdoor in the floor of the building.

Chapter 48
STEPHEN

With Barney nearby, eyes wide and panting, Stephen kneels on the floor, inspecting the trapdoor and the second padlock. This one is trickier, needing a combination to open rather than a key, so his trusty thin wire won't be of much use this time. He thinks for a moment before pulling out the note he found on Frank Hammel's body.

There are four numbers left over from the grid reference. He enters each one slowly, ensuring the dials are lined up. The padlock clicks open. Graham reaches over, helping him lift the heavy trapdoor. Graham takes the padlock and slips it into his pocket.

Barney barks, but doesn't attempt to jump into the hole they've uncovered. He whines and lays down, staring at it intently.

Stephen's heart almost stops as he peers into the darkness below. The mind-numbing fear he once had threatens to unleash itself once again. Being outside in the dark is one thing, but climbing down into a hole beneath the earth is quite another.

Graham seems to sense his hesitation. 'I don't expect you to climb down there. Not if you're not feeling up for it.'

Stephen shines his phone light into the hole. 'For once, I'd like nothing better than to stay behind, but I'm afraid my conscience just won't allow it.'

'Fair enough.' Graham turns to the dog. 'Sorry, old boy. You're going to have to wait up here.' Barney barks in response, but doesn't move from his spot. Graham takes a look inside the deep pit. 'Looks like there's a ladder attached to the inside wall.'

'How old do you reckon this tunnel is?'

'Hard to say, but my bet is that this building was built over the top of it to conceal it once upon a time. It could be hundreds of years old, but the ladder looks fairly new.'

They both raise their eyes to meet the other's. They don't need to speak another word to understand, but the prospect of what they might find down in the dark is one that's overriding any apprehension or fear they may have.

After Graham's inspected the ladder, convinced it's strong enough to support their weight, he manoeuvres himself into position, turning his back to the hole. Stephen watches as his head disappears and waits several seconds before peering down after him.

The darkness has already swallowed Graham whole.

Stephen attempts to dislodge a lump in his throat by swallowing, but his mouth is like sandpaper. None of his bodily functions seem to be working the way they're supposed to. His lungs, for one thing, appear to have forgotten how to inhale oxygen. Either that, or all the oxygen has been sucked from the room.

'All good down there, Graham?' he calls out, unable to stand the silence for another second.

'Just about,' comes the reply. Gosh, it sounds as if Graham is miles away already.

Stephen glances over at the dog. 'Fancy swapping places?' Barney whines in response. 'Didn't think so. Well … here goes nothing.'

Stephen sucks in a rattly breath and holds it as he positions his body over the ladder, facing it, the way Graham had done. As he descends, his brain does its best to force him to return to the light, to the surface where it's safe, telling him all sorts of horrible lies.

There could be bugs the size of dogs down here.

If you fall, you'll die.

What if the trapdoor blows shut? You'll be trapped down here forever.

Down here in the darkness is where the demons live …

'Stop it,' he growls to himself.

'What was that, Stephen?' comes a voice from below.

'Nothing, Graham.'

Stephen continues down the ladder, pushing his inner demons to one side, ensuring he always keeps three points of contact. Halfway down, his right knee clicks and threatens to buckle. He slips, grasping the sides of the ladder in time. His palms are sweaty as he clings to the metal bars for dear life.

If you fall now, you'll probably only break your legs.

He closes his eyes and counts to ten, then continues. And there he was, thinking he'd conquered his fear of the dark.

Stephen touches solid ground a few moments later, landing next to Graham who has switched on his phone torch. He scans the small area around them, hardly enough space to do a full turn on the spot without bumping into each other.

A dark tunnel leads off to the east.

Graham's phone torch grows dimmer, then dies completely. The darkness that follows is so thick that Stephen almost chokes on it as he scrambles around in his pocket for his own phone, which he'd pocketed to allow him to climb down the ladder.

'How much battery do you have left?' asks Graham.

Stephen checks. 'Not enough.'

'Then let's move fast.'

Stephen turns and directs the beam of light into the darkness ahead. Despite their need to be hasty, he is forced to keep his pace slow, because the earthy, damp tunnel is so dark, cramped and low that he's at risk of injuring himself. The tunnel twists and turns, making it seem much further than it probably is. Luckily, there doesn't appear to be any different choices in direction to take, so Stephen continues onwards, safe in the knowledge that his old friend is close behind him rather than any lingering demons.

After several minutes, he stops in his tracks.

'Something the matter?' asks Graham.

'I'm not sure ... I thought I heard something.'

Both men stand in silence, holding their breaths. 'You're right. I hear it too,' says Graham. 'Someone's down here with us ...'

That short sentence is enough to make Stephen's stomach perform a flip. It certainly sounds like footsteps; a dull thud, thud, thud, but it isn't coming from behind them. It's ahead of them.

Creeping forwards, Stephen keeps the beam directed at the ground, so he doesn't blind anyone or make it obvious he's approaching. The light is bouncing off the dark walls, casting eerie shadows.

As he rounds the next corner, he walks straight into a blockade of iron bars.

'Bloody hell,' he mutters. 'What is this?'

Graham joins him at his side. 'An underground prison by the looks of it.'

Stephen can't fault his guess. It's exactly what it looks like. He grabs the bars and shakes them, feeling for any loose ones, but they are solid iron.

'Hello?' he calls out into the darkness beyond the bars.

The sound of approaching footsteps make him gulp back another lump in his throat, one that causes his eyes to water as he attempts to take a breath.

'Who's there?' comes a small, female voice.

Stephen raises his phone light as a young woman steps into view. Her clothes are stained with dirt, shabby and hanging off her. As the light illuminates her face, she shrieks and raises both her hands to cover her eyes.

Stephen lowers his phone, quickly putting his hand over it. 'My apologies,' he says to the woman. 'My name is Stephen Mallow and this is Graham Williams.' He pauses. 'You must be Sophia Hammel.'

The woman coughs and lowers her hand from her eyes. 'Y-Yes. Oh my God. Are you here to rescue me?'

'I suppose we are.'

Sophia shuffles forwards and stops when she reaches the bars. Stephen keeps the beam off her face, but even the residual light is enough to make out her features. The poor girl is skin and bone, her face pale, gaunt, but still holds the delicacy of youth. He's sure that underneath the layers of grime and dirt is a beautiful young woman, by now in her mid-twenties.

She's been down here all this time. No wonder the torch light hurts her eyes.

'How long have I been down here?' she asks.

'Ten years,' answers Graham.

Sophia shakes her head. 'That's impossible.'

'I'm afraid it's true. You disappeared ten years ago, almost to the day. Your father has been keeping you locked down here.'

Sophia's head nods. 'Yes. He did it to protect us.'

Stephen tilts his head to the side, like a listening dog. 'Did you say *us*?'

'Yes, my mother's down here too.'

Chapter 49
STEPHEN

'Your mother has been trapped down here too?' asks Graham, stepping forwards.

'Yes, I had no idea. My dad told me she left us after my brother died, but it wasn't true. He kept her down here to save her.'

Stephen scratches the back of his neck. There's a strange, tickling sensation which is sending his internal radar humming, like someone has just brushed his skin with a feather. Not only that, but the walls of this underground bunker, or cave, whatever the hell it is, feel as if they are getting closer and closer. Are the walls moving? He's seeing stars, twinkling stars.

While Graham asks Sophia a few more questions, Stephen takes the opportunity to look around the area, but there's not a lot to see other than the dancing stars. Sophia has walked up to the bars from a different room further into the tunnel. This is merely the outside barrier, blocking the path, ensuring she doesn't escape any further. Frank must have spent a long time building this cave for his wife and daughter. To protect them. Trap them. Because, whether he did it out of love or not, he's still kept them locked up against their will, but Sophia doesn't appear angry with him. She's grateful. Stephen thinks of Stockholm Syndrome; a very real possibility in this scenario.

Stephen refocuses his attention on Sophia, who is still talking.

'My dad was one of the relatives of the founding members of the council,' says Sophia. 'I followed him one night and walked into a secret meeting. Turns out, the other council members wanted to sacrifice me, no matter what it took. All of their farms were failing and they were close to losing their livelihoods. That's what happened to John Hammel. His own father and his brother killed him. They strung him up by his neck one day while he was sitting underneath the tree, drawing a sunset. They made it look like John did it to himself.'

'But why? Why would members of the council kill their own son and brother? What did John do to deserve that?'

'The same thing I did. He found out too much and got too close to the truth.'

'Which is?' asks Stephen. He can barely draw breath.

Sophia pauses a moment. 'The members of the village committee are, and always have been, a bunch of sadistic murderers. For over a hundred years, they've run this village and they'll do anything to stay on top, including scaring the rest of the community into believing in a curse. They created it. Haven't you noticed how only four farming families are still thriving around here? The other farms and businesses in the area are dwindling each year, eventually having to close up, which ensures the remaining farms and businesses continue to thrive.'

Graham mutters a few indecent words under his breath.

Stephen clears his throat. 'Let me get this straight because I'm a little confused. You're saying that the founding members of the village council, including your father, have been controlling this entire village going back generations? That they've been killing anyone who's got in their way and covering up deaths somehow, all while remaining undetected by everyone else around them?'

'Pretty much, yeah. They have control over a lot of things, including what gets leaked to the press and what doesn't. They've got everyone scared. Even the police. They killed one of them too, and they've been getting away with it for over a century.'

'But your father ... he's hidden you and your mother down here to keep you safe. If he's one of them, then why didn't he allow you both to be sacrificed for their gain?'

Sophia sniffs loudly. 'Turns out he does love me enough to not want me dead, but not enough to turn his back on the council. He's scared too. They wanted to sacrifice my mum to start with, so Dad hid her away, but everyone's farms and businesses started declining. They got it in their heads that the curse was real. They had to sacrifice someone, someone close to one of the council members. And since John Hammel started it all, they set their sights on me, a pure Hammel family descendant, but Dad couldn't let them do it, so he grabbed me too.'

'No one else knows you're down here? The other village members have no idea that one of their own has been betraying them for over a decade?'

Sophia shakes her head. 'I don't know, but that leads me to my next question. How did you guys find us?'

'Your father. He … left us a clue. A message. He said he was sorry and then … we found him hanging in the tree. I'm sorry,' says Graham. 'Stephen managed to decipher his code, managed to take the clue before the council members found him and took his body down.'

Sophia sinks to the floor, using the bars for support. Her body shakes as she sobs quietly.

'I'm sorry,' says Graham again.

Sophia sniffs loudly again, wiping her streaming nose and eyes with the cuff of her filthy shirt. 'Do you think he did it to himself?'

'I believe so, yes. He tried to right the wrongs, sacrificing himself for you and the community. He even tried to provide Stephen and I with other clues, including hiding a sketch and a missing person poster of you in the scarecrow's jacket.'

Sophia frowns. 'Ah, so that's why he took John's jacket from me.'

Graham nods.

'There's something else I don't understand,' says Stephen, interrupting the conversation. 'If your father isn't the main man in charge of the council, then who is? Who's been leading the story of the curse? Is it Ceri Griffiths?'

Sophia opens her mouth to respond, but as she does, a loud bang echoes from behind them, sending cascades of dust and soil down upon their heads.

Stephen's whole body freezes.

'I think we may have just been locked down here too,' says Graham.

Chapter 50
GRAHAM

As soon as the loud thud appears from above, Graham knows they are trapped. He turns to Sophia, whose eyes have turned to saucers. She grasps the bars, her knuckles white, shaking her head side to side in quick succession.

'Sophia, is there another way out? How did your dad get in and out all the time?'

'As far as I know, he used the ladder every day, but as he's got older, he's been making the trip less and less. We have stores of food down here, but we have run out once or twice.'

'Where is your mother?' asks Graham, looking behind her into the darkness.

'She's resting.'

'Who knows we're down here?' asks Stephen.

'We must have been followed after all,' says Graham. He grabs the bars, noticing the padlock. 'Where's the key?'

Sophia sighs. 'Dad always kept it on him.'

'Stephen, time to put your lock-picking skills to the test once again. Did Frank have any means to communicate with you from the surface while you were down here? Are there cameras?'

'Cameras no, but yes, he has a radio set up to talk to us.'

Graham nods, remembering the radio he'd spotted in the building above them. 'Please fetch it. I have a feeling that those above us may wish to talk. They won't get away with trapping us all down here. The village will talk. The last thing they'll want is to draw attention to two more missing people.'

Sophia nods and runs down the dark tunnel.

Graham looks at Stephen, noticing his trembling hands. 'Have faith, Stephen. We'll get out of here.' He doesn't mention Stephen's once crippling fear of the dark or the fact he was trapped in his basement by his own father many years ago. The similarities between Stephen's childhood and Sophia's are unsettlingly uncanny.

'Just promise me something, Graham,' says Stephen, stepping forwards to the padlock. He takes out his thin wire.

'Anything.'

'Never ask me for help ever again.'

Graham chuckles, knowing Stephen isn't being serious. In fact, he's proud of him for making a humorous comment at a time like this.

Fast footsteps approach. Seconds later, Sophia appears at the bars and passes Graham a walkie talkie. Graham takes it and switches it on, crossing his fingers that his gut instinct is correct and whoever is above them, is waiting by the radio he saw on the side, ready to talk to them.

The radio crackles.
And they wait ...

Chapter 51
STEPHEN

Static splutters from the walkie talkie, filling the eerie silence around them.

'Are you ready to talk, Mr Williams?' comes the low voice of William Davies, the butcher.

Graham presses the button on the side. 'What do you want? You can't keep us down here. People will talk. Think about it, Davies.'

'We only want the girl. We know she's down there. We've been looking for her for a long time.'

Stephen shudders at the impersonal way Davies is describing Sophia, like she's an object, not a human being. Stephen glances over at Sophia. She's not a girl anymore. She's a grown woman, having lived the past decade down in the dark and damp earth. She and her mother have finally been found. She deserves to have her voice heard. Stephen doesn't know what the village committee have planned for her, but they do seem to think that she's the answer to ending the curse.

But now that Frank is dead, surely his sacrifice is enough to satisfy them? According to Sophia though, the curse isn't even real. Merely a spooky story the council has created to control everyone.

Stephen holds his breath as Graham continues to speak into the radio, taking full control of the situation.

'No deal,' he says.

'Give us the girl and this is all over,' comes the curt reply.

'There has to be another way around this.'

There's a long pause on the other end. Stephen wonders if they've given up, deciding to let them all starve to death down here, but then it crackles again.

'Send up the journalist instead.'

Graham's eyes swivel to his. Stephen gulps hard, sweat beading on his top lip and forehead, then nods once. He doesn't know what awaits him, but he knows it's the right decision. He can't let them take Sophia. He'll do whatever he needs to do to keep her safe.

'Fine,' says Graham, then switches off the radio. 'I don't like this, Stephen. It's a trap.'

'Don't worry. I can handle myself.'

'Somehow I very much doubt that.'

Stephen ignores Graham's swipe at him and turns to Sophia. 'You were about to tell us if Ceri Griffiths is the person in charge before the trapdoor slammed shut?'

'Yes, she is.'

'Who is she though?' asks Graham. 'I don't recognise her name.'

'That's because she's known as Karen. In Wales, it's tradition to use your middle name. Her name is Ceri Karen Griffiths. My first name is actually Cariad. Sophia is my middle name.'

Graham's mouth drops open.

'Isn't Karen the name of your friend you mentioned, Graham?' asks Stephen.

Graham closes his eyes and mutters, 'I'm losing my touch. She never told me her surname. It's never even come up.'

Stephen ignores Graham's bitter tone and turns back to Sophia. 'I need to know what I'm up against. Is there anything else you think I should know? How will they play this? Is this Karen woman dangerous?'

'She's the worst there is. She pretends to be all nice, but my dad's told me stories about her family. They're all psychos. I'm pretty sure her family started the whole curse thing and twisted and used it to control everyone in the village.'

Stephen pauses for a moment, his brain working on super speed. 'With your father now dead, that makes you the last Hammel in the family, does it not?'

'I guess so. My little brother died when I was young and now dad is dead … and Mum is only a Hammel by name. Perhaps they think if they kill me, they can end the curse once and for all. Protect the members and their families at all costs.

I'm not sure why they'd want you in place of me, but it can't be for anything good.'

Stephen brushes off a spiderweb from his shoulder. 'You let me worry about that. They're panicking, that's all. I reckon they plan on killing all of us. It's the only way their secret will remain safe. They want to tie up all the loose ends before the truth gets out into the community.'

'What's your plan?' asks Graham. 'Take into account that the police are corrupt in this village. No one is coming to help us.'

Stephen nods. 'Don't worry, I have a plan.'

'And that would be?'

'I don't know yet, Graham.'

'Are you telling me that you're about to make it up as you go along; the man who always plans everything in detail, who doesn't go anywhere without a step by step outline of how to proceed?'

Stephen grins. 'There's a first time for everything.'

'Hmm. Our lives are in your hands. If you fail, we're going to be trapped down here.'

'I'll try and wedge the trapdoor open while they aren't looking. You'll need to try and find a way to get Sophia and her mother out from behind the bars. Here.' Stephen hands Graham the thin piece of wire.

Graham takes it. 'I'll get them out.'

'It's settled then.'

Graham extends his hand for Stephen to shake, but Stephen just smiles at him. He steps forward and embraces his old friend, squeezing him into a hug like he wished he could have hugged his own father. He doesn't like being physically close to people, but now isn't the time for his personal preferences.

'You're a good man, Stephen,' says Graham, slapping him on the back.

'You're going to need this too,' replies Stephen, handing Graham his phone.

It looks like he's going to have to make his way back to the ladder using only touch.

Less than five minutes later, breathing heavy and clammy with sweat, Stephen reaches the top of the ladder. The trip through the darkness has rendered him almost catatonic, but his nerve endings are on fire. Every sense is alive and kicking, on overdrive.

He's made it.

He knocks on the underside of the trapdoor. It takes a few moments, but then a crack of light appears in a square shape above. He blinks, shielding his eyes as he emerges from the dark depths. His body craves the light like it craves oxygen.

'Hello, there, Mr Mallow.'

Stephen looks up at the face of William Davies. 'Call me Stephen,' he replies, climbing the rest of the way up. As he passes the floor, he quickly sticks a stone into the crack of the hinge of the trapdoor. A quick slight of hand and it's done. He's grabbed from behind and shoved to his knees by Diane, who's much stronger than he gave her credit for. The trapdoor slams shut, but it's not completely flush with the ground. No one notices. They're too focused on Stephen who puts up a fight, a ruse to draw their attention.

It works.

Stephen glances around for the dog, but he must be hiding.

Once they leave the area, Graham will be able to push open the trapdoor. How he plans to get Sophia and her mother out, Stephen doesn't know, but they have their own parts to play in this rescue mission.

Stephen is kicked in the side. He grunts and rolls over into a foetal position to protect himself from any further damage. A sharp pain pierces his skull.

'Hmm … not exactly part of the plan, but you'll do,' says Davies. 'Since Mr Williams is down there keeping Sophia company, how about we get Stephen here ready?'

Stephen forces his eyes to focus on Davies who has two heads that swim in and out of focus. 'Ready for what?' he asks.

'You'll see.'

Stephen tries to force back a cough, but it erupts from his chest. Once he catches his breath, he says, 'It won't work, you know. There's no such thing as the curse. It's all been fabricated over the years. You do realise that, right?'

Davies laughs. 'I'm afraid it's a little too late for that. What goes around comes around.'

Before Stephen can answer, a large fist connects with his face and he plunges into darkness.

When he peels his eyes open, a large group of people are standing around him in the yard. He knows this place. He's back at Rosemore Cottage. The sun is beginning to set now. The Hanging Tree stands proud atop the hill in the distance, surrounded by yellows and oranges that magically dance across the sky. The group of people in the yard are all dressed in black robes.

The village committee members, he presumes. But something doesn't quite add up in Stephen's mind. There are a lot more of them than Stephen had first thought. For all he knows, the entire village has turned up, but turned up for what? He can't see any of their faces, thanks to their oversized hoods. They each hold a lit torch in their hands.

Stephen feels as if he's travelled back in time.

Wait ... that's exactly what he's done ...

It's then that he realises. It's a mirage of a long-forgotten time. A hundred years back in time, to be precise. Davies and Diane make no move or remark that tells Stephen they are aware of the group of villagers. Only Stephen can see them. It's in his mind. He's seeing things again.

He's close to the end. He can feel it. The tumour is pushing deeper and deeper, harder and harder. His brain is breaking down.

Between them, Davies and Diane drag him up the hill towards the tree. Stephen's legs have lost all coordination and strength. He knows he should be trying to fight for his life, but there's a feeling deep down inside that's telling him he needs to allow this to play out.

He accepts his fate.

The black-robed villagers chant and follow the trio up the hill. This is it. He's doomed. He's going to be strung up a tree and hung, just like John Hammel all those years ago. And his body can do nothing to stop it. He has no fight left in him and that's okay.

His only thought is of Graham, Sophia and her mother trapped down in the dark. What if the stone wedged in the hinge doesn't work and they are trapped down there forever?

Stephen is shoved to the ground at the base of the tree, fallen acorns digging into his knees. Stephen stares into its branches as the orange and yellow sky lights it up like a beacon.

'I'm sorry, John,' he says. 'I'm sorry you died here like this. I'm sorry I couldn't make things right.'

He closes his eyes as a loop of rope lowers over his head and tightens around his neck. He tries to gulp, but it's so tight, his Adam's apple gets stuck. Tears brim through his closed eyelids as he takes what he knows to be his final breath.

The rope tightens.

It tightens some more.

He's forced to stand, but he never opens his eyes.

'Any last words?' says a voice nearby.

Stephen feels the life, the words of the man from a hundred years ago enter his head. 'The darkness is my friend. I shall live on.'

A loud smack echoes around him.

Hands grab at him.

Still, his eyes stay closed.

'It's all right, Stephen. I've got you, my friend,' says a voice in the darkness.

Chapter 52
GRAHAM

Thirty minutes earlier …

Stephen disappears into the dark tunnel, leaving Graham with his phone light, which only has twenty-two percent battery life left. He doesn't know what Stephen has planned, but he knows he must hurry to rescue Sophia and her mother from behind the bars and then race to save his friend too.

He gets straight to work, using the thin wire Stephen gave him to jimmy open the padlock. Stephen made it look easy. Sophia holds the phone light for him so he can use both his hands. It takes several frustrating minutes, but eventually, the padlock pops open.

Graham wrenches open the bars. 'Fetch your mother,' he says.

'I … I can't. I'm not strong enough to carry her. You'll have to do it.'

Graham opens his mouth to ask what's wrong, but it'll only waste time they don't have. 'Take me to her,' he says.

Sophia leads him along the tunnel. The further along he gets, the stronger the foul smel becomes. It's a mix of damp, rot and sewage. To think, these women have been down here for all this time. Sophia's mother has been down here close to fifteen years. It's unthinkable, unfathomable that a so-called loving husband and father could do this to the people he loved, even if it was to save them from certain death.

Sophia runs ahead, disappearing round the corner. There's a faint light ahead. Somehow, Frank must have rigged up a lighting system, but when Graham arrives at the light he finds only a flickering lantern with a candle inside.

He stares around the small cave; the one room where Sophia and her mother have been living together. There's a filthy mattress on the floor, covered in a dark blanket with a pillow, along with a couple boxes of vegetables and plastic bottles of water. A black bucket sits in the furthest corner, covered with a flat piece of wood; the origin of the rancid smell, he presumes.

That's all there is here.

'Jesus Christ,' mutters Graham, not usually one to take the Lord's name in vain. He looks around, searching, but something is missing.

'Where's your mother?'

Sophia points to a corner that's shrouded in darkness. The candle's light can't quite reach that far. No sound or movement is coming from the area.

'Sophia,' he says solemnly. 'Is your mother …'

'She's there. She's just sleeping.'

Graham's eyes flood with tears as he swallows down his overwhelming grief for the poor girl who's been trapped down here in the dark with the body of her mother for God only knows how long.

'I promise you that she will be brought to the surface, but right now, I need to get you out of here. Do you understand? I can't take your mother with us, but I will personally see to it that she is taken care of once you are safe and I've rescued my friend.'

Sophia glances towards the dark corner where there's a noticeable bump underneath the blanket. A cold shiver runs down Graham's spine as Sophia approaches the body, kneels beside it and whispers a few words.

She joins Graham at his side seconds later.

'Let's go,' she says.

'Brave girl,' says Graham.

They reach the bottom of the ladder. Graham climbs up first as he's unsure if Sophia will have the strength to push open the trapdoor above. He hopes Stephen was able to wedge something into the hinges, enough so that it doesn't form a tight seal.

The closer he gets to the top, the harder his heart thumps. He can't hear voices, but he reckons he knows where they'll be taking Stephen. He doesn't have a lot of time. Sophia climbs silently behind him. He can hear her heavy breathing, but she doesn't utter a word.

Higher and higher he climbs in the pitch black, having to keep his phone torch off because he can't climb and hold it at the same time. He pauses on each step, checking his grip. The metal is slippery, cold in his hands as he nears the top.

He waits a moment, listening for any sounds. There's scuffling above, sniffing. He thinks he knows who the culprit is.

A thin strip of light signals the end of his climb. It means the trapdoor hasn't shut all the way. It's still going to be heavy to lift, but he reckons they won't have locked it again because Graham pocketed the padlock earlier.

Awkwardly positioning himself under the trapdoor, he lifts his arms above his head, pushing against it with his hands. His aging muscles and joints pop and scream in annoyance, but with enough effort, he lifts the trapdoor and pushes it open, ensuring to stop it before it crashes down against the floor.

The building is empty – bar a very excited collie dog who is waiting for his master's return.

Graham climbs out of the hole, then turns and reaches out his hand for Sophia. A few seconds later, her head emerges, her eyes blinking against the light of the fading sun. She's trembling as she emerges from the dark hole and wraps her arms around herself like a shield.

But then the dog yaps and lunges at her.

'Barney!'

Sophia collapses to the ground as the dog throws itself at her frail body, licking frantically, wagging his tail so hard that

Graham's half convinced it's going to fall off. Barney yaps and whines while Sophia smothers his furry head in kisses, tears rolling down her dirt-stained cheeks.

'Look how grey you are!' Sophia strokes his head, staring at the silver hairs around his eyes and muzzle. She looks up at Graham with tears in her eyes. 'He was just a pup when I last saw him.'

'He led us straight to you,' replies Graham. He watches the happy duo for several more seconds, but he can't hang around.

'Sophia, I need to go and help Stephen. I'm going to hide you in the main house, but then I'm going to have to leave you for a while. Will you be all right?'

Sophia nods. 'I can come with you.'

'No. It's you who they really want. I can't guarantee your safety.'

'But ...'

'Please. Stay here with Barney.'

Sophia stands up on wobbly legs. 'Okay,' she says.

Graham nods and, with Barney close at their heels, they race across the yard to the farmhouse. Graham quickly checks over his shoulder. He can't see or hear anyone else around. She'll be safe here now that she's out of the hole.

'Stay quiet. I'll come back for you. If I haven't returned in an hour, then head into the village and speak to the police, or failing that, speak to someone you know you can trust. Can you do that?'

'Yes. Please. Go and save your friend.'

Graham races to Stephen's car, praying, hoping he's not too late.

Chapter 53
GRAHAM

Now …

'It's all right, Stephen. I've got you, my friend.'

Graham arrives in the nick of time to see Stephen being strung up from the tree. He grabbed one of the planks of wood by the back door of the cottage before heading up the hill after parking the car in his yard.

He uses it to subdue Diane who's too busy holding on to the end of the rope, keeping Stephen's airway restricted, to notice Graham charging up behind her. Davies is nearby, but he too, is taken by surprise and Graham knocks him sideways with a swift blow to the body.

Neither of the perpetrators are going to die from their injuries, but it's enough to keep them down, writhing on the ground while Graham unties the rope that has Stephen's limp body hanging from the other end.

Stephen's on the verge of unconsciousness, but at least he's alive. Barely. Graham lowers him to the ground, ensures he's safe, then turns to the two people still moaning on the ground.

'You don't know what you're doing,' says Davies, frothing at the mouth, clenching his teeth.

'No. You don't know what you're doing,' Graham replies as he grasps both his wrists and binds them together. 'Did you seriously think sacrificing a mild-mannered journalist was going to help you regain control? Face it. You're done.'

'Someone needs to die,' cries Diane. She's bleeding, having cut the side of her face on the sharp end of a stick as she collided with the ground I. 'It's a ritual. It has to happen in order for the village committee to continue to prosper.'

'Are you listening to yourselves? This is the twenty-first century,' snaps Graham. 'Even an old fart like me knows that sacrificing a human being isn't going to help the local community continue to harvest a decent crop. You're being manipulated and controlled.'

Diane laughs. 'It doesn't matter. She wants you, Graham. She'll come after you next. If we don't do as she says then ...' Diane spits blood onto the ground, coughing as she looks up. Graham sees her eyes refocus on something behind him.

'Hello, Graham. Didn't I warn you not to stick your nose where it doesn't belong?'

Graham's skin bristles with goosebumps as he turns and comes face to face with Karen Griffiths; the lady who he's casually flirted with since moving here.

'Karen,' he says with a sigh. 'I was wondering when you'd turn up.'

'Oh, you've already figured out who I am?'

'Ceri Griffiths. If I'd known that most traditional Welsh people go by their middle names, then I may have put it together sooner or if you'd ever bothered to tell me your surname.'

'Hmm,' she says. 'There's always a reason for everything. The Griffiths family were the main farming family in this area a hundred years ago. Did you know that? The Hammel family were indebted to us. We were the ones who bailed them out time and time again. My great, great, great grandmother was Carys Griffiths, the girl who John Hammel was planning on marrying. You see, when John died, she was pregnant with a child, but that child isn't the offspring of John Hammel.'

Graham's brain tries to work overtime to unravel what she's saying, but he doesn't get there quick enough as Karen continues. 'John's father and brother killed him that day. It's John's brother, Rhys, who is the direct descendant of the Hammel family. He was the father of Carys' unborn child. It seems she was somewhat of a slut back in the day and was seeing both brothers at the same time, but only Rhys managed to take her innocence. Poor John.' Karen chuckles. 'I think the poor lad was actually planning on proposing to her that day; the day she was due to meet him on top of the hill underneath the tree to watch the sunset, but instead, she found a hanging body.'

Graham shakes his head. 'So that's the secret you've been trying to hide all this time; that the Hammel family and the Griffiths family are one and the same? What about the so-called curse? All the deaths, the scarecrow, Sophia Hammel … where does she fit into all of this?'

'The curse was never real, but the Bevan, Hammel and Davies family never knew that. My family are the original founding members of the council and the creators of the curse. If my family disappears, then so does my livelihood. I'll do anything to keep my family on top and if that means killing and manipulating some of the others, then so be it. I'm the only Griffiths left now, so I'm having to improvise.'

Graham glances at Diane and Davies, who are now struggling to their feet, but with their hands bound, it's proving difficult.

Karen smiles devilishly at him. 'You see, Graham, it never bodes well to stick your nose into someone else's business. I did try to warn you.'

'And Stephen … why try to kill him?'

'Simple. He was getting too close to the truth, just like dear Sophia was.' She laughs out loud. 'And to think, Frank actually managed to hide her away for all these years right, under my nose.'

'He hid more than that.'

Karen narrows her eyes. 'Don't tell me his wife is down there too?'

'Her body is, yes.'

'Even in death, Frank continues to surprise me. We never wanted his wife, not really. She wasn't a Hammel by blood, but Bevan and Davies both got it into their heads that they needed to kill the whole Hammel family. That's the thing about curses, Graham. They grow and fester all on their own if you let them. I barely had to do a thing, but I'm afraid your time has now come.'

Karen reaches behind her and draws a hunting rifle, which is on a sling, hidden by her body. She aims it at Graham.

'Don't worry,' she says softly. 'I'm a good shot. Some say the souls of the dead live within its roots.' She glances at the canopy of leaves above, then locks her gaze back on him.

Graham reacts fast, but not fast enough.

Bang!

A white hot pain pierces his shoulder as he throws himself to the side. As he turns, he sees Sophia lunging at Karen, rugby-tackling her in the torso. They both crash to the ground, rolling around among the acorns and brown leaves.

Diane screams, 'Nooo!'

Another bang.

Davies charges at Graham, having managed to wriggle free of his restraints. Ignoring the shooting pain in his shoulder, he kicks Davies in the stomach as he tries to grab him. Davies goes down, so Graham follows his attack up with a kick to Davies' face, knocking him out cold.

Sophia and Karen are still grappling on the ground, both grasping the rifle with their hands. Diane has made a run for it, down the hill. Graham lets her go for now and rushes to Sophia's aid. He grabs hold of Karen and punches her square in the face, then yanks the rifle out of her grasp.

Sophia lets go and lays on the ground, panting, exhausted.

Karen spits blood at him, seething. 'You'll fucking regret this, Graham! Mark my words. Nothing good ever comes from sticking your nose in …'

'Oh, shut up,' mutters Graham, just before slamming the butt of the rifle into her nose, breaking it. She howls, covering her face with both hands as blood pours into her mouth and down her chin.

How's that for irony, he thinks.

Graham grabs the rope that had been used to string up Stephen and quickly binds Karen's and Davies' wrists together; tighter this time.

Sophia is kneeling next to Stephen, who is still unconscious, his face pale.

'I need to get him to a hospital,' says Graham, reaching to check Stephen's pulse. It's weak, barely there.

'I … I don't think he's going to make it,' says Sophia softly. She's crying, her cheeks streaked with tears.

Graham shakes his head. 'No, he'll be fine. I got to him in time. He's still breathing.' He reaches into his pocket, removes Stephen's phone and dials for an ambulance.

Sophia and Graham sit beside Stephen while help arrives, shaded by the canopy of the tree while the night creeps closer with every passing minute.

The darkness arrives to collect its old friend.

Epilogue
GRAHAM

Six months later ...

Graham sits beneath the tree on a wooden bench he built himself. The branches above are mostly bare, but tiny spring buds are beginning to bloom, ready for another year. Sunrise is in precisely eleven minutes. He's waiting for someone. They'll be here soon.

Barney rests at his feet. The old dog doesn't always manage the trip up the hill with him, but today is a special day. Graham has spent the past six months looking after the canine and has come to enjoy the warm, furry body on his lap of an evening. Just two old dogs, enjoying each other's company.

The view is spectacular. He makes the journey to the top of the hill every single morning and evening without fail; rain or shine. It had been particularly difficult during the winter months, especially when two feet of snow made an appearance on Christmas morning, but it's worth it.

It's a very special place to be. Watching the sunrise and sunset has become his twice daily ritual. Yes, there are times when he has to break it, like a couple of months ago when he succumbed to a nasty cold and then developed a stubborn chest infection that wouldn't shift without blasted antibiotics, but otherwise, he makes the effort to visit the bench under the tree. His overall health and fitness has improved (other than the cold and chest infection) thanks to his trips up the hill and his cutbacks on junk food and whisky. In general, Graham is feeling good.

The bench has turned out well, and is now showing the signs of wear and tear from the harsh Welsh weather. It's often covered in dirt, fallen leaves and bird droppings, but Graham brushes it down and keeps it in decent condition.

Resting on his lap is a notepad and a pen, ready for when inspiration strikes. He closes his eyes and breathes in the cool air. Spring is well and truly here; the temperature rising with every passing day.

'Sorry I'm late,' says a friendly voice.

Graham opens his eyes as Barney jumps to his feet and greets the new arrival. 'Not at all. In fact, by my watch, you're right on time,' replies Graham.

Sophia ruffles Barney's head and kisses him before taking a seat. Barney leaps up and lays across her lap. 'The bench has turned out great.' She shifts slightly, careful not to disturb Barney and runs a finger over the small, gold plaque attached to the back of the bench.

In memory of Stephen Mallow and John Hammel.
Two souls. Two lives. Two incredible legacies.

'Thank you,' replies Graham with a sad smile. 'How are you? You look very different than when I last saw you.' Her face is fuller now, a bright spark to her eyes and she looks to have put on several pounds in body weight, making her look healthy and strong. She's chopped off her long hair, which had been limp and knotted when Graham had rescued her. Now it's cropped and shiny, shaved on one side above her ear.

Sophia faces forwards, staring at the view, at the sun beginning to crest over the horizon. She strokes Barney's soft coat while she speaks, curling his long fur between her fingers. 'I've been good. Therapy has been going well, and I'm ready to move back home.'

'Are you sure?'

'Yes. I've thought about it for a long time. I needed to get away and recover, but I'm ready to come back and try and take over the farm. I'm gutted I missed Mum's funeral though.'

'It was a lovely service. She's in the graveyard when you're ready to visit. I've been taking care of John's grave and hers and your brother's too.'

'Thank you, Graham. I'm sorry about Stephen.'

Graham looks ahead at the now-rising sun, its yellow and orange hues cascading across the sky. 'Thank you. He's back in Cherry Hollow next to his girlfriend, Rachel. The coroner said it wasn't the loss of oxygen that killed him. It was his brain tumour. I wrongly assumed that it was all in his head, especially since he'd been seeing things that weren't really there. I suppose I wasn't ready to accept that I was going to lose another friend, so I believed it was something else that was causing him to see things.'

'I've read about Cherry Hollow. I've had a lot of time to read while I've been recovering. It sounds like an interesting town.'

'That's one way of describing it.'

'There wasn't anything you could have done,' says Sophia. She's carried a shoulder bag up with her and has put it on the ground. Shifting Barney ever so slightly, she reaches down and fetches a sketchpad and a pencil.

'No, I suppose there wasn't,' replies Graham. 'I think Stephen knew his time had come. He was never going to be able to outrun death. It's one of those inevitable things we all have to come to terms with eventually, but I like to think he's at peace now.'

Graham and Sophia share a smile. 'I think he is,' says Sophia. 'He was a writer?' She nods at the notebook in Graham's hands.

'Yes, a fine journalist. Rather skilled at finding out the truth behind a story.'

'Is that what you're doing now?'

Graham sighs. 'It doesn't happen every day, but I'm sure he'll make an appearance when he's ready. I feel like he has one more article left to write before he says goodbye.'

'It freaked me out the first time it happened to me too,' says Sophia, taking the pencil and pressing the tip against a blank page. She holds it there a moment, then, slowly, she begins to draw.

The sunrise is brightening the sky all around them now, warming the air. Graham closes his eyes, breathes in deep and exhales slowly, until his lungs are empty. He looks down at the writing pad, picks up his pen and begins to write.

Graham and Sophia sit in silence, channelling the spirits of the dead.

'Nice of you to join me again, old friend,' he says into the breeze as the light of a new day draws closer with every passing minute.

The Light Within The Darkness
By Stephen Mallow

Yes, you're reading this correctly. It's me. This is a little unorthodox, I'll admit, especially because I'm no longer a part of this world. Some of you may be sceptical and I don't blame you for that. As I said, it's a little unorthodox, not to mention nearly impossible, but I'm afraid there's no other way to explain it.

I would have died eventually, thanks to the brain tumour that had developed in me, but I find it rather poetic to have gone out the way I did. Please know, I am at peace. I am happy. I am content. I am with my love. This means this will be my final article. It isn't a long one, but it may be the most important one I've ever written.

In the past, I've talked a great deal about the darkness and how it can affect us in different ways, even mould us into people we don't recognise if we let it. The darkness is a very powerful and often misunderstood emotion and presence.

I've been hiding within its shadowy corners for too long, like many of us tend to do when life gets too difficult and throws impossible challenges our way. It's human nature to retreat to a safe place inside, whatever that may look like.

But today, for my final article, I want to talk about something else, something different.

The light.

Like the darkness, the light can often be misinterpreted. We often try to fake the light inside, pretend we are happy, thriving and content with our lives, while ignoring the impending darkness closing in. This is a dangerous game to play.

Everyone has a light side and a dark side. It's a known fact of life. It's simply not possible for a human being to be blissfully happy forever, but lately, I've noticed a gradual decline of lightness, especially on social media and the news.

Every day, I'd turn on the news or scan through social media, only to see so much darkness, so much negativity and evil. I've always thought of myself as a positive person, but seeing all the hate and violence everywhere I looked, began to eat away at my soul, as it would with anyone.

I can't help but think that if we, as humans, stepped out of our inner darkness and turned on our lights, it would make the world a much more beautiful, hospitable and wonderful place for future generations.

If only we had that ability, though. If only it were as simple as switching on a light.

Before the rise of the internet and social media, life was simpler, I'm sure, but evil and hate still existed and it has done since the beginning of time.

Take John Hammel, for example.

One hundred years ago, John Hammel was hung from a tree by a rope at the hands of his own father and brother. Even his girlfriend betrayed him.

Since then, years have gone by, yet we haven't learned a thing.

Hate. Evil. Darkness. It still exists in every one of us. In some more than others.

I am no longer a part of this world, but I implore you all to consider something before you let out your inner darkness against another person.

Consider this ...

What if you didn't let your darkness control you? What if you switched on your light instead?

All of us are capable of making our own decisions. That's the beauty of the human race. But it's also a curse. Yes, it's easier to let the darkness win, but I promise you that a little kindness and generosity goes a long way. A little light can make a huge difference.

I hope that by writing this final article from beyond the grave, it can help you to realise that you do have a choice. You do have the power. I never set out to change the world with my writing, but if this article changes the life of even one person, then I consider it a job well done.

Don't let the darkness win.

All it takes is for you to step out of the shadows and into the light.

Take care of the world and your life because it's the only one we have. Don't waste it by destroying others. Use it to help them instead.

To my good friend, Graham Williams: thank you for allowing me to write my final article and for showing me the meaning of true friendship.

It's time for me to sign off now. Indefinitely.

Take care.

Stephen Mallow.

****

If you've enjoyed reading The Hanging Tree, please consider leaving a review wherever you bought the book or tag me on social media using my handle @jessica_reading_writing.

****

Fancy reading what Graham and Stephen are talking about in Cherry Hollow?
"The Darkness Within Ourselves" is OUT NOW on eBook, paperback and audio and available to read for FREE on Kindle Unlimited.

Did you like this book?

I really hope you enjoyed reading The Hanging Tree.

If you have, please consider leaving me a review on Amazon and Goodreads, share a review on your social media pages and tag me, share my book to any book clubs you may be a part of or recommend my book to friends and family.

Reviews are massively important, especially to self-published authors. They help find other readers who may enjoy the book and spread the word to a wider audience.